THE COOKS

Charles Facas

for Orson

Chapter One

SHE AWOKE instantly, fully rested and ready to go. It sounded like a helicopter or a jet outside, but whatever it was, it had done its job. In the early morning darkness, she found her clothes and quickly threw them over her slender figure. He was still passed out and looked like he wouldn't wake for another day. She grinned as much as the morning would allow as she admired his slumbering figure. Noticing a plate by the bedside, she dipped her finger into what was left of the sweet meringue and had one last taste. Shaking her head in satisfaction, she whispered, "It'll find you soon, Mr. Sebastian." With that she grabbed her purse and left.

Hours passed before John's body stirred. He rolled onto his back and slowly opened his eyes. His rough, leathery skin felt softer than he remembered. Age was catching up to him, he thought. His fifty-first birthday was right around the corner and he felt he didn't have much to show for it. He wasn't a bad man, never committed any serious crimes, never hurt anyone. But then again, he wasn't necessarily a good man. He was the main focus of his life; he didn't have family, children, more than a couple of close friends, or even a steady girlfriend (or a clue if girlfriend that was the correct term to use when you're fifty). But he did have a love: cooking.

John believed it must have began when he was a youngster, living on the outskirts of Paris in one of the many areas known as wine country. His grandmother, his mother and his sister were all his teachers. It had started simply enough, with soups and stews, cheese and fruits, some pastries. He'd had enough stew in his childhood, John thought, that he could make it in his sleep. Once a week, under the watchful eye of the household women, little Jean would make the family dinner. This was at age nine. At first, John thought they made him do this because they were too lazy and wanted to put him to work. Later he determined that what they really wanted was to make him a woman. But he eventually gave up on that theory when he entered adolescence (they encouraged dating women). It was then that he'd at last found the true reason: Cooking *impresses* women.

His theories changed routinely, but since they also entertained him, he never found the time to complain and soon enough began to enjoy the art of cooking. (Not until a publicly drunken, mildly philosophical adventure in Manhattan, which saw him spend a night in jail with fellow chef and friend, Pierre Albese, was he to learn that it was also a science.) By the end of his high school education, John Sebastian was a formidable chef specializing in rural French cuisine. With the help of a guidance counselor and a full scholarship, he enrolled into the premier French cooking institute of the time, L'Ecole des Bon Chefs. Upon graduation, John decided to go to America. He had fared well at school; he was able to bring the peasant food he grew up with to new levels in gourmet, and now he wanted to see the world (and all the women therein). He had some money in his pocket, a skill in his hands, and curiosity in his mind.

Before he embarked on his journey, his mother told him two things he'd never forget. One was that his father (whom he had never known) was an American, and one of the best chefs in New York City. Or, at least, he had been. He'd come to Paris one spring to relax, to sample some restaurants, and to meet some fellow chefs. That's when they had met. The affair lasted one night and that was the last they'd seen each other. He probably didn't even know he had a son. His name was David. That's all she knew. The next thing she told him was that she was a prostitute. Or, at least, she had been.

The grand American tour began in New York City. After a quick sampling of the city's loveliest women, John had decided that the grand American tour was over. He had crashed at the apartment of an old cooking school classmate. The guy, Morrows was his name, had some contacts in the city and helped John find work. His first job was preparing salads at a tiny French bistro on the Upper East Side. That led to his first apartment; a small, dark cave. Home. He worked his way up to hors d-oeuvres, and three years later, by the time he was twenty-five, he was cooking the entrees. Life was pretty good back then: He was fortunate to have skills, he enjoyed the American women, and they seemed to enjoy French men. He recalled some of their names: Carol, Mary, Patricia, Elizabeth. There were many others.

John continued as head chef at the tiny French bistro for years, eventually developing a reputation of respect around the city. When he reached his early 30s, he knew it was time to start his own restaurant. There was no trouble finding investors; they ate at the bistro three times a week. "J. Sebastian's" opened up a year later in Greenwich Village. The food, of course, focused on rural French dishes: soups and stews, cheese and fruits, some pastries. The restaurant was successful and things couldn't have been better for him. He had established himself as the chef du jour and his peasant style was the local rage. He noticed that different women were coming around, too. They had names like Samantha, Georgia, Gretchen, Wendy.

By his fortieth birthday, John had three restaurants in Manhattan. All were consistently doing well, so well that he didn't have to cook anymore. His chefs were trained, and they could handle things just fine. And always, when John would introduce something new, he would invite the three chefs to his cooking studio and have a little cooking party. After a case of wine and hours of culinary dementia, the three chefs would have the recipes committed to memory and then they'd all pass out.

John never wrote down recipes; something he attributed to his childhood. His family had taught him how to cook with cooking, not paper. John knew that he could've learned cookbookery, but old habits are hard to break.

Life was good for John. He never had serious trouble with anyone, never had serious health problems, never had serious financial woes. All this, however, did not prevent the mid-life crisis. It had happened in his mid-40s, although he couldn't recall the exact day. *What was he doing with his life?* A horrible question. Sure, he had three successful restaurants in New York City. Sure, he had a beautiful apartment to live in. Sure, he'd had hundreds of gorgeous women throughout the years. What, then, was so wrong? Nothing. But the pressure of nothing was tearing him apart. At first he changed some of his menus, adding sleek nouveau dishes, zipping up the taste with more spices and outré combinations. But that didn't do the trick, nor did his patrons appreciate the gesture. Then he thought about buying a car, but Manhattan was no place for a car. Perhaps a girlfriend? So John met a lovely woman named Alyssa and actually stayed faithful to her for four months. In the beginning it felt wonderful and John thought he'd found what he needed. But then he came to the conclusion that he didn't really like Alyssa. He found her to be a pain in the neck.

A year passed and John wasn't feeling any better. He was forty-six and miserable. Of course, he'd have his good days when all would seem fine, but then came the bad days which erased every little sparkle of hope. It was during one of these funks that he came up with the solution. He was in the park, nibbling on a deli sandwich for lunch, and the answer dawned on him: Food is life. Initially, this sounded too simplistic for him to take seriously. But John had worn out his options for peace of mind, so he decided to go with it.

John's family had given him the gift of the culinary arts. They knew how much of an impact it could have on one's soul as well as on others. It's not often that something so necessary to survival was also so therapeutic. (Was sex? John thought. He figured his mother had covered both.) John knew that he had to do something new, something that he'd never done before, something his family had done for him: Teach. He already shared recipes with his chefs, but they were already culinary experts. John needed to teach those who didn't know. He needed to share his knowledge, plant his cooking seeds in some fresh soil. He knew that this was it. This was what was missing from his life. This was why his family had taught him. You share this knowledge with those who don't know it even exists, and you're sharing the gift of life. John wondered if the mustard in his deli sandwich was laced with something funny.

Thus at age 46, John Sebastian turned his attention to teaching. He rearranged his cooking studio to accommodate a class. It took some time and a bit of money, but John knew it to be the answer. He was so excited that he finished outlining the curriculum weeks before class even started. They would meet once a week for eight weeks and there would be only one level: Whether you were an expert or afraid of the kitchen, you would get the same instruction. He would teach simple soups and stews at first, outlining basic ingredients and cooking techniques. He would also instruct the class on cheese and fruits, and which wines were appropriate. He would then lead up to some pastries.

The class filled quickly and John couldn't remember being so excited for the first day of school. But this first day of school was different. He had the jitters, didn't sleep the night before, and he just prayed that his broken English would be understood. The first class was comical. At the end of the two hours, all the students were drunk and hungry. Not one of the dishes came out properly and yet the entire case of wine was gone. This is not to say that the class was a failure. The students had a great time and they were all eager to return the following week. Over the next few years, John honed his teaching skills. At one point he decided to add a second class, but that was a little too much, so he went back to one.

He focused more on discovering an entertaining pastime than on cooking techniques. No grade was given, no credit earned. The final judgment came personally to each student, who in his or her own mind knew what he or she had learned. Most left the course with confidence in their newfound ability and a fresh culinary outlook. They were able to find the pleasure and satisfaction that came with preparing food. From this, John was content. After years of filling his own emptiness, he was finally sharing the secret life with others.

That first class was just over five years ago. In that time, his restaurants stayed prosperous and he remained a name chef in the city. Some called him "that crazy French cook," others called him "Napoleon Joe." He didn't mind them. Publicity is publicity. He felt a tinge of loneliness last year upon turning 50 alone (although he had spent his birthday night with Grace and Monique). The classes he taught filled a certain void for him, but there was still a hole in his mind, or perhaps in his heart. He had found comfort in his life, he had found contentment with his work (a word he had never used), but true happiness seemed to elude him. He knew you could not go out and just buy happiness in an automobile, or even in a fine Italian supper with a robust Chianti. Happiness, for some reason, had to find you. That was why when Natasha had said, "It'll find you soon, Mr. Sebastian," he knew exactly what she was talking about.

Chapter Two

JOHN SEBASTIAN rolled out of bed with a grunt. Half his morning was spent thinking and rethinking about the night before and the woman he was with and how he felt about the whole situation. After hours of dizzying analysis, John had no logical conclusions to explain his emotions, at least, none that he was brave enough to admit. He stood in front of the mirror. It took a few seconds to focus, but when he did, he grinned. He wasn't a thin man, yet he wasn't obese. He was definitely large, though. Large without obesity. The thought of that made him smile. Most of his gray hair remained on his scalp, even though he sported a "buzz" cut (it made cooking easier). The gray look was satisfying; he felt like the seasoned professional he was.

His apartment was of decent size and decor. There were three bedrooms, two and a half baths, living and dining rooms, a den and, of course, the kitchen. His "Custom Cuisine" boasted Italian marble counters, maple cabinets and a terra-cotta floor. All of his appliances were new with the exception of his antique cast-iron stove, which he had shipped from a small town in Scotland. His knives were old, but his "babies" were better built than anything sold today. Pots and pans and skillets lined the walls on steel racks, and below them were rows and rows of herbs and spices. A scarred chopping block sat in the middle of the kitchen, with a wine refrigerator serving as its foundation. And finally, John had his set of old blue jars, a cooking school graduation gift from his mother, filled with assorted necessities; sugar, flour, tea, lollipops.

The quiet and private West Village was always good to him. John was not much of a decorator, but he managed to make the apartment look mature. What made the place memorable, however, was the abundance of plant life. Every room had at least five plants in it. The dining room had about twenty; it was like eating in the rainforest. The plants kept him company. He couldn't remember when the plant addiction started (with the exception of the occasional Thai stick), but over the years, more plants started appearing until the apartment was covered and smothered. John was thankful that he had Delores. Delores was an old Dominican lady that he had met ten years earlier through Paul Pastor, another chef in the city. Delores came by once a week to clean and dust and to feed the plants. John had the feeling that she brought a new one in every once in a while but he had never asked her about it. The mystery was much too fun to ruin with fact. John had never bought a plant in his life.

He went into the kitchen to make some coffee, and then went out to the den, where he spent most of his waking time at home. He opened the drawer in his desk and retrieved a joint. And so began his day; a cup of black coffee and a puff of marijuana. The restaurants didn't need him today, so he could take it easy. He'd stop by one or two to administer his daily checkup, but that's it. All there was on the agenda was to prepare for tonight's class.

What should they cook up tonight? The eight-week course didn't have a syllabus; John would think of the dishes right before the classes. Maybe some chicken. Whenever he had a pot-smoke, every food seemed ultra-appealing, giving John the freedom to think of quirky ideas that he would normally discount. As the thought of a chicken dish bounced through his mind, somehow his thoughts transferred to the night before.

Mon Dieu!

Natasha had been coming to the bar at Sebastian's for a while now. She was in her early forties, worked in advertising, was a former model and divorced. Last night was the third night they'd spent together, and it again left John in a completely satisfied state. There was something unique to Natasha that he couldn't place. He had met her the year before as she'd become friendly with the staff and had her own "seat" at the end of the bar. John had been in the kitchen most of the night, trying to cook all the dinners with just two burners. After the last entree had been prepared, he'd come out to the bar to reward himself with a cocktail. He had, naturally, noticed her there sitting alone (he was, after all, a man, and a single man at that). He maneuvered behind the bar, had Felix fix him a gimlet, and made his way toward her. He had no plan, but figured something would intervene if there was potential.

Sure enough, Felix quickly responded to her request for another chardonnay and, noticing that John was standing two feet from her, introduced them.

"John, Natasha. Natasha, this is John Sebastian, it's his restaurant."

John laughed to himself. It wasn't such a bad way to be introduced. They talked for a couple of drinks, and she left. He was impressed by her love and knowledge of food, her dry sarcasm and the fact that she didn't seem to want to jump his old French bones. She had long, straight auburn hair and beautiful green eyes. How this woman was single, he didn't know.

A few nights later, John was back at Sebastian's although he wasn't quite sure why. As he was secretly hoping, Natasha was at the bar. John again came out of the kitchen (a bit earlier this time) and they shared another entertaining conversation (as he'd hoped they would), but this time over a few drinks as well as some appetizers. Once again, though, she left him wondering.

Finally, after some serious debating, he asked her out on a date. Much to his nervous delight, she agreed, and for once in his life, John Sebastian didn't have only one thing (sex) in mind. The date went as smooth as it could have, considering that the 50-year-old man felt like a bashful teenager, and more proper (sexless) dates followed. After about two months of this conservative behavior, John realized two rather surprising things. One was that this had been the longest he'd maintained a relationship with a woman without sleeping with her, and two, he was actually enjoying it. It was then when she suggested he make her dinner at his apartment.

They both knew what that meant. He quickly agreed.

That Saturday evening, she arrived at eight. She didn't dress any fancier than before. Perhaps she even dressed down. She looked fantastic. He served some vodka martinis and put on Tchaikovsky.

He had made a peasant stew with lamb, and it came out perfectly (as it should have). They drank a soft merlot with dinner and then moved on to the champagne as he brought out the crème brulées. Natasha passed on espresso afterwards and opted for more wine. They took care of two more bottles, and that's all they collectively remembered. They didn't have sex that night, but somehow they ended up in his bed. The next morning they woke up in each other's arms a bit puzzled; it took a few moments to size up the situation. Then they made love.

That was months ago, but the memory was still strong. Since then, they'd seen each other on many different occasions (usually at the bar), and had developed a solid friendship (it was the first time John couldn't use his mother's prostitution as an excuse to not become friends). During this time he'd seen various other women (and there was that summer solstice incident with the twins), but Natasha knew of this. If she cared, she didn't express it. Perhaps she was alternately involved, too. Last night was the third night she had stayed at his apartment. Three nights in seven-odd months. What struck John was that he thought about her a lot, and not even in the carnal sense (although there was plenty of that). Her image would pop up at random moments; if he burnt the chocolate cake, if Harry DeSoro didn't pay his tab, if he cut himself shaving. Not that her image would set his mind at ease, he knew that didn't happen, but for a split second he could relax and manage a subtle moment of la.

This meant something and John knew it. Did Natasha? He only hoped it didn't imply something he wasn't ready for. Sitting on the couch in the den, drinking some coffee, smoking some Thai, he wanted to call her.

Are you high, little Jean?

Chapter Three

MAYBE CHICKEN Francese, John thought. The class shouldn't have much trouble with that and thankfully there were no vegetarians. Not that he disliked vegetarians, but most of the dishes created in his kitchen involved some type of meat. Some herbivores in his past classes were reluctant to handle the carnivorous recipes, although they rejoiced on "Plate de Vegetable" day. Chicken Francese was simple enough. They could easily make it on their own, too, unlike the seven-hour "Back-Country Soup." He had to pick up some flour, eggs, white wine, butter, lemon, parsley and, of course, some chicken. That shouldn't take too much time; he'd order the wine and get the rest on his own. John picked up his phone and called a familiar number.

"Hello, you've reached Natasha Williams at Wilson Advertising. I'm either on the phone or away from my desk. Please leave your name and number and I'll get back to you as soon as I can."

Lost for a moment within her voice, he quickly hung up. Leaving a perfect message was something John couldn't do. He figured he seldom left "perfect" messages. Maybe one out of ten times. It was all about knowing what to say, and he really didn't know what to say. He didn't like it when his mind was consumed with her. Sip of coffee. Natasha. What kind of wine should I get? Natasha. Where did all these plants come from? Natasha. It was never like this. Well, maybe once, long ago. He'd been twenty-five or so at the time. Whatever. It didn't work out. But this was the only other time he could remember being so obsessed with a woman. He had to leave his apartment. Now.

John threw on some faded jeans and a gray button-down and left. Ten minutes later, he approached Neuf-Cinque, his third restaurant in Manhattan. He had set it up a few years ago, ecstatic that he finally had a bistro close to home. It was the smallest of his eateries, but perhaps the most comfortable. Steps from the sidewalk led down to the little restaurant (it was a converted brownstone basement). The first room was long and narrow with room for ten tables. In the back and to the left were the restrooms and to the right was smaller dining area holding six tables. Straight ahead was the kitchen. The decor was relaxed: teak wood walls and floors, candle lighting, soft jazz in the background, humble bistro tables and chairs.

"What's up, Boss?" asked Henry, head chef at John Sebastian's hippest restaurant.

"Henry, how are you? Just stopping on by. Have any lunch back there?"

"Mais bien sur, monsieur," replied Henry, brushing up on his four French words. "I'll fix something up."

Let's see, John thought as he waited for lunch, he had flour and butter and lemons already at the studio. All he needed to get now was chicken and parsley. Maybe he should add a vegetable. Then he could give the class a lesson in cooking management. String beans. John paused for a moment, picked up his phone and dialed.

"Hello, you've reached Natasha Williams at Wilson Advertising. I'm either on the phone or away from my desk. Please leave your name and number and I'll get back to you as soon as I can."

Click. John didn't know what to say. He needed to eat something, get his mind off of her. Oh, but that thought just made it worse. What power did she have that he couldn't stop thinking about her? She had some sort of chokehold on him. Who's in control here, anyway? He had to be stronger than that.

"Where's my lunch?" he mock demanded.

"Hold your horses!" was the response.

John had hired Henry almost seven years before as a souse chef at his second restaurant. When Neuf-Cinque opened, he brought Henry in as head chef. John felt somewhat like a father figure to him, guiding him through the pitfalls of love and cooking. He'd helped Henry become something of a cooking Casanova, but now he wondered if that was the best direction he could give. Did he really want Henry to be alone at age fifty? John let that thought swirl around. It was then when he realized that at the end of the night, after dinner had been served, after all the cocktails and champagne, after all the hoopla went home, that maybe he, John Sebastian, didn't want to be alone.

Platter in hand, Henry came out of the kitchen with a satisfied grin.

"Lunch is served. Mind if I join you?"

"Sure, what are we having?"

"Super sandwiches."

Henry placed the platter on the table. Two sandwiches with lettuce greens, tomato reds and bread browns lay before them.

Henry spoke, "Never underestimate the sandwich."

"Never," agreed John.

John was hungry. It was about noon and he hadn't had a bite all day. As they ate, they talked about the inventory, the menu, and Henry's social life. As they were finishing up, Henry dropped a question.

"Fallen in love yet?"

John froze. "What do you mean?" was the only response he could muster.

"You know, are you seeing anyone?" Henry asked innocently, not knowing what had just gone through John's brain.

Slowly, John answered, "Actually, yes, I have been. Things are going well." There, that was good, he thought. Nice and relaxed.

Henry paused for a moment, and then another. He had a sip of water and looked into John's eyes.

"Is there something going on that I should know about?" Henry asked, but didn't stop. "You just said, 'Yes, I have been. Things are going well.' I've known you for seven years, John, and you've never said anything like that. Ever! What happened?"

John was in shock. He started sweating. He had to cool off. Water. He guzzled his water and caught his breath.

"John, are you all right?"

"Yeah, yeah, yeah, I'm fine. Sorry. Didn't get much sleep last night."

"Okay, so what's going on?"

John tried to calm himself. It took a while, but he finally slowed down his heartbeat and breathed deeply. He cleared his mind and waited until he reached a mild state of meditation before speaking again.

"Henry, have you ever been in love?"

Whoa! Out of meditation, right back into chaos. Did he just open his mouth and say that? No, no, no, hold on. Breathe. Again. Breathe. Okay. You know exactly what you're doing. You're in complete control. Okay, great, here we go. Wait until Henry stops laughing. Okay. He's almost done.

"Henry?"

Henry's laughter subsided, but he kept smiling. "I never thought I'd see it happen, but I always hoped it would."

John played dumb. "What do you mean?"

"Oh, come on, John. It's all over your face. Who is it?"

John grimaced and shook his head slightly. "Her name's Natasha."

"Natasha?" Henry asked and thought for a moment. "Oh, yeah! From Sebastian's. So she's the one, eh?"

"You know her?"

"I've never met her, but Felix told me all about her." A quick laugh. "This is the best news I've heard in a long time. But I see you're not so 'comfortable' with it."

"I never said *I* was in love."

"True, you didn't. But you did almost pass out."

Resigned, John smirked. "So what about you? Have you ever been in love?"

Henry took a deep breath, his smile faded just a bit. "Once. Sure. Once it happened to me. Back in high school."

"High school? Does that qualify?"

Henry wondered the same thing.

"I'm not sure. But if you remember it, I think it does."

"Okay, go on."

Henry continued, "It really wasn't much. It was your typical teenage romance. She and I were inseparable. We took on our entire high school for three straight years. It does sound a bit silly, talking about high school love, but that's the only time I think I've felt it. It was fantastic."

"So what happened?"

"What happened was that she went to college and I went to cooking school. She was in California, I was in New York, then Paris."

"So you lost touch?"

"Yeah. We kept in touch for a couple of years. But then we lost touch. She ended up marrying some guy right after school. I ended up sleeping with every woman in France. But seriously, John. What's going on? How do you feel?"

"I feel like I'm not in control," he said.

"Do you have the feeling that you need to be within three feet of her at all times?"

Pause. "Sure."

"Okay, can you think of anything else at the moment?"

"No."

Henry nodded his head in understanding. "Alright. I want you to prepare yourself."

"For what?"

"Just prepare yourself."

"Fine! I'm prepared."

"No, you're not, John. You're in love."

Another pause. "Dammit."

Though John was afraid of the words he was hearing, he was thankful that he had someone to speak with. It seemed Henry didn't know too much about love, but his younger, sharper perspective helped. Still, John didn't know if he now felt better or worse.

"So what do I do? …What *can* I do?"

"First of all," Henry stared him down, "relax. These feelings are normal. You'll have difficulties eating and sleeping. That's completely normal. What you should do is what feels like the right thing."

"I don't understand what you're talking about."

"All I'm saying is do what feels right. That means if you feel like calling her, call her. If you feel like seeing her, go and see her. If you feel like doing something else, do something else. You know what I mean? It might sound stupid, but it's true."

"Hmmm."

"Yeah, just do what you feel. Put it this way, you're not going to ruin anything that wasn't meant to be by being yourself."

"So if I want to call her, I call her?"

"Exactly."

"What if I don't know what to say?"

"Doesn't matter. Whatever you say, you'll say. And she'll say something back."

"Where'd you learn all this?"

"And the best thing about this is that if it's real, then she's probably feeling the same way."

"Hmmm. I suppose that does make sense."

"Of course it does. And just remember one more thing. You can't make something happen that won't. I mean, you can't make this relationship work, and you can't push these feelings away. What happens will happen. So the best thing you can do is relax, take a deep breath, go about your day, and give her a call if you feel like it. Better yet, when you're ready, tell her what's going on in your head."

They both sat there in silence for a bit. John was letting everything soak in. Relax. Do what feels right. Tell her how you feel. Henry was a good kid. How did he learn this stuff?

"So where did you pick up this stuff from?"

"John," Henry answered in disbelief, "I got this from you."

Chapter Four

JOHN TOOK a stroll down Sixth Avenue, processing the advice from Henry. He was in a slight daze because of it. Usually a grinning pedestrian, John wore the face of a solemn ditch digger. When he came to, he was staring at a bunch of Italian parsley.

"Mr. Sebastian, how can I help you?" One of the many butchers was eager to serve the local hero.

"Jerry, I'm going to need some cutlets for class tonight."

"Say no more. Just give me a few minutes."

John left the counter and explored the culinary jungle. Vegetables everywhere, fruit everywhere else, fresh bread, fresh fish, aged cheeses from around the world. John likened his comfort in a fresh produce market to the regular man's comfort in a hardware store. He meandered about the premises, eventually winding his way back to the butcher. He failed to recognize, probably to his benefit, the three women (and the one man) who were eyeing him the whole time.

"Here you go, Mr. Sebastian, fifteen cutlets."

"Thanks a lot, Jerry."

"Sure thing, Mr. Sebastian," he said, adding, "Hey, are you okay?"

The question didn't even faze John. "Yeah, sure, of course. I'm fine. Thanks, Jerry."

"Sure thing, Mr. Sebastian."

Taking advantage of the beautiful day, and a truckload of thoughts, John decided to walk to the cooking studio. It was twenty-blocks, which meant approximately twenty minutes, but a good walk would serve him well. He wondered, would a good relationship serve him well, too? He immediately blocked that thought out and focused on the streets of Manhattan. Soon he wasn't in much of a fog anymore and his mind started to function normally again. He even had a slight sensation of sureness and showed it with a crack of a smile. Along the way, there were some familiar faces. The ones that recognized him, he acknowledged, but he didn't go so far as to engage in small talk. He just kept moving. He was doing what felt right.

By the time he arrived at the studio, it was about 2 o'clock. John placed the chicken in the massive refrigerator with the parsley and the string beans. The studio looked healthy; it was clean, it smelled fresh, and the midday light gave it some charisma. There were three long counters facing the front of the room, and one smaller counter facing the others. Each counter had three workstations (the smaller counter had one), and each workstation had two burners, a sizable built-in cutting board, a small sink and a smaller drawer with some necessary utensils. Hanging above every counter was an equally long rack that housed a variety of pots and pans and larger utensils. John had helped design the student kitchen and was proud of the outcome. That was five years ago, but the kitchen had stood the test of time and was still the best he'd ever come across. John moseyed to the only table in the room. It was by the smaller counter in the front of the classroom from which he taught the class. The table and chairs were from Neuf-Cinque. John thought it a great idea to put them in the studio; he could sample the students' cuisine at a candlelit table with a glass of wine. He pulled out one of the chairs and sat down. Staring into space, he took out his phone and dialed a number.

"Hello, you've reached Natasha Williams at Wilson Advertising. I'm either on the phone or away from my desk. Please leave your name and number and I'll get back to you as soon as I can."

Click. He hung up again. He had to think. He had to think of what to say. What did he want to tell her? "Had a great time with you last night!" "You know, I've been thinking…" "Hey, how's your day going?" Nothing felt right. He was afraid to say anything to her. He was afraid to open his mouth, not because of what would come out, but what might not come out. He paused that thought and recalled Henry's words. "Do what feels right… relax." Yes, relax. That's good for starters, John thought and then for no apparent reason decided that he should go to Sebastian's to see how things were going there.

Locking the door behind him, John left the studio and wandered out of the building. He walked to Sixth Avenue and hailed a cab. Sebastian's was on the Upper East Side (where name chefs were "supposed" to have their own restaurants). Caught in some midday traffic, John calmed a bit and tried to enjoy the ride, if that was at all possible in a New York City cab. They slowly passed by "Plant Row" on 28th Street, which was the official rainforest of the city. It reminded John of his apartment and he wondered if this was where Delores bought all those plants. Maybe she was a regular here.

They knew her as "Lady D." She got the royal treatment every time she walked down the block with the shopkeepers bowing as she strutted by, hoping she would choose their plants on that beautiful day. But even if she didn't, they would still adore the enchanting Lady Delores. Well, that was as good of an explanation as any for where his forest came from, he thought, and it kept his mind off of relationships (that is, until the exact moment he realized it).

The cab made its way uptown and pulled over in front of Sebastian's. It was about 4 o'clock and much of the staff was already there. For an instant, John forgot why he was there. Was he there to check the books? The kitchen? The bar? He greeted some of the waitstaff eating a pre-shift dinner. John went back into the kitchen to take a peek. A couple of the chefs were there, laughing about something, and welcomed him. Felix was back there, too, readying a plateful of food for himself. John always preferred to eat afterwards, but he figured that perhaps it was better to work on a happy stomach. Felix looked up and blushed red. Then John saw why: He had double-filled his plate with food, making the plate disappear. John started laughing with the other chefs as Felix cracked a smile.

"You're a growing boy, yes?" mused John.

"I guess so," Felix replied. "I'm heading out to the bar to eat. Want to join?"

"I just had a bite downtown, but sure."

John and Felix left the kitchen and saddled up at the end of the bar towards the front of the restaurant. Felix was the unofficial assistant manager; he was the one who could best communicate with the chefs, who were mostly of Latin descent (Felix, himself, was Portuguese). On his plate was a lot of rice. It took John a few seconds to see what else was going on. There was also some chicken, as well as some onions and green peppers. John could smell the garlic, which was probably the flavor of the sauce that filled in the spaces. It smelled great.

"Everything all right up here?" asked John.

"Yeah, we're all up to speed," answered Felix, with his mouth half full.

"Where's Lara?"

"She's coming in at five. Had some kind of appointment or something."

John paused for a bit as Felix continued his binge. A little reserved, John asked, "So things are going well at the bar?"

Felix took a break from his plate and look at John quizzically. "Yeah, things are fine. They're very, very good."

"Great." Pause. "And the regular people are coming in still?"

Felix put his fork down and once again looked at John.

"Yes. The regulars are still coming in." Felix grinned.

John appeared to be satisfied with that response as he nodded his head. After a lengthy pause, he spoke again. "No 'D' lister's coming around?" A 'D' lister was the name they gave to the troublemakers, the ones who they encouraged not to return.

"No, sir, they haven't come around in a while," he said, deliberately slow.

John wondered what he, himself, was getting at. Did Felix think of him as a complete kook? Maybe he should bring up what he actually wanted to talk about. Not just yet. "That actor still coming in, tipping big?" John inquired.

"Oh, yeah. He's still coming in. Tippin' big. Nice guy." Felix glanced at John. "Likes martinis."

What did Felix mean by that? What was it about martinis? Felix was almost finished with his plate and John knew he had to get there somehow.

"John?" he asked.

"Uh-huh?"

"You were here three days ago."

"I know," John replied with caution.

"So what's going on?" Felix asked with some concern.

John started a mild sweat and stretched his back, which had suddenly tightened up. He knew that the unknown caused fear; things like death and snakes. In a rapid moment of thoughts, John reasoned that he never really contemplated death and there were no snakes in the city, therefore those fears had eluded him. However, he concluded, his fear of love, the greatest unknown to him, seemed to have made up for the lack of others. He took a deep breath and knew it was time to jump in headfirst. "You know that woman who comes in? Her name's Natasha?" There. He had said it.

"Sure, Boss, she comes in all the time."

"Hmmm," was all John could sound out.

"You got something going on with her, Boss?" Felix asked as he looked the other way and pretended to cough. This comic conversation was finally making sense. John thought he was disinterested.

Eventually John thought of a response. "Well, yeah. Kind of."

"What's 'kind of' mean?"

After an anxious pause, John let it out. "Well, we've seen each other a few times now and then."

"Oh yeah?" And things are going okay? You like her?"

Feeling a shade more comfortable, John tried to mellow his voice even more. "Yeah, things have been rather good. And I think I kind of like her, you know?" What the hell? Was he sixteen years old again? John figured sometimes you just say what you say, and it's what you meant to say but not the way you wanted to say it. Felix didn't seem too interested, though. Maybe he doesn't understand what was going on here. Should he press him for information? John wasn't sure, but he really wanted to. Talk about being juvenile, but it was too tempting. If Felix is so passive, then he just might give some insight or whatever and never even think to tell anyone. John concluded, it was worth a shot.

"So, Felix," John began, "has she ever, you know, ever mentioned me before? You know, when you're talking at the bar, or anything?"

That was too much.

Felix burst out laughing, cackling like a giant bird. He was almost crying. In fact, John thought he saw a tear as shook his head in exasperation. Felix hopped off his barstool, picked up his plate and ran back to the kitchen, leaving John for a torturous moment. John wasn't shocked, and in the back of his mind he almost expected it (although he'd thought that Felix was somewhat oblivious to the situation). But he had hoped for something else. John was smiling now, laughing at himself. For the first time that day he was enjoying the giddiness of this romance. The almost overwhelming fear had started to retreat, and with every second his smile became wider and wider. It was good to feel sixteen again. Then he had an awakening of sorts: He really liked Natasha. He more than liked her. He wanted to spend a lot of his time with her. He wanted to spend most of his time with her. For the first time that day, and maybe in his life, John Sebastian was comfortable with the idea of being in love.

He left the restaurant before Felix could return. John no longer wanted any information Felix might have. And he didn't even care that the restaurant would be talking about it all night. Then, of course, the news will trickle down to the other restaurants, and probably to all the patrons and all the chefs in town. But right now, John didn't care. He got a cab and went home. He knew what he had to do.

Chapter Five

MAKE SENSE out of this life. That's the thought that accompanied John on the way back to his apartment. He didn't even notice the cabby's over-aggressive, swerving back and forth, slam on the brakes style of driving. John didn't think he could ever make sense out of this life. Perhaps, though, he could make sense out of parts of it. Cooking, for example. Now that made sense. That brought him a great deal of happiness and he could see how it fulfilled his life, but was cooking part of the "life making sense" equation? What kept resurfacing, though, was the way he felt about Natasha. Somehow the feeling didn't make too much sense to him, yet it made perfect sense out of his life. Natasha gave him something that cooking didn't; she filled in a void that had always been empty. He felt she wouldn't become just a part of his life. Rather, she'd become his entire life. These thoughts were all strange to John, having never entered this locked room. Was he crazy, or was he just in love? Given the two choices, he preferred the latter (and smiled at the thought of it). Natasha. She could make sense out of this life.

Closing the front door behind him, John headed into the kitchen. All this love philosophy opened up his appetite. He was going to call her, but he wanted to eat something first. The last thing he wanted to do was to talk on an empty stomach. For a premier chef, John didn't have much in the fridge. There were a dozen condiments; ketchup, mayo, three types of mustard, butter, garlic butter and dill butter, soy and teriyaki sauce. His fresh produce consisted of a couple of pears, some romaine lettuce and two tomatoes. John bought food as he needed it. If he wanted to cook something, he'd go out that day and get the necessities. But he ate out so much that he rarely cooked at home. Being a well-known chef allowed you to eat anywhere, and when you're in the business of food, there's nothing more that you'd like to do. A lunch menu finally clicked in John's head: a basic grilled cheese sandwich.

He reached up to the pots and pans hanging above and brought down a flat skillet. Out of the refrigerator, he took the garlic butter, some Gruyere cheese and a tomato. He sliced the Gruyere thin and did the same with half of the tomato. Then he turned on the burner and put the skillet on it with a tablespoon of the garlic butter. While waiting for the skillet to heat up and the butter to melt, John sliced some French bread. He then placed some cheese on the bread and put it open-faced on the skillet. As the cheese began melting, John placed a few slices of tomato on top. Five minutes later his sandwich was complete. John put the sandwich on a plate, filled up a glass with ice and poured in some homemade iced tea, and then brought it all into the den. The dining room was only used for dinner parties or impressing dates. Maybe he should sell the table.

Don't be bizarre, little Jean.

John ate silently and tried not to think about his upcoming conversation with Natasha. He knew he couldn't script what he wanted to say, so he blocked any thoughts of it. Or, at least, he tried to. He didn't know what to tell her, but he *did* know how he felt. "It'll find you soon, Mr. Sebastian." Did she have some sort of super-human intuition? John thought that a lot of women possessed it, but Natasha seemed to have it strong. (Yes, Natasha, I think it did find me.) He had to finish his sandwich quickly; he had to make the call. He was becoming overworked with excitement and nervousness. Why didn't he just call when he got in? Was he really hungry? Making that proverbial leap of faith was something he'd never done before, and something he wasn't even sure how to do. And now just the thought of doing it was making his anxiety scream. What if she didn't feel the same way? What if she saw him as an occasional fling? Was karma going to finally bite him in his big French ass? If he was feeling it, then she must be, too. Right? Doubt was growing and John started shaking. He hopped off the couch and brought his plate into the kitchen. He wrapped the cheese and the leftover tomato and put them back in the fridge. He quick-rinsed the skillet, dried it and returned it to its proper hook. Then he paused and closed his eyes. That sandwich was playing football in his stomach. Another pause. Okay. It's time.

He marched back into the den, grabbed his phone and dialed.

"Hello, you've reached Natasha Williams at Wilson Advertising. I'm either on the phone or away from my desk. Please leave your name and number and I'll get back to you as soon as I can."

Click. Not yet. He was shaking too much. In a second. Hold on. All right, do it again. Being nervous and tongue-tied is fine, right? Isn't that how it's supposed to be? Like Henry said, 'Relax.' Okay, relax. Relax and breathe. Okay. She could change your life instantly. She could give you a new life, one you never thought of having, one you've always avoided. She could give you, perhaps, the life you've always wanted. Relax now. Relax and breathe. Don't put so much weight on this. If you care too much, then you might get hurt, and then where will you be? Stop it, John. Don't think like that. Be a man. Be a man and make the call.

"Hello, you've reached Natasha Williams at Wilson Advertising. I'm either on the phone or away from my desk. Please leave your name and number and I'll get back to you as soon as I can."

Click. Dammit. Okay. He knew what he was going to say. He couldn't just call up casually; that approach had backfired with Felix. He had to be straight up. He had to be honest and let it flow. "Natasha, with you in my life, everything makes sense. Being with you explains who I am and all that I do. I know that sounds confusing, but I can't say it any better. You are the great explanation and I just wanted to tell you that."

"Hello, you've reached Natasha Williams at Wilson Advertising. I'm either on the phone or away from my desk. Please leave your name and number and I'll get back to you as soon as I can."

Click. He couldn't say those things. Was he out of his mind? That grilled cheese sandwich was still bouncing around in his stomach. Just make the call and get it over with. What's she going to do anyway? Hang up? Call him a fool and laugh? Say she never wants to see him again? He hit redial closed his eyes.

"Hi, John."

Her voice was beautiful. He could've just hung up the phone and lived the rest of his life in happiness after hearing those two simple words. He could tell that she was on to him, and that was a good thing. Maybe it took off some of the pressure. Why did he bother himself with so much paranoia? Her voice was the most comforting sound he'd ever heard, pushing all of his worries aside. Did everyone have to go through a mental junkyard to find peace? He quickly assumed they did, but really didn't care about it now. It was his turn to speak.

"Hi," he finally managed.

"Something on your mind?" Natasha grinned.

Chapter Six

"WELL, YOU know, I was just thinking about you," John said, squeezing his eyes shut.

"Judging from the amount of times you called today, you've been thinking about me a lot," Natasha coyly responded.

Pausing for a moment, John solved the mystery. "You knew?"

"Yep."

"I don't know why," John said, trying to play it cool.

"You don't?" Natasha pretended to be surprised.

"Listen… I don't know… I guess I was just, you know, trying to call you." A wave of fear knocked John down.

"John?"

"Yes?"

"Did you want to tell me something?"

Was she on to him? His fear turned into panic, and then panic turned into nausea. He was not in a comfortable position, but this was Natasha. Relax, John. Just say what you're going to say.

"I wanted to see you."

Great, she mused, he's over the first hurdle. Let's see how far he'll go. "But we just saw each other this morning."

"I know, I know." John paused. "It's kind of more than that."

"More than what?" Natasha feigned curiosity. At the same time, though, she wanted him to say it, to tell her that he felt the same way she did.

"Well… I've just been thinking about you a lot." There, that wasn't so bad, John thought as he exhaled.

Part of her wanted to respond with: "You've already said that," but she didn't want to discourage this little boy. "I've been thinking about you, too."

"Really?" John asked, but thinking he asked a bit too quick.

"Really."

"Oh."

'Oh?' Come on, John! You can do better than that. How about, 'Well, that's excellent, or 'Neat'?

John shook his conscience and continued, "I really need to see you."

Wow, that's some confidence, thought Natasha. Was he snapping out of it so soon? We'll see. "Well, you have class at seven… and it's only five. How about now?"

"Now?" John thought fast and then shut off his thinking. "Yes! Great."

"Great, I'll be there in twenty minutes."

Click. She hung up. Now she had the nervous reaction. She was going to go to his place right this moment and… what? She thought her experience and posture were all intact, but now she was feeling weak, even a bit faint. What? Get in control, Natasha. She grabbed her purse and left.

John was pacing. He had to breathe correctly. He had to flex the muscles in his shoulders and then relax them to make sure they wouldn't stiffen up. The place was clean, almost exactly how it appeared when she'd left that morning. But thinking about the apartment's cleanliness was irrelevant. He didn't care, he was just trying to fill his mind with something other than what might unfold in less than twenty minutes. The possibilities were terrifying. What was he going to tell her? What was she going to tell you? John didn't want to puzzle over that one. He told himself not to worry, but that's all he kept doing. Then he reversed it, telling himself to worry about it a lot, hoping that might calm him down. It didn't. He dared not sit down and trap himself in a chair with the anxiety dancing around him, swirling up and strangling him. No, that wouldn't be good. Keep moving. Pace to the other rooms. Pace there and back. John wanted her to be there now, but also didn't want her there at all.

This could be the end, little Jean. She's a good woman, just like your mother.

Did he really want to alter his life? In a few words, he could do just that. How many words had that ability? That thought lingered. A few words, a long time. There were some words John had never spoken before in his life. Sure, he'd realize later, there were millions of words he'd never said, but this was big. Okay, you have a plan; you know what you have to say. All you have to do is step up and say it, and then you'll be done. Have some water. John went into the kitchen and poured himself a tall glass of water. He drank it without stopping and then washed his face in the sink. That's a little better. He felt refreshed, but soon the fear came back. He shook his head. He could give up the whole thing right now.

Buzz!!!

She's here.

John buzzed her in without saying hello or asking who it was. He was sweating. And shaking. And dizzy.

Knock, knock.

John let out a deep breath, paused, and opened the door.

Natasha stood there staring at him. She looked like she ran the whole way. She slowly walked in and he closed the door behind her. He didn't know what to do and she was silent. Neither could speak. As the fourth awkward moment passed, she inched towards him. As she threw her arms around him she managed to softly say, "Hi, John."

They hugged for what seemed like days as well as only a brief second. John held her strong against him. Their eyes were tightly closed as they felt shivers climb their spines and branch out across their bodies. He he'd never felt so content in his life. Without thinking, he finally spoke. "I love you."

She started to cry, and he was a bit confused, but for only a moment. "I love you, too."

He couldn't help it, he was crying now, too.

Chapter Seven

THE WAIL of hard rock music in her ear was a rough way to start the day, but at least it convinced her to get up. Her name was Amanda Myers, but people called her Mandy. She was a small-time fashion designer for a small-time, yet trendy, online apparel company. It was a daily laugh that her closet, uniformly filled with gray and black (exception: one brown sweater), belonged to a fashion designer.

She didn't know the band, or even what station the alarm was on, but every weekday morning at 7am it seemed like the same song woke her up. It made her wonder if she had ever truly liked rock 'n' roll. She remembered how important music used to be to her, but it was now mostly background noise: dance music at a club, classical at a wedding, R&B at a bar. She could hear it, but she just didn't listen to it. Some days she just felt older. On this Tuesday morning, Amanda couldn't make sense of her alarm's rock overture, so therefore she didn't like it.

She took her usual quick shower to wash off the morning sweat and then made her usual cup of tea to wash down her usual yogurt breakfast. These routines, along with the others that punctuated her typical day, gave her stability and balance. Balance kept her world together; it gave her answers, it gave her glue. Balance was everywhere she looked, throughout her childhood and into now, in her relationships and within her solitude. A solid morning routine was essential for a good day. If she messed up her morning schedule then her theory of balance would provide her an unfortunate mishap by day's end.

The balance theory was only relevant when things weren't going well, in which case it could often help explain the situation. For example, if she was finishing the design for a new pink sweater for the winter catalog and someone, say Geoff, the irritating new copywriter, came into her office and by accident spilled his mocha latte all over her designs which had taken three weeks to create, then she would, naturally, get angry. But then she would look back and see if the balance theory could provide an explanation. Was there a time when she, herself, had spilled coffee (or anything) on someone's work? Think hard. Yes. Indeed, she had. When was it? In grade school? Yes. She had spilled a carton of fruit punch on Gretchen Gruber's "Toys I Want For Christmas" collage. There. Balance.

Incidents that couldn't be explained immediately, she determined, were setting up future events of balance; one day they would even out. She knew this was really the old "What comes around, goes around" axiom, which she knew to be karmic in nature (so she felt kind of cool), but she turned the cliché into a credo. She looked at every action of the day, from waking up to watching an old man cross the street, and knew that all of them were balancing something out or foreshadowing an event to come. They had to be. How is an old man crossing the street balanced out? That was tricky, but she knew something would and that she would one day witness it. Every human (and animal) has its own balanced life before it. Amanda could stay up all night thinking about balance and probably solve just a fraction of the events, but she really only remembered her theory during bad times.

Amanda enjoyed her wardrobe, the racks of blacks and grays. She liked to keep it simple and no one seemed to mind or notice. She had changed her dress code a few years back shortly after moving to New York City. At one point in her life she didn't own any gray or black. She remembered it as her Easter Egg phase. Her clothes looked like they belonged in a large yellow wicker basket with fake grass. Most of the dresses and skirts bore some sort of flower pattern, and there was that huge neon green dress that made her look like a fairy godmother. Then one day in New York, a day Amanda couldn't remember, she wore black slacks and a gray shirt that she'd received courtesy of her company. From then on, she'd changed. She proceeded to purchase, at a 50 percent discount, seven more of the exact same shirt and three more of the slacks. That was the birth of Mandy Manhattan. The colorful fabrics in her closet found their way to the thrift store and the street corner (a speedier, less arduous method of dispatch), and in marched an army of gray and black. Within the year, her underwear had been replaced, her sweaters, and even her shoes, although she already had some in black. Curiously enough, the only one who seemed to notice the change was her mother.

Amanda was fully aware of what she was doing; she was simplifying. She had started with her wardrobe. She reasoned that in a city of a million distractions, you had to simplify everything you could. She also reasoned that her dark clothes were balanced by her colorful personality. Or maybe the new clothes gave her incentive to become more colorful. She had also noticed that she wasn't the only one in New York to dress like this. She blended into the masses; she had done away with one of the million distractions. Before she was a fragile, pastel egg. Now she was a shadow, and she liked that.

Most of her friends were in the fashion industry. There were other designers, some managers, some marketers. She had a crowd of about 15 and a few nights a week they'd all go out for drinks or dinner. At the moment, Amanda wasn't dating anybody. She called it a self-imposed dry spell. She felt her last few love affairs had been out of convenience, not out of love, and maybe not even out of like, or at least not out of like-a-lot. The root of the problem was the crowd she was in. The crowd was incestuous. Everyone had dated everyone else: Jared had gone out with Kimberly, Kelly and Sutton; Kimberly had hooked up with Stephan, George and Peter; Kelly had gotten together with Walt and Stephan; George had paired up with Margo and Liza; Margo had messed around with Walt, Peter and Tasha; and Peter had seen Kimberly, Margo and Tasha. Amanda left herself off this mental list. She knew who she'd dated and vowed next time to go outside the circle.

She didn't have to be in a dry spell. She was attractive, intelligent, creative and had a great personality (this would be in her future online profile), and every day she felt some guys' eyes on her. But the thought of another date seemed like a chore. Amanda could see why some people chose careers over relationships, although that seemed horrible, too. She had met so many different types of men that she knew what she wanted. And she didn't want to settle, either, though that was a distinct possibility. She had done the "Sleep with him the first night" relationship, the "He's kind of a jerk, but there's someone wonderful inside" relationship, the "We really don't connect, but I'm getting used to it" relationship, the "This is a great guy and I can't believe he's breaking up with me" relationship, and the "This is such a nice guy, but there's something odd about the way he eats" relationship; none had worked. Amanda had been all over the love map (though it seemed without a compass), but now she knew what she wanted in a lover. More importantly, she knew what to look for in the beginning of a relationship, not to mention in the first conversation.

Love was a learning process, or rather, relationships were. And the reward, she knew, was well worth the emotionally tiresome education. She wondered how folks of generations before, who married at age 16 or something, endured and sustained their bond. As far as she could see, the ultimate achievement in one's life was going through it with someone else. But what happened to her generation? Long-lasting, fulfilling relationships were subservient to personal development. Her peers were more concerned with professional success and financial stability than meeting the right person. At least, that's how she felt this morning.

Wearing a thin gray shirt and black slacks, Amanda left her East Village studio. Her office was up in the 20s and the walk was a comfortable distance. There weren't any sensible subway options, but in harsh weather she sometimes elected to take the bus. Cabs were out of the question; there was something wrong with taking a cab just 10 blocks. Besides, when the temptation for a cab showed itself (like in a rainstorm), there were no cabs to be had.

The walk to work was more exercise than the walk back. It could have been the fact that she was going uptown, which is perhaps psychologically more difficult than going downtown. The path she took never varied. Once she had found a way she liked, she stuck to it. This enabled her to have visual checkpoints, something to make the journey have meaning. There was the block-long sporting goods store, the antique furniture showrooms, the movie theater, the park, and finally her office. She'd been tracing the same route for years now and she still never saw a familiar face. This struck her as odd, but she was thankful. She didn't need any more distractions.

Chapter Eight

BEING A designer was perfect for Amanda. She had trained at a local fashion institute and had learned how to make sense out of the sketches which she'd been drawing since she was a kid. Through the school's career placement center, she found work at a giant online company. She was at the bottom of the designer ladder but was able to witness how political the fashion industry could be. She wisely kept a low profile, making no allies nor enemies. Once she felt comfortable in this new fast-paced environment, the idea of leaving the company was made into a goal. She appreciated the experience but the atmosphere was frustrating. She wanted something a little more casual, a little more laid-back. She didn't see fashion as a world dominating force the way the others seemed to. She enjoyed participating in the industry ("fashion was her passion"), but she never did (or could) adopt the "our new line of Capri's must be worn by the masses" mentality. Fashion was like painting, she thought. A good painter didn't sit down at their easel and say, "Today I will create something that will move continents." What they probably said was, "I really love to paint, and today I think I'll do just that." Amanda didn't paint, but that's how she thought it'd go if she did.

When she'd had enough of "so and so big company," she began probing for new opportunities. One of the first options she found was the company she now worked for. Through a friend of a friend of a friend, she'd heard about this startup looking for new designers. Having only gotten her feet wet with her current employer, Amanda didn't mind the idea of a lateral move. She still had more to learn and the possibilities with a new company sounded like a step up anyway. After three interviews, the job was hers for the taking. She thought about it for two seconds and accepted the position.

The new environment was bliss (as much as work could be). There was no tension, no looking-behind-your-back paranoia, no snooping-around-what's-the-other-guy-doing jealousy. It was simply, "Here's your job." If everyone was competent and productive, then a day at work was almost pleasurable. Sure, there were bad days (Amanda knew that the rosy feeling would somehow balance out), but the definition of "bad" was different there. All "bad" meant was that some work was backed up or they had run out of bottled water. Amanda enjoyed the people around her; Margo and Stephan, the other lower-tier designers; Missy, the head designer; David, the other head designer; Lily, the boss. They had, for the most part, a stress-free attitude with the young designers, letting them make mistakes and grow at their own tempo, which was something Amanda wasn't used to. In her previous position, a mistake meant turned heads, fuming bosses and patronizing glances from everyone down to the interns.

This new company wasn't concerned with starting trends. They tended to produce what they liked (another unusual twist). Amanda sometimes wondered where and when trends started in fashion. She knew that celebrities could set one off, but the plain-Jane trends were more puzzling. Did every woman in the country decide one day to wear bright blue jeans? Who got everyone to wear black tights with jean short-shorts? Amanda wanted to know the answer.

Amanda arrived at the office fifteen minutes late. Right on time. She and Margo and Stephan worked in one of the corners of the office. They had an area approximately ten feet by ten feet that housed a desk for each of them, as well as a couch and a coffee table for creative thought. There was also a beanbag chair by the window that Stephan was currently sitting in. At her desk, Amanda had all she needed: sketch books, fashion books, a thousand plain and colored pencils, erasers, rulers, drawing guides, and a phone. The three of them shared a computer that sat upon a fourth, smaller workstation. In a "don't tell anyone, but I really don't like disco" way, Amanda enjoyed the fact that there was only one computer. She much preferred thinking and drawing without the glare of the computer monitor blinding her. The computer could be a distraction if you let it. The old-fashioned way of design, simply picking up a pencil and rubbing it on a piece of paper, was how Amanda liked to work. The designer's corner, often called "D.C.," had a slight separation from the rest of the office. They had some tall plants and a couple of cubicle walls dividing their area from the others. It was kind of like a clubhouse. Amanda was amazed how relaxed she felt there. Perhaps having the freedom to take a nap on the couch contributed to that.

Her job was rather simple. She and the others would receive instructions from the boss regarding what styles to design, and then they would design them. They would research previous trends, they would take into account non-fashion influences, and they would close their eyes and create. When they had compiled a handful of options to choose from, they'd hand them in and wait for the next assignment. Often (actually always), the bosses would want them to expand on a particular design; to flush it out in a certain direction. Revisions were a part of the deal. Even though all three of them griped about it, the results were often impressive. The way the head designers handed back material was saintly compared to the old company. Back at her first job, everything handed back (which, again, was everything) came with a "You know you're wasting my time" scowl or an "I can't believe you really thought someone would wear this" snarl.

"Morning, Mandy," Stephan said as he tilted his head from the window. He was enjoying a sunlit daydream in the beanbag chair.

"Hey," Amanda replied. "When'd you get in?"

Stephan, still in a daydream mood, answered, "About a half hour ago." He paused to reset his gaze out the window. "I woke up a little early and couldn't get back to sleep, so I figured a private Mush session was in order."

Mush was the name they had given to the beanbag chair. Sessions with Mush were, at first, more of a comic event. But the chair grew on them so much from the relaxation and comfort of the sessions, that it was no longer a laughing matter. It was on the same, more serious level as "I'm going to my therapist today."

"Well, I'll let you can get back to sleep," Amanda offered.

"Sleep?" Stephan echoed, "Nah! I'm merely in a state of rest. I'm ready to take on the day... and the entire Metropolis!"

With that, Stephan stood. He was only five feet tall, but he was flexing his body and swaying his arms in spirals so he looked like he weighed about two hundred and fifty pounds. He was doing his superhero imitation. Somewhere along the way, Stephan had adopted a superhero character. One day, pretty much out of nowhere, Stephan said he "couldn't finish his design by five, but SquidMan could certainly do the job, along with all the other's work." Margo and Amanda gave each other a look of confusion but didn't stop Stephan from his premeditated delusion, and surprisingly enough, SquidMan finished all of the tasks. SquidMan didn't show up too often, but he (or it) usually did at crunch time, and Amanda and Margo usually played along. Why not? It wasn't too distracting, and it even inspired them from time to time; "Hey Stephan, I'm really stumped on this project. What would SquidMan do?" (Though, it was true that this didn't help their image of being professionals.) Once, SquidMan inquired if there were any other superheroes in the vicinity. Amanda and Margo quickly and wisely responded no. They would enjoy his game and do nothing to discourage it (they knew better than to interfere with the creative process of an aquatic superhero), but there was no way that they'd participate.

"There is much to be done today," Stephan continued in his SquidMan voice as Amanda settled in at her workstation. "Opposing forces will try to oppress the small, tiny nation, but they did not count on me being here!"

Amanda didn't know what was so pressing today that required SquidMan to emerge from the Sea of Mortal Hope. Their current assignment was designing next summer's line, and they had plenty of time to do it. Maybe he was just bored.

"Great," Amanda offered, low-key enough so that Stephan would keep going with it. After some trial and error, that was how Amanda and Margo had agreed to handle Stephan. If they were enthusiastic and overly encouraging of SquidMan, then he (or it) would lose interest in his mission. However, if they downplayed the whole thing, then SquidMan would triumph.

Chapter Nine

AMANDA ORGANIZED her desk. Her goal was to complete an outfit by the end of the day. She could probably handle five or more rough designs, but to finish one was a better goal. When she dedicated herself to one a day the results tended to be of higher quality. Sometimes, though, the creative forces could inspire a dozen outfits and you had to go with it (she had learned not to suppress creativity). She surveyed her pencils and picked out a handful of summer colors and then went to the file cabinet to retrieve the last five summer catalogs for reference. Although she knew what most of them were, a visual hardcopy was always helpful. Amanda approvingly noted the balance of the seasons and the fashions that accompanied them. The cold of the winter balanced the warmth of the summer; the cotton shorts of the summer balanced the wool pants of the winter; the snug-fit cut-off shirts of the summer balanced the thick heavy sweaters of the winter; the dark, earthly colors of the winter balanced the brighter, cheerful summer colors. A voice prevented Amanda from getting too deep.

"You think this is a challenge for SquidMan? Wrong again, fool! I will set loose an armada of pain upon you!"

Stephan was at his workstation, madly scribbling drawings and notes. What made SquidMan so endearing was that he was so protective of Stephan (although he assisted others in times of dire need). Yet Stephan was hardly aware of SquidMan's super heroic shouts of bravery (at least that's how it appeared). SquidMan helped Stephan cope with the day (we all have our own coping methods, Amanda figured) and it seemed like Squidy had eaten a fully balanced breakfast, though it was more likely that he didn't get enough sleep. Aggressive creative behavior at this time in the morning usually came from sleep deprivation. Amanda was tempted to probe Stephan about it, but decided that it might wither SquidMan's machismo.

"You will pray for mercy! You will beg for mercy!"

"Wow, he's in high gear today," someone whispered in Amanda's ear. It was Margo, who was her usual twenty-five minutes late. Amanda was glad she was finally there. SquidMan days were lovely, but they were incredibly more special when she and Margo could share them together.

"Hey, there," Amanda chimed before noticing an odd scent. "Someone went out last night."

"Oh, is it that bad? Damn." Margo slinked into her chair and started moving things around.

"So what'd you do? Hot date?"

Margo paused just enough to reveal that the answer was yes.

"Ooh! So who was it?"

Margo took a deep breath. "Oh, you don't know him. I met him online."

"Well, tell me about him."

"Maybe we should get some work done first," Margo said, trying to change the subject. A date was priority news; it wasn't often that either of them had one. It was such a rare occurrence that they were both a bit shy discussing it (even though that's all they wanted to do). Once the door opened, though, it wouldn't close all day. Not even SquidMan could shut it.

"Okay, that's a good idea," replied Amanda, rolling her eyes. "So what happened? Who is he?"

"All right," Margo began as she sneaked a look at Stephan to make sure he was preoccupied. The last thing she wanted was to have him involved with her private romances. She and Amanda had a drilling process when it came to things like date-talk, so she started preparing herself. It required a cool tone of voice, relaxed breathing, and verbal precision.

"His name is Tim."

"Uh-huh."

"He doesn't like to be called Timothy."

"Uh-huh."

"Blond hair, brown eyes."

"Uh-huh."

"Six-foot-one, maybe."

"Okay."

"All-American."

"Uh-huh."

"Eagle scout."

"Alright."

"Climbed Kilamanjaro."

"Got it."

"Met him at a dive bar on the Upper East."

"Hmm."

"He was wearing a gray suit with a blue shirt, no tie."

"Okay."

"Works for some financial whatever."

"Yep."

"Lives on the Upper East."

"Hmm."

"Doesn't have a dog, but wants one."

"Okay."

"Insisted on buying my drinks all night."

"And?"

"No, didn't let him. Well, just a couple."

"Good."

"Definitely conservative."

"Hmm."

"Quite conservative, actually."

"And?"

"Gives money to political campaigns."

"He told you that?"

"Yeah, but I thought it was kind of cute, you know, that he would even tell someone that."

"Okay."

"When I first saw him, I thought it was going to be a long night."

"Right."

"But he started to grow on me, and I don't know what it was."

"Go on."

"So we had a bunch of drinks."

"Dinner?"

"We went to some falafel place next door."

"What'd you get?"

"Falafel."

"Him?"

"Gyro, no onions."

"Hmm."

"So drinks were great, food was necessary. Then we decide to go for a walk."

"Where?"

"Well… we were heading to his apartment."

"Hmm."

"Well, he wasn't doing it on purpose. It wasn't like that. In fact, he fully admitted we were walking in that direction and that maybe it was getting late, so we should say goodbye. It was kind of romantic, you know, saying goodnight on the corner of Lex and whatever."

"Hmm. Okay."

"So he tells me that he'd like to see me again, 'If that was cool.' He said, 'If that was cool.' I kind of thought that was cute."

"Yeah, that is."

"So then I gave him a kiss goodnight and caught a cab."

"You kissed him?"

"He was so nervous, he wouldn't have done it. And I kind of wanted to, and I was a little tipsy."

"On the lips?"

"Yeah."

"French?"

"No, I wasn't that tipsy."

"Got it."

"Yeah. So that was that. Got home at around one, fell asleep trying to remember the name of his first dog."

"Think of it?"

"Yeah," Margo nodded, "Junior."

Amanda and Margo had learned a lot about men together. Talks like these were enlightening; a continued study of the male species. Between the two of them, they had dated all sorts, from lawyers to musicians to computer programmers. They were slowly getting to the end of the line where they'd once and for all be able to solve male behavior. No one had ever accomplished that but Amanda and Margo were sure that they would, and perhaps even win some kind of award.

"Oh, one more thing," said Margo with a mischievous look. Amanda knew that this was the moment Margo had been waiting for. There was always "one more thing."

"Okay," Amanda said. "What is it?"

"Well." Pause. "Tim, you know, from last night?"

"Uh-huh."

"Well, he has a friend."

"And?" Amanda snickered in the back of her head. This was going to be good.

"And, well, Tim was such a nice guy that..."

"That what?" Amanda demanded.

"Well..."

"Stop saying 'well.'"

"Sorry. Okay, uh..."

"Margo?"

"I set you up on a date."

"You are no match for me, weakling! I will shred you to bits with all my might!" SquidMan was winning the battle (not that they'd ever seen him lose). It was the perfect distraction for Margo to hop up and disappear, letting her last words seep into Amanda's subconscious. A date? There was a lot of explaining to do. Did she really do that? You were supposed to ask the victim first; those were the rules. Maybe she didn't want to go on a date, maybe she was enjoying a life without dating. Amanda wasn't kidding anyone, but she was really trying.

"Okay, who is it!?" Amanda asked as soon as Margo returned.

"Are you mad?" Margo asked carefully.

"No, not yet. Who is it!?" Amanda shot back.

"Okay, he's just a friend of Tim's, like I told you."

"You met a guy for four hours, and you're setting me up with his friend? Are you nuts!?"

"I don't know. I just had a good feeling about it."

"You're saying that, after one night, you trust this guy Tim?"

Margo paused a moment and pondered the question. "Yeah, I do trust him. Listen, it's no big deal. If you don't want to do it, then you don't have to. I just thought of you when we were talking about being single and all of our single friends."

"What, am I the poster child or something!?"

"No, but he told me about this friend of his. He called him one of his best friends, and I thought that you might hit it off, maybe."

"Hmmm."

"Listen, he's going to call me today, and if you don't want to do it, then whatever, no big deal."

Amanda was feeling both annoyed and excited and didn't know which emotion to gravitate towards more.

"Okay," she said, calming herself down, "so when? What night?"

"Well, how about tonight?" Margo asked with a bit of a smirk.

"What!!?? I can't do it tonight!"

"Why not? I think tonight's good for his friend, too. And if all goes well, then maybe we'll go on a double-date this weekend."

"Are you drunk!?"

"No! Come on, it's a good plan."

"Listen, I'm not opposed to going on a date. But not tonight. Definitely not tonight."

"Why not? What's the difference between tonight and some other night?"

"Because tonight means today!"

"Yeah, well. Whatever. No better time than the present, right?"

"No way."

"Come on, just think about it. You never know."

"No, I *do* know. I don't want to do it tonight."

"What else are you gonna to do? Start blogging?"

"No," Amanda pouted, but then recalled something vital. "Wait! I have my cooking class tonight. Ha! I couldn't do it anyway."

Margo paused a moment and squinted her eyes just a bit. "And why exactly are you taking this cooking class?"

"Hello? So I can learn how to cook."

"Oh, really?"

"Yeah, so I don't have to get take-out every night."

"And that's the only reason?"

"I'm not taking the class to meet guys, if that's what you're getting at."

"Ah, hmm… okay. Whatever. So when's your class?"

"It's tonight. So there's no way I can go on a blind date."

"I know. You've already said that. What time tonight?"

"Seven," Amanda replied slowly, knowing that Margo would find some sort of loophole.

"Well, well, well, that'd be perfect. You could meet this guy right after work for a drink and then go right to class!"

"No way," Amanda said with absolutely no conviction.

"Yeah! And if he's a total dork, then you'll have a great excuse to leave! And if he's not a total dork, then you could either blow off your class, or quit while you're ahead, which will make the next time you see him that much better," Margo concluded with pride, then added for good measure, "And you'll make him wait."

Once again, Margo had defied the natural system of human behavior and changed the rules to her favor. Amanda wished that she could just abandon common sense like that and free her body and mind from her standard discipline. Of course she was going to agree to it; why the hell not? Margo was right; if the guy was a dud, then she'd have a legitimate way out. And the guy seemed to have decent references, or at least a good friend. They could just go to a crowded bar and there shouldn't be a problem.

"Okay, I'll think about it," Amanda said with a hint of disinterest (just how she wanted to sound).

"Great! Tim will probably call right before lunch."

"Fine."

"What are you guys talking about?" Stephan was back.

"Nothing. Just girl stuff," Amanda and Margo both replied.

"Hmm." Stephan knew he had missed out on something and he didn't like that. He vowed to find out what was going on by day's end (even if it meant getting down on his knees and begging).

Amanda sifted through the old summer catalogs. It was essential to review past patterns in order to not repeat them. But sometimes you could improve on an old idea, which was actually commonplace. One of her ultimate dreams, besides starting her own clothing line and becoming a world-famous tennis player, was to design something that was timeless.

Amanda had determined that a mere fraction of a fraction of fashion had remained constant over the course of history. If you wanted to talk about a long-lasting item, talk about the sandal. Whoever invented that, thought Amanda, was definitely near the top of the fashion hierarchy in heaven. He probably had the inventor of moon boots getting him coffee every morning. Coming up with timeless fashion would be amazing for her now, and in the afterlife.

She spent the rest of the morning hours tooling around with some sketch ideas. By mid-afternoon she hoped to have some solid direction for the outfit, but the morning was for brainstorming. Through the motions of a designer's life, Amanda had learned that the most important skill to have was the ability to make decisions. Once you could do that, then the designs would follow. With all the options available (shorts, short-shorts, long shorts, sport shorts, Bermuda shorts, cut-off shorts, skirt-shorts), you had to make decisions. You had to pick one thing and go with it. If you thought you could handle a few ideas at once then you were wrong, and you'd find out when the room was spinning at the end of the day and your sketchbook was blank. Amanda had learned the decision-making secret from an old teacher (perhaps the best lesson she'd ever learned). Amanda's decision was made after about a ten minute complete daze: summer slacks and a casual top.

Perhaps the slacks decision came from the underlying thoughts of a blind date; cover up those legs. As for the style, she could go with pleated, Capri, drawstring, elastic-stretchy, zippered. She thought a stretchy waistband style would be best. Simplifying the dressing (and undressing) process was always beneficial. She decided to go with a full-length, almost bell-bottom look. That would be it; she'd think of the shirt later. She started sketching some ideas based on that criteria, and by noon she had about twenty different designs down on paper. They ranged from loose fitting to snug, from a 1970's look to a modern look to a 1970's modern look, from extremely girlish to rather handsome, from six pockets to one to none. She loved her job. Every sketch was in a different color, enabling her to envision what might look best with any style. Amanda enjoyed the fruity summer tones and lived vicariously through them. After surveying her morning designs, she knew she wanted to go with a dark peach. on paper. They ranged from loose fitting to snug, from a 1970's look to a modern look to a 1970's modern look, from extremely girlish to rather handsome, from six pockets to one to none. She loved her job. Every sketch was in a different color, enabling her to envision what might look best with any style. Amanda enjoyed the fruity summer tones and lived vicariously through them. After surveying her morning designs, she knew she wanted to go with a dark peach.

Chapter Ten

AMANDA KNEW the person calling was Margo's new beau. It was just after 12pm and the red dot on the phone was blinking in sync with the subtle ring. Margo looked down, studied the flashing light, then glanced at Amanda with raised eyebrows. It was amazing what you could communicate with facial gestures. Amanda simply nodded her head, whereupon Margo snatched up the receiver, much like a snake striking at its victim, and greeted the caller. What followed were a series of "Yeps" and "Uh-huh's," ending with an "Okay, great, talk to you later." Amanda tried not to appear interested in the discussion, forever playing it cool. But this time she couldn't hold it in. (Had she waited, Margo was prepared to hold the information all afternoon.)

"Okay, so what happened?"

"Well," Margo began slowly, as if she was in some old snail's-pace Western, "it seems like you got yerself a date, little lady."

Amanda was silent, already starting her mental preparation.

Now back to normal speed, Margo was excited. "Well, hello? Aren't you psyched?"

"Ah, yeah," Amanda began. "Yeah, we'll see, I guess."

"You're psyched! This guy is going to be cool. I just know it."

"Yeah, we'll see." Amanda tried to sound enthusiastic, but she really didn't have much confidence in this type of dating system. "So what's his name?"

"Jesse."

"Jesse," Amanda quietly echoed, "I don't think I know any Jesse's."

"See? That's a good sign! Maybe one will be enough."

51

Or maybe one will be too much, Amanda thought, although intrigue was starting to maneuver through her nerves.

"You're to meet approximately eleven blocks away at the Boomer Bar."

"The Boomer Bar? What!? Are you kidding me? You know we never go there. That's not our crowd… or our generation!"

"Easy, easy. I know you're nervous and I know the bar is lame, but it's a good meeting spot and it's pretty equidistant, so why not? You're meeting him at 6."

A starting gun fired in Amanda's head; the countdown had begun. She knew it was normal to feel nervous, but she went from nervous to anxious to terrified then back to nervous before Margo could continue.

"He already knows what you look like. And Tim says he's like six feet tall, with short red hair and a suit. Of course, everyone there will be in a suit. But there's the red hair bit, so I think you'll recognize him."

Amanda paused before responding.

"Red hair?"

Her position had suddenly changed; curiosity had pushed aside fear. Amanda couldn't recall ever dating a redhead. Maybe this could be exciting. There was something about redheads… they were like a different breed of humans.

When Amanda was satisfied with her basic design of the day, she took off to grab some lunch. Most days she'd leave with either Margo or Stephan or both, but today she was on her own schedule. Often they would bring lunch back to the office and eat at the coffee table, or if it was a light lunch, just sit on Mush. (When it was crunch time, they'd get delivery.) Amanda wasn't incredibly hungry, though; she usually wasn't until the evening. Her body was accustomed to the "tiny breakfast, small lunch, decent dinner, couple of drinks" diet.

Not sure of what to eat, Amanda walked around for a while. If anything, at least she'd get some exercise. It was one of those eighty-degree days when the New York humidity had forgotten to show up, making the walk all the more refreshing. She finally came up to the Happy-Salad-Pizza-Bagel-Deli and got a turkey sandwich on wheat bread with shredded lettuce and mustard. She then made her way to the small park around the corner and found a mostly empty bench. She grinned at her five-dollar lunch. In New York, that wasn't such a bad price.

She finished up and, on a post-turkey high, let her thoughts drift. Staring blankly into the sun-scattered trees, she saw herself meeting a redhead named Jesse. He was tall, handsome, and had a beautiful body. She arrived at the bar and he cleared three bar-stools for her, somehow convincing three others to abandon their seats. She graciously thanked him and sat down, and her drink was already there; he knew what she liked. He asked her many questions about herself and could eventually finish her sentences for her. He spoke of his life, what he believed in and what was worth fighting for. He was a real man. He'd make a wonderful father and a devoted husband. He paid such close attention to her and she felt like she was the only woman in the bar. It was finally time for her cooking class, but she didn't feel it was so important anymore and she let it slip out of her mind. They ended up going back to her place, which she had just cleaned that day, and talked about silly things over a couple of drinks. He then had her sit down on the couch while he cooked her favorite dinner: pan-seared salmon in a lemon-dill sauce, grilled asparagus, and roasted new potatoes. And then, for dessert, he spoon-fed her chocolate ice cream while massaging her scalp. There was soft, romantic music playing and candles creating intimate shadows… she couldn't imagine being more relaxed. But then he had to leave. He wanted to stay, and she wanted him to stay, but he didn't want to rush into anything. He stood in the doorway and they embraced. The embrace grew into a long passionate kiss, but the kiss was so strong that her dreamy date never made it out the door. They had sex twice that night and once in the morning.

Amanda awoke to a homeless man standing before her, jiggling a small coffee cup full of change. It took her a moment to come out of her fantasy and shake her head no. He walked on, leaving her to decide whether she should return to the office or continue with day two of the wonderful redhead adventure. Reluctantly, she determined it was probably time for work. At least she'd quit while she was ahead.

Finding your dream lover, Amanda had figured, was not something you could just go out and do. It had to happen naturally. This was all good news, though; sometimes it's easier when things are out of your control. She knew other women sometimes tried to trap a guy into a relationship via sex or over-attentiveness or whatever. That wasn't the way she operated, but she could definitely relate. Amanda wasn't so keen on the man's perspective but knew there had to be some kind of balance. She'd already determined that all the guys that women called "jerks" probably balanced out all the women who tried to sabotage men into commitments. But were men desperate to have a loving woman in their arms? She didn't know the answer to that. She assumed that the answer was yes, but she hadn't seen much proof of that. There were, as she had witnessed, many "normal" men out there looking for comfortable relationships, but they never seemed to give out that aura. And the men who did make that obvious tended to be dorks. Amanda knew there was much to learn, but she had already spent too much time thinking about it today. It was probably spawned by her blind date. What kind of man was this guy Jesse going to be? Would he be the "Desperate to have a girlfriend" type, or the "Why does he keep staring at my breasts?" type, or the "I'm a jerk because I've been conditioned to avoid meaningful relationships" type, or maybe (and hopefully) the "Down to earth, normal" type (the type that didn't need to be defined as a "type").

Amanda returned to her desk in a daze. Too many thoughts had interfered with her meager lunch. The truth, though, was that she was nervous about the blind date (she couldn't believe she had agreed to it). Margo was gone, probably getting lunch, but Stephan was once again relaxing on Mush, gazing out the window.

"What's up, Stephan?"

He was slow to translate the question, but started nodding his head. Amanda wasn't sure if he'd finally understood something that'd been on his mind for days, or if he'd finally understood the meaning of 'What's up?'

"Oh, Mandy, it's such a small world we live in."

"Are you hitting on me again?"

"Do you often hear something like, 'My friend from high school met this guy from Russia who knew this gal from the club who worked with twin brothers at a museum, one of whom dated this divorcee who modeled for us last fall'?"

"Umm… not so much?"

"There must be a solution, an answer. Something that explains this sort of phenomenon. Something better than, 'It's a small world.'"

"Maybe you can think of it," Amanda proposed, to which Stephan raised his voice.

"That's what I've been trying to do!"

"Any luck?"

"No."

"You know, maybe you should, and this is just a suggestion, just find the answers that are a little more attainable."

"And just give up on the essential ones!?" asked Stephan in mild disgust.

"I wouldn't call the 'Small World Phenomenon' essential."

Stephan thought about it for a second. Amanda had a good point. "Perhaps you are the wiser of us, fair lady of the south." Stephan rose from the chair named Mush and gave Amanda a sincere bow. "It is time for lunch." With that he glided away. No wonder his brain was working on fumes; he hadn't eaten all day (nor had he slept the night before).

Motivation hadn't surfaced yet, so Amanda just started doodling. It was a simple way to warm up the brain (although it wasn't thrilling to have the head designer sneak a look and find a couple of kitty-cats dancing under a rainbow). Just as she felt some inspiration coming on, Margo returned from her lunch hour.

"I know you didn't have much for lunch, but please, please, don't eat any more pencils." Margo quickly summed up the situation and continued like a concerned mother. "They're just not good for you."

Amanda smirked. She was thankful to have friends who helped her see the enormity, or non-enormity, of many a crisis. And it wasn't as though she was having one, but Margo could probably tell that the blind date was lingering in her motor skills department.

"But you already know that. Don't you, sweetie? The last time you had some, I believe it was last July, you treated yourself to some tantalizing summer colors; yellow, orange, cherry red… but then you ended up sick for three days. We don't want that to happen again, now do we? No, we don't."

"Okay, okay, okay, I get it. I won't eat any more pencils."

What Amanda was really saying was that she'd stop worrying about the blind date and get some work done. When she was a child and cut herself or got a boo-boo, her mother would always start talking to her about ice cream, and it always worked.

Chapter Eleven

AS THE afternoon evolved, Amanda tried to focus on her designs but became more entrenched with her mystery date. She couldn't help but look at the clock every ten minutes and watch the day ticking by. Margo snuck her an occasional look, always wearing a tight-lipped grin, which Amanda would promptly return. Across the room, Stephan had finally succumbed to his exhaustion and let SquidMan finish the day for him. He had forgotten about the morning's girl talk so at least Amanda didn't have to deal with that. For the most part, the office was uncomfortably quiet all afternoon. The only energetic moments came from Squidy. Twice he jumped out of his seat; once to issue an ultimatum to the evil sketching demons, and once to declare that the world would soon be safe.

Every time Amanda felt the thought of the date entering her consciousness, she started sketching something. She was meeting the guy at 6pm, but she'd probably be done with work at around 5pm, so she tried to come up with a plan for the hour in between. But even that made her uneasy because it always led to the date. However, despite the pseudo-romantic distractions, she had somehow thought out her daily design.

Her loose slacks with a zippered back pocket and snug, thin-strapped top went well together. She finished the basic black-and-white outline just after 4pm, and then it was time to color it in (always a fun activity). She photocopied the black-and-white sketch so she could apply several color schemes to it. By 5pm, she had settled on two. The first was a dark peach and the other consisted of black slacks and a gray top. She was happy with both but had a fashion instinct as to which her bosses would choose. If the company only sold clothes in New York, then it'd be the gray-and-black design. But they outfitted people from the Midwest to the Far East, so dark peach would probably be favored (and it was, after all, her first choice).

Stephan jumped out of his seat for the last time, apparently content with some recent conquest. Margo also got up from her desk. It was time to go and Amanda, in her day of work and worry, had not come up with a plan for the next hour. She was hoping that Margo would keep her company.

"I bid thee farewell," announced Stephan, who was already walking away.

"See you tomorrow," called out Margo, then looked at Amanda. "Amanda, darling," she began in a deep British accent, "are you going to be alright, dear?"

"Yeah, I'm fine. I'll be fine. Just a little nervous, I think."

"It's good to be nervous, darling. But I wouldn't worry so much. It'll happen as it will."

"I know. You're right. What are you doing now?"

"Why, I'm off to me flat," Margo responded, then quit the accent and sat back down. "Do you want me to stay for a while? You're not supposed to meet until 6, right?"

"Yeah."

"Hmmm. Probably a little too much time to think it over, eh?"

"Yep."

"Sorry, sweetie, but I gotta go. Wish I could stay, but relax, go and have some fun. The guy might be great, or the guy might be lame, so don't worry about it. You'll be fine."

"What do you mean, 'The guy might be lame!?'"

"Whatever. You know what I mean. He's definitely not going to be lame. He's going to be totally cool."

"Alright, just go. I'll tell you all about it tomorrow."

"I'm counting on it," Margo said as she grabbed her things and left.

Amanda would leave at 5:45pm, so she had about thirty-five minutes to kill. She rested her head on her desk and closed her eyes; she would just wait there, she thought. She tried to fill her mind with thoughts of her cooking class; something stress-free that she could look forward to. Even if the date was a dud, then at least she'd have her class. Her positive mind power then came back. This guy wasn't going to be a dud. She was going to have a really good time and that would be that. And if so, then maybe she'd see him again. Amanda let those and a hundred other thoughts invade her while she waited silently and still. Then she wished it was time to go. The thinking bit was getting to be too much. When she looked at the clock for the seventeenth time, it was finally 5:45pm.

Amanda walked with determination through the rush-hour pedestrian wall, her body was like a bulldozer. She felt good and ready for what was ahead, her anxieties fading with every step. The Boomer Bar was packed, as it usually was at happy hour. Amanda may have been the only one without a suit on but she paid no attention to that. She found an opening at the end of the bar and shimmied into it, giving her a clear view of most of the drinkers. She slowly panned her head, scanning the crowd for redheads. As she was finishing her first search, she saw him. He was at the opposite end of the bar, doing his own scan. Their eyes met and he smiled. She smirked. Oh boy, here we go. He was definitely cute, at least from a distance, so that was a good sign. But as he gathered himself and made his way over, she noticed something strange about his movements. It seemed like the people he walked by were glaring at him.

"You," he began, stretching the "oo" sound, "must be Mandy."

He's drunk. Great. "Hi," Amanda replied uncomfortably, not quite sure what to say, but sure that she wanted to leave.

"I'm Jesse," he slobbered, emphasizing the "Jess."

"Yeah, I figured you were," Amanda returned, wondering how to make an exit.

"You wanna drink?"

"Ah, no, that's okay. You know, I don't really feel…"

"Come on," he urged, just as the bartender noticed Amanda didn't have one.

"Drink?" the bartender asked.

"Ah, sure." She didn't feel strong enough to say no. "White wine, thanks."

The bartender fetched her drink and placed it on a napkin in front of her. "On your tab?" he asked Jesse, who nodded without even looking at him.

"Cheers!" Jesse declared. "To new friends!"

Was this guy for real? Amanda couldn't believe she'd spent most of her day stressing out about this. She figured it served her right; a tiny bit of punishment for being consumed by it. The date turned out to be nothing like she expected, even though she'd drawn up a dozen different scenarios. She was thirty feet from the door.

"Cheers," Amanda whispered, taking a sip from her wine. Then she thought she might as well have some fun. She knew she'd never see this chump again, so why not go with it for a while.

Amanda amended her "cheers," this time in a grandesque voice. "A toast to everyone! Big and small, old and new, smart and dumb, and to you!" She surprised herself with not such a bad poetic toast (she'd have to remember that). She even took Jesse by surprise, leaving him temporarily speechless and perhaps a bit stunned.

"Yes, cheers," Jesse softly agreed. Amanda wondered if Jesse was now afraid of her.

"Cheers to strange encounters and close encounters, bringing us all together!" Amanda was starting to enjoy herself. Maybe this was a game show somewhere. "Big Toast" would be it's name.

"Yes, cheers," Jesse agreed again, but was not sure what to make of this woman. He'd had a solid strategy for this date, but it kind of disappeared.

"A toast to the beginning, and the end, and to all in between!" Amanda declared, catching some other folks' attention.

"Cheers," Jesse offered. With every toast, she was wearing down his drunken verve.

"A toast to the bottom of the glass, a mysterious sight, may it never be seen!" Amanda thought she might be losing her edge.

"Salud," replied Jesse, raising his glass in the air. There was a bit of silence after that. Amanda wanted to leave and Jesse wanted to drink. He spoke up right before Amanda could give her departure speech.

"So you draw fashion?" He barely got the words out.

"Uh-huh. I draw lots of fashion," Amanda replied.

"That just sounds really cool," Jesse managed. "So how do you get the ideas?" He sounded like he was reading from a pamphlet.

Amanda had had her fun and now it was time to go. She looked at her half-full glass of wine and then shifted her gaze to Jesse, looking at him straight in the eyes. "Jesse, I'm sorry, but I've got to go. I have a class this evening and I don't want to be late." Sometimes the choice between self-improvement and social disaster wasn't so easy to make, but it was right now.

"Oh," Jesse said, kind of surprised. "Okay, yeah, I think Tim told me that or something."

"I'm sure he did. Well, it was nice meeting you. Thanks for the drink," Amanda said as she started walking away.

"Hey, wait!" Jesse called out. Oh boy, here we go again. "We should do this again some time. Maybe I can have your phone number or something?"

Amanda knew her phone number wasn't going to end up in his hands, but she decided to use a proper brush-off technique for this situation. "Why don't you give me yours?" she asked assertively, not allowing a rebuttal. He paused for a moment, not sure if that was a good thing.

"Yeah, sure, sure. Let me write it down," he said as soon as he could determine that it was a good thing for a woman to have his phone number. He got a pen from the bar and sloppily jotted down his name and number on a napkin. "Okay, here," he said. His hand was shaking as he handed it to her.

"Thanks, Jess. It was nice meeting you," she lied, though she made her voice ambivalent so he wouldn't know it.

"Yeah, definitely," he replied, but by then she was halfway down the bar with the exit door shining like a beacon of freedom. The mobbed bar was full of men, and their eyes paid close attention to her as she maneuvered through. As she approached the door, she saw that a group of guys were blocking it. She excused herself and slipped between them, feeling their stares up and down her body.

Rush hour traffic had mostly scattered as Amanda took to the streets. The midtown breeze helped wipe away the horrors of dating and all the men involved. If only she could create the right man. She had no problems with cotton, wool, silk, or any synthetic fabric, so why couldn't she do it with men? She'd make him six feet tall, maybe six-two. He'd have a strong physique, but wouldn't be too big. He'd have the capacity to be ten pounds overweight, but no more than that. She couldn't decide on his hair, but narrowed it down to either blond or brown (one red head was enough for now). Amanda was beginning to look forward to the male creation process when she realized that she'd forgotten one essential element: The brain.

She needed the perfect brain. She needed one with a sense of humor, with kindness and fairness, with strength and sensitivity, with complete and uncompromising love, faithfulness, and devotion for her whenever she wanted it. She'd give him a servant's mentality; he'd be there for a mental challenge when called upon and he'd stay dutifully silent when ordered to do so. He wouldn't need to engage in any male-bonding activities, and at her request, he'd leave her alone or go out and get her treats.

Designing the perfect man was an age-old fantasy, but as Amanda walked confidently to her class, she thought she just added some finer points to the blueprints. She knew that her super-male creation would never be, but she held on to the hope that he already existed and that maybe one day she'd find him. The world just had to have more to offer than drunks and players.

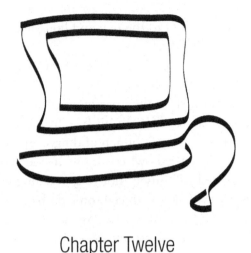

Chapter Twelve

AN UNBEARABLE ray of sunlight seared through the window, slowly cooking two motionless figures on the king-size bed. Clyde Casino hated himself every morning when he'd forget to pull down the shades the night before. He rolled around until he couldn't take it anymore. He was starting to sweat, and combined with a raging hangover, the feeling was horrid. He carefully got out of bed and tried to focus. When Clyde remembered where he was, he moved to the window and pulled down the shade. In the corner of his ear, he heard his cell phone ringing. After a sigh and a circus clown effort, Clyde finally found it under the living room couch and said hello. It was a woman named Claudia Vixen (at least that's what she called herself) who Clyde had slept with a few weeks before. After a series of "Hmm's" and "Uh-huh's," Clyde finally said, "Sorry, no can do tonight," and hung up. It was something he'd love to do, but yet something he didn't want to do. At least, not anymore. Shaking his head, he looked back towards the bed and saw only a long mop of hair; he had forgotten her name and just about everything about her. Did she like Chinese food? Yeah, maybe Moo Shu.

He didn't have to be at work until 9; that is, if he felt like going. He didn't really have to go at all. But lying back down on that hot skillet was the last thing he wanted to do. So instead he threw on some clothes and walked to the deli and bought an iced coffee, his standard summer breakfast.

"Rough night?" Deli Guy asked him. Clyde might have answered in the affirmative.

When he returned to the apartment, the previous night was starting to come back to him. In his bare living room there were a few empty bottles of wine, a bunch of dinged-up beer cans, a glass bong, and a big kitchen bowl coated with double-fudge brownie mix. Clyde nodded to himself, not fully recalling what happened, but aided by the evidence, deduced some probable activities.

The only furniture in the room was a small, mangy, uncomfortable couch and a scratched-up side table. There was a portable radio in the corner with a handful of CDs splayed around it, and next to that was his computer. At times he was amazed, at times disgusted, that a multi-millionaire lived like this. Surely, he could be in some five-bedroom penthouse anywhere in the city (as long as he could sneak by the co-op board), or a sweet country spread in Jersey, or on his own private yacht. But for some reason he just couldn't leave this small, relatively unfurnished one-bedroom apartment in Chinatown. Clyde was okay with this, though. After all, he only slept there; most of the time he was either at work or at play.

Clyde sat on the floor with his back resting against the couch and sipped his coffee. He found a half-smoked cigarette and lit it and debated whether or not he should take a shower. Normally, an early-morning shower would be out of the question, a complete waste of his time. But after an epic night on the town, which last night clearly must've been, he thought he'd spare the office his smelly memories. The coffee helped charge his brain. It did not, however, clean either of his two towels, so he picked the one without the suspicious stains. After a five-minute rinse (he didn't want to go overboard), he dried off and got dressed. Whoever it was in his bed was still there and hadn't moved. Clyde was bored and didn't want to stick around (his apartment wasn't outfitted for sticking around), so he spoke to the limp figure, "Just close the door behind you when you leave."

She was just another one-night stand (though one who managed three impressive bong hits). Clyde knew her type. Clyde also knew all the other types out there; he had slept with them all. There was only one kind of woman that had eluded him and Clyde knew that if he ever found her, then it just might be his final conquest. This woman had the potential to change him into someone stronger, smarter, and more powerful, and maybe into someone who didn't need to sleep with every female in the city. This woman had a deceivingly simple title, too. (Perhaps to fool us men, Clyde thought.) She was the girlfriend, the mysterious girlfriend.

Clyde had never had a girlfriend, nor had he ever been in love. The longest he'd dated someone was approximately three and a half weeks, but even then it wasn't monogamous. Clyde was beyond content living a life devoid of emotional commitment and thought that was all he'd ever need. But then something strange happened.

Just a few months before, while the winter chill was subsiding, Clyde was busy with his usual "A Gal A Day" lifestyle. It was a Monday and the gal's name was Jasmine. Clyde had secretly dubbed her "Hot Pants" even though she wasn't wearing any sort of pants at all. On Tuesday he was with Linda (an older woman), and soon decided to call her "Hot Pants," too. Wednesday brought Jane, and she was immediately called "Hot Pants." After Jane, Clyde had forgotten their real names for about a five-week stretch. They were all "Hot Pants." It was during this time when it hit him. He didn't want any more cheap imitations; he wanted the real deal. He wanted his own "Hot Pants." He wanted her to be there every morning and every night. He wanted to say, "Hey, Hot Pants, do you want to go see a movie tonight?" Or, "Hey, Hot Pants, do you just want to stay home and get delivery?" Clyde could not deny the feeling. He wanted a girlfriend.

The offices of TheLoveliestPlaceAround were on Broadway and 21st Street. Clyde walked into the building, greeted Doorman Wally, and took the elevator to the 19th floor. Fumbling with his key chain, Clyde finally found the one key he didn't recognize and unlocked the door with it. The lights were off but he could still see because of the incoming sunlight (causing him to cringe). He flipped on the lights and watched as the entire office lit up under nauseating fluorescents. There were a handful of desks with computers and a couch and water cooler off to the side. At the far end of the room was a door, and behind that door was his office. It was rare that he arrived at work before anyone else, so he was not sure of what to do. He sat behind his desk in his comfy leather swivel chair and spun around to take in the view. Clyde figured that would be a good activity until Marge showed up. He was very opposed to actually doing any work until 9 o'clock, because that's when work started.

From the 19th floor, the city looked harmless. Little people slowly gliding to and fro, cars and trucks bumping about, other executives doing the same thing he was doing; life didn't seem so bad. Clyde allowed himself to drift off into a philosophical dreamland, pondering how all the people and machines weaving in and out of each other were connected, if they were all parts of a grand device; a giant, functional, well-lubed complexity of science and nature. He had a gut feeling they were, but no human could ever come up with the right equation (perhaps a computer could, though). There must be some sort of connection, he thought. There were just too many things working simultaneously for there not to be. But then he went deeper into the thought; if someone like, say, himself figured it out, would he tell anyone? What if the world's population knew the answer to this mystery? Would they stop what they were doing? Would there be total pandemonium? Would there be world peace?

Just as Clyde was finishing up his thoughts, he heard a voice (unfortunately, not a deep omnipotent one, but a thin, tiny one). "Oh! Good morning, Mr. Casino. You're here early!"

It was Marge, the mother of the office, the savior of Clyde's schedule. She was in her 50's or 60's (Clyde wasn't sure), and she usually spoke with little exclamation marks.

"Hey, Marge. Yeah, I got an early start." Clyde spun his chair back, facing his desk. "What's the day lookin' like?" he asked, like he did every day.

"Lookin' good to me," Marge replied like she did every day. It was a ritual they began when Marge had started working there. Clyde had asked the question, she had given the response, he had politely laughed and told her that that was funny.

"I'll be right back," Marge said and disappeared for a while. She still had to boot up her computer and get organized.

Marge was great. Clyde knew that he'd be in big trouble if she ever left, he also knew that one day she would (by then, he hoped to be retired on a beach in Bora Bora). He didn't have to think too much when she was in the vicinity; he just had to do what she said. (He would never, of course, let her know she held so much power, though the fact that she was probably the highest-paid secretary in the city might've given her a clue.)

When he first needed assistance five years earlier, Clyde had hired friends of some of his employees. His first secretary was Natalie. She was an attractive brunette with a 'go to the gym five times a week' figure. Her appearance lit up Clyde's day, but her capacity to work was nonexistent. Clyde had seen this scenario on T.V., but never thought it would happen to him. Natalie was there for no more than a week before she and Clyde had sex.

After that, Clyde didn't feel comfortable with her right outside his office. He soon let her go, saying that he couldn't work with a lover. She didn't seem to mind and was out of the office that day. Their relationship (which was purely physical) dismantled a few days later.

Heidi was his next secretary, and they had sex on her second day of work. She, like Natalie, was not a marquee administrator, but she sure did look good. Clyde had taken the office gang out for "Hump Night" (Wednesday night) cocktails, and by the end of the night Heidi was sitting on his lap, feeding him Buffalo wings and singing Southern rock songs. No one in the bar minded the sexy out-of-tune blonde. They went back to her place and Clyde had the best sex of his life. The next morning, Heidi wasn't feeling so great and told Clyde that she didn't want to go to work. Clyde told her that that was okay and if she didn't want to work at all, then that was okay, too. She quickly agreed and they had sex again. That was the end of her career at TheLoveliestPlaceAround, but not the end of the relationship, which lasted four more days.

Clyde thought that he'd finally figured out how to make a good hire: Make sure they have the ability and drive to do the job. Veronica seemed to be bright and motivated during her interview and so she was hired. It was just accidental that Veronica was gorgeous. She worked extremely well for a couple of weeks, which gave Clyde a satisfied feeling. But after another "Hump Night" cocktail session, Clyde and Veronica found themselves in his sparse apartment, rolling around the dirty parquet floors with no clothes on.

Veronica stayed on at work for another few weeks but became bored with her duties and left, which was good news for Clyde, who had a difficult time working with someone he was sleeping with (though the lunchtime quickies were nice). After Veronica left, Clyde knew that he was closer to finding the secretary that he needed. He had learned a few lessons by then about whom one should hire and how one's relationship should be with them. He was confident that he wouldn't make another mistake. But with Bethany, Clyde learned his most valuable lesson: You're going to make mistakes.

Bethany was a bombshell with long blonde hair and a voluptuous body; a dream for every man. She showed up on time ready for work and actually did a fairly decent job. By day's end, however, she and Clyde were having sex on his desk. Afterwards, Clyde was half kicking himself and half in bliss. Bethany left him stunned. She was amazing. The next day he couldn't concentrate on work; she was only 15 feet away. At the end of the day, she came into his office with a smile and tray of fresh tropical fruit. Once again they had sex and once again she left him there tranquilized. This kept up for three weeks. In that time, Clyde got zero work done and was no longer sure what his company was called and what it's purpose was.

It was a Monday morning when he remembered that he had to make a living. When he saw Bethany (in a sheer white dress) he told her she had to leave, that he couldn't work in this environment, that he'd love to continue whatever it was they were doing, but that if they did, there soon wouldn't be a business (or an office) to do it in. She understood and accepted his reasoning. As she was leaving, she told Clyde with a smile that if he ever needed her again to just give her a call. (That gave him something to think about, and as it turned out, he did give her a call, and she did come to the office at the end of the day, and they did, once more, have sex on his desk.)

He found Marge online. Deluged with résumés responding to his simple ad, Clyde weeded out all the administrative riffraff, leaving him only but a few candidates. Clyde was going from one extreme to the other. After his recent spate of seductive, yet typically inexperienced candidates, he was now going to hire the best. He scrutinized every résumé, looking only for extensive secretarial experience. Marge's résumé was exactly what he was looking for. As soon as she walked in his door, he knew she was the one (and not only because he didn't find her attractive). He just had a good vibe. She was ready to work and knew what to do without anyone telling her. She was an instant success and created an environment for Clyde that he hadn't known could've existed. Marge made Clyde more productive, and for that he was thankful. The only problem, if it could be called a problem, was that Marge initially disapproved of TheLoveliestPlaceAround. But it only took a few minutes of convincing, and a whole lot of cash, before Marge opened her eyes and realized there was nothing really wrong with an online brothel.

Chapter Thirteen

CLYDE CASINO was born and raised in New York City. Growing up in his crowd, if you had a weakness it would be exploited and you'd have to run for cover. It was Darwinism in action. Clyde was never a muscle man and didn't know how to fight, but no one ever knew that. What he did have was attitude and intelligence. His attitude alone got him through puberty. As he started drifting from his neighborhood in his late teens, he discovered that most people he met had nowhere near the attitude he had. It was then when he realized his power. Clyde knew he could get his way whenever he wanted and no one would ever challenge him. But he didn't want to just be a tough New Yorker hanging on the corner drinking tallboys. He dreamt bigger than that. He wanted to take advantage of the gifts he had. It was no secret when he was growing up that he was good at "them computers." Luckily, Clyde had managed to show that computer geeks could be cool, and he'd proved that by holding some "hacking" seminars in the school library at lunch.

Clyde was also a closet porn fan. He loved porn. He loved photos, he loved videos, he loved gentlemen's clubs, he loved it all. His bedroom walls were smothered with large-breasted women with pleasurable expressions. He knew all their names, all their dimensions and what sexual positions they enjoyed the most. He had a vast pornographic film collection, ranging from the classics to obscure foreign titles in black and white. He kept tabs on most every porn star, current and retired, and knew their best and worst work. Clyde couldn't recall when he first ventured through the porn door, but he remembered as a child when a friend came over with a nursery rhyme book. The friend had asked Clyde if he had any of his own books, at which point Clyde pulled out an issue of *Big Mama's*.

In time, the initial thrill of pornography dissipated and Clyde became a passive connoisseur. He still used porn for fantasy but no longer obsessed about the women. To him it was a sign of maturity. He started seeing pornography as worldly, something vital to the human race. He started intellectualizing it. With this new mentality, Clyde reached a whole new level of appreciation for the industry, a place he was sure very few had visited. Clyde never had any trouble with his peers and pornography; enjoying it was seen as "cool." But eventually his friends couldn't comprehend or relate to his deepened appreciation, and so he began to keep it more and more to himself. He could no longer see porn the way the common man did. He was beyond that. But Clyde never thought to do anything with his library of knowledge because it was just a hobby, like whittling. He just thought that it could, one day, be entertaining cocktail-party chatter. But when it came down to Clyde choosing a profession, he had to look at his own traits and areas of expertise: attitude, intelligence, pornography, computers. It was then clear what he had to do.

An online brothel. There were sex sites galore out there already; there was a sex site for nearly everyone. But Clyde knew that an online brothel was the answer, the answer he'd been searching for since he was one. Clyde wanted to create a place where people could go from the comfort of their computers and have their most beautiful or dirtiest fantasies come true.

The first thing to do was change his name. His family name wouldn't be wise to use, so for the greater good of the ones he loved, he legally changed his name to Clyde Casino. He couldn't recall how he'd chosen it (maybe because he wanted to be called "C.C.," which never happened, or maybe because he enjoyed a similarly named seafood dish), but it was perfect. It instantly made him sound established and it boosted his attitude ten notches. It was a name with potential, a name he could grow into, a name that would live on after he was gone. And he really liked the sound of that.

The second thing he had to do was actually start the company, which was the hardest thing he'd ever done in his life. He needed hardware, he needed software, he needed operators, he needed money,. Clyde began with the hardware and software, buying or borrowing what he didn't already have so he could get his idea on a computer screen. Clyde did the front-end and back-end programming himself but had some friends design and build the website. Finally, he needed a few computers to handle all of the potential traffic. The website construction was mostly done on favors and friendship, but the hardware needed cash. For Clyde, there was only one safe place to turn: Mom and Dad. And so Clyde filled most of his time with chores; cleaning, errands, taking out the trash. Suddenly Clyde was twelve years old again but soon he had amassed enough cash to buy 'this really cool computer.' He hadn't yet told his folks the purpose of the new system. (And he wasn't sure if he was going to.) Clyde now had everything he needed to start TheLoveliestPlaceAround.com.

The first page of the site was the welcome page. From there, you could either enter the site or leave (it was the page you weren't supposed to go past if you were underage or offended by sexually explicit material). Once you officially entered and your payment information had cleared, you were ready to participate. The brothel patron could then see what sex operators were available and choose who he or she wanted to be with. The sex operator, via hi-def webcam, would then take the patron on a minute by minute love tour. The only rule was that there were no rules. Anything goes.

After weeks of developing, building, and planning, Clyde knew it was time: He had to hire some operators. After a delicious home-cooked dinner of roasted chicken and mashed potatoes, he went out into the city's nightlife. His first stop was The Jug Hut, a prominent Midtown strip club. Clyde walked in and felt an instant flash of depression. Ever since he'd expanded his fondness for pornography, what really got him down at these places was the clientele. They just didn't get it. But even though his personal appreciation was so much more advanced, he knew it wouldn't be appropriate to stand on a podium and lash out at others.

Clyde found himself a seat in front of one of the many stages and tried to enjoy himself. After about twenty seconds of the first dancer, he was enjoying himself. But that wasn't why he was there, and he had to keep reminding himself of that. He was scouting for operators. When he had woken up that morning, he just knew that the site would be successful, but a voice in his head told him that he wasn't prepared for that yet. A strip joint was the first place Clyde thought of to find help. After all, they surely knew what men wanted. Clyde was giddy all day, realizing that his job was going to be kind of fun (going to strip clubs and all). But when he arrived at the first club, it dawned on him that he might have made a mistake.

The Jug Hut had many attractive dancers, most of whom, Clyde assumed, would be perfect for the job. Sheila was the first private dance of the night. She was a petite woman with gigantic breasts who seemed to know what she was doing. After the dance, which was in a discreet area in back, Clyde proposed the idea to her, asking her if she'd be interested in something like that. She first asked if it was some kind of scam and if he was some kind of jerk, to which he responded "no" and "no" (and wondered if anyone would ever actually answer "yes"). She then asked how much money she'd make, to which Clyde responded that she'd pull in upwards of three hundred dollars a day. She said that she already made that much, to which he replied, in triumph, that she wouldn't have to leave home or take off her clothes (unless she wanted to). Clyde gave her his phone number, told her to call if she was interested.

"ONLINE COMPANY SEEKS CUSTOMER SERVICE REPS — EARN $300 A DAY OR MORE — NO KIDDING!" The ad went online that night. Clyde realized that perusing strip clubs was probably the wrong way to hire competent operators. Instead, he was going to let them come to him. With the advertisement, anyone interested could reply and he could weed out the jokers. The future operators didn't have to be voluptuous sexual machines (though it'd be okay if they were). They had to have the desire to please. That's all he was looking for.

Clyde received almost a hundred responses the first day. As the week came to a close, he had compiled a master list of forty-six qualified candidates. He then gave them all the true job description. After that, twenty-one were still interested enough to interview for the position. Sheila the stripper had also called and wanted to know more so the list grew to twenty-two. Clyde then set up a mass interview the following Sunday at a nearby bar. When that Sunday rolled around, Clyde didn't feel quite prepared to interview potential sex operators, but he was more than ready to turn his dream into a reality.

Clyde had never interviewed anyone (unless Sheila the stripper counted). He knew what he needed his operators to do, but didn't know what questions to ask. Clyde talked to his dad, who was very excited about TheLoveliestPlaceAround.com, as was his mother, though they still had no idea what the site was for. His dad told him that he should ask what their strengths are, what they'll add to the company, and what their hobbies are. He told Clyde to pay special attention to the way they answered and not to the answers themselves. Clyde understood this and started developing a clear idea of what kind of employees he wanted. He was looking for someone with several qualities, one being that they had an open mind; someone who wouldn't mind taking their clothes off for strangers and perform both traditional and untraditional acts on camera. The second quality needed was someone to be creatively compelling; one who could adapt to the clients' needs, one who could make any situation sexy. This second criterion was critical. If his operators weren't creative, then the clients would become bored. If the operators weren't compelling, then the clients would detect a fraud and never return. This was of paramount importance because Clyde knew that client retention would be the key to his company's success.

Beer Bellies was a dive bar. Clyde had first walked in to enjoy some suds at age fifteen when all the other local kids were starting to drink. That was a long time ago, but Clyde knew everyone who worked there and almost everyone sitting at the bar.

"Hey! The kid's found a new church!" Rodney yelled as Clyde walked in. The bar patrons, numbering about a dozen, erupted in laughter, during which Johnny D. belched, which kept the laughter going. "No girlfriend these days, kid?" joked Big Benny Blue-Plate Special. Clyde ignored the common question, but the bar added some more happy noise. They were all good people, and some were like family (albeit like the distant uncle who started drinking every afternoon at 2pm).

"Listen up!" Clyde commanded, because his attitude told him he could. The bar quieted down, sensing that Clyde had something important to say (although most were just looking for another reason to laugh). Clyde continued, "I've started a new business!" And then he paused, knowing this crowd and knowing that he had to wait in case someone had a wise-guy comment. There were none, though. In fact, whether it was due to Clyde's reputation as an entrepreneur or as one of the brighter kids in the neighborhood, he had silenced the crowd. They were listening.

Clyde continued. "This afternoon I'm interviewing twenty-two people."

There was still no sound save for the lounge music on the jukebox, which was a good thing because he needed everyone to cooperate and not do anything stupid to any of the interviewees. Clyde kept going, figuring that he was on some kind of roll. "And I've decided to hold all the interviews here!"

There were only twelve-odd boozers in "The Belly," but the excited roar sounded like a stadium crowd. Their shrine had been chosen for something noble by the smartest whip on the block. That was surely reason to celebrate. They howled and hollered and toasted with their mugs. They even started the "Yeah" chant where they all start whispering "Yeah" while simultaneously clapping their hands until the whisper turns into a yell and the hand claps turn into bar slaps and foot stomps, climaxing in a wild frenzy of shouts and percussion until everyone makes eye contact with each other and then in sloppy unison yells "Drink!" at which everyone chugs their entire beverage and slams their glass down on the bar. Clyde supposed it was the best news they'd had in a while.

Dom, the elder, was the first to speak (and the first to refresh his drink after the chug). "We're here for you, son. Just let us know what you need." The rest of the patrons enthusiastically agreed and waited for Clyde to speak again.

Clyde was pleased by the reaction. "I'm going to need the back table so I can have some privacy, and I'm going to need everyone to make these people feel at home."

The patrons enthusiastically agreed, some with nods of the head, some with, "No problem, kid," type of responses, and some with raised drinks and a chorus of "Cheers!"

Thinking on the spot, Clyde added, "And I need a volunteer." He paused and cast a glance about the bar, watching everyone get fidgety with anticipation. "Someone who's friendly, responsible, and who wants to help out."

At that point, everyone started talking at once, explaining why they should be the volunteer and forcing Clyde to make a decision.

"Okay!" he shouted, silencing the crowd once again. "I think, and I know you'll all agree with me, that since everyone seems to be interested, I'll have to go with seniority, which means that, Patty, if you're willing, I'd like you to do it."

At first there were mumbled sounds of disappointment, but it soon turned into sounds of approval as they realized that Patty was the right choice. She, like Dom, was one of the elders at Beer Bellies, and she was "untouchable" in the bar sense, which meant that she never had to pay for her own drinks and no one was allowed to sit on her barstool (or if someone did, they had to move when she arrived). She was just a bar-soldier when Clyde was fifteen, but had eventually earned one of the top spots.

"How about it, Patty?" Clyde asked. "I could sure use some help."

Patty looked at Clyde with pride, the way a grandmother would, and Clyde thought he saw a tear form. But that brief look evaporated as Patty snapped back to herself, the leader of "The Belly."

"The kid knows best," she assured her troops with a touch of comic arrogance. She looked at Clyde and winked. "Of course, I'll help you out, Sweetie. That's what I'm here for."

Chapter Fourteen

CLYDE HAD about twenty minutes to prepare. The back table stragglers at Beer Bellies graciously moved and Georgie the bartender wiped the table clean of all the stale liquor. Clyde pulled out a laptop from his satchel, put it on the table and powered up. He then took out the master list of interviewees and brought it to Patty. He instructed her to check off the people as they came in, to have them wait at the bar until their turn, and maybe offer them some water or a soda. Patty was with it, though, already knowing what to do and shooed Clyde away.

Clyde returned to the back table and waited. He thought perhaps these interviews should've taken place online so he could see the operators in action, but he truly wanted to weed out unqualified candidates before doing so. Even he, Clyde Casino, shuddered at the thought of going through a sex show twenty-six times. Sure, he could do it in maybe four or five days, but that would take a lot of energy. Clyde figured that meeting them and asking them to type out responses would almost be an equally effective way to judge. He looked back down at his questions then closed his eyes. After mentally reviewing what should happen in the interviews over and over again, Patty walked towards him, waking him from his trance.

"Ms. Katie DeTrecca is here," she said in a surprisingly comforting voice. Maybe Patty was a secretary in the past, Clyde thought. She seemed to have done this before.

"Thanks, Patty. Send her back."

Patty smiled and winked at him as she disappeared back to her spot at the bar. A moment later, an attractive young woman approached. He stood up to greet her. "Hi, Clyde Casino, thanks for coming down," he said, holding out his hand.

She shook it and responded a bit nervously, "Nice to meet you, too."

Clyde paused for a second, trying to recall if he'd just said, 'Nice to meet you," or not. "Please have a seat and we'll get started."

Clyde sat down opposite Katie and started the process. "Well, I'm glad you're still interested in the position after we discussed it's true nature."

"Sure, that doesn't bug me at all."

"Great. Now, before we get into the testing part of the interview, I'd like just to talk for a while and ask you some questions," Clyde said, not entirely sure what the questions were going to be.

"Sure," Katie agreed.

"Okay," Clyde started. "What are your strengths, and what do you feel you can bring to TheLoveliestPlaceAround.com?" Clyde felt out of character asking these questions, but he wanted to try it once.

"Well," Katie said and then paused, obviously not quite sure of her strengths. "I think I work well with people, that I'm easy-going and friendly, and people like to talk to me because, well, I don't know why, but it seems they do, and I think I'm a good listener and know what people are really thinking." Clyde noticed that she was turning a bit red in the face. "And I really like making people happy and…"

She stopped right there. Clyde waited a moment before he spoke.

"Hmm, well, that sounds good. It sounds like you'd do pretty well at this."

Katie looked as though she had something else to say, and Clyde realized, perhaps, that he had interrupted her. "Was there anything else?" Clyde asked, trying to make her feel comfortable.

"Well, yeah, I think so," Katie shyly answered.

"Oh, I'm sorry, go ahead." Clyde knew he was learning on the job, so he made a personal note to himself: Be patient.

"Well, it's just that, along with all those other things, well… it's just that I also really like sex." She was red now, and Clyde felt his face burn up a little, too. He supposed he should be prepared for comments like that; it was part of the business (another note to himself).

"Great," he said to no one in particular while nervously nodding his head. "So maybe we should start the testing part thing," Clyde stumbled, no longer able to make eye contact with this honest, attractive woman.

Clyde turned the laptop around so that the screen faced Katie.

"All right," he began, "we're going to do a practice run just with typing, okay?"

"Sure," Katie answered as she concentrated on the blank screen.

"You're going to be the operator and I'm going to be the client, and I'm going to talk to you, but you just type in your responses, okay? Just type what you'd say or what you'd do."

Clyde knew that this was the segment of the interview that would ultimately determine who was cut out for the position. He'd come prepared with a list of questions he was going to ask every candidate.

"All right… oh, first type your name at the top of the page," Clyde instructed.

"Done," she reported.

"Okay, here we go." Clyde paused, gathering his confidence and breath. "Hi, my name is Richard." He paused again, as he would between each line so that she could type in her response.

"I'm a wealthy man with houses all across the world."

Katie was typing furiously. Click, click, click.

"What do you look like?"

Click, click, click.

"What are you wearing?"

Click, click, click.

"I'm in town for one night and I'm feeling kind of lonely."

Click, click, click.

"Are you getting excited?"

Click, click, click.

"I want you to do things to me."

Click, click, click.

"Do you like doing that?"

Click, click, click.

"What's your favorite movie?"

The clicks stopped momentarily as Katie looked up at Clyde with a puzzled expression. She then resumed her typing.

"What do women really like?"

Katie paused again, but she was starting to understand the new line of questioning.

"Where do you live?"

Click, click, click.

"What's your favorite restaurant?"

Click, click, click.

"If you and a man and a trampoline were in a room together, what would you do?"

When she had completed her answer, Clyde spoke again. "Okay, so that's it! That wasn't too bad, was it?" he asked, half talking to himself.

"No, not at all," Katie said, and Clyde believed her.

"So are there any questions you have for me?"

"Ah, yeah, I kind of do."

"Okay."

"Well, one, what's the actual pay?" Katie asked in more of a business-like tone than a girly one. Clyde anticipated many different questions and had tried to come up with some convincing responses even though he knew that nothing was definite.

"The operators will earn a minimum of one dollar per minute for each minute they work."

Katie seemed satisfied with this answer. "Where are the offices?"

"Well," Clyde began, "I haven't set them up yet. Right now, they're in my apartment." He didn't mention that it was actually his parents' apartment. "But when we get off the ground, I'll be getting a space somewhere in the city."

"And you're sure of that?" Katie asked rather assertively (which Clyde kind of liked).

"Yeah, absolutely. But the operators will be able to work from anywhere they want, from the beach to the North Pole."

"Cool," Katie said.

"But again, we have to get off the ground first, but I don't think that it'll take so long. Is there anything else?"

Katie pondered something for a moment but then said, "Nothing right now, I guess."

"All right, great. I guess that this is the end of the interview, so... I'll review your performance test and... I'll let you know. Okay?"

"Great, sure, yeah, thanks," she said as she walked away, giggling while she did.

"Thanks for coming down," Clyde said, not knowing what else to say at the end of an interview. That really wasn't so bad, Clyde thought. One down and twenty-one to go.

"Brenda Brucer is here," Patty said, again waking Clyde up from his thoughts. He was beginning to like this job.

"Thanks, Patty," he replied with renewed energy. "Send her back!"

At the end of the day, after all the interviews (and a few cold beers), Clyde already had a clear idea of which candidates were in the running. He could just tell from the way they carried themselves (although he was also quite sure that Angie had aced the performance test even though she was so shy that she began to cry when her interview started). After reviewing the tests, most of his predictions were true, leaving him eleven solid candidates. Of the most impressive performers, there was Ms. DeTrecca, who answered some of the questions so well that Clyde had trouble sleeping. Sheila the Stripper, though she was a half hour late, also made the final cut because of some of her own unique responses.

Clyde made his callbacks and had everyone meet at a nearby park (he wanted to avoid Beer Bellies because he didn't want the local public to know his business idea just yet). Along with a few pizzas, he brought a handful of newly leased laptop computers with hi-def webcams, which was a big deal for Clyde because it signified that he was really going through with this.

When the group was settled on the grass, Clyde stood up and addressed them. "Okay! Welcome everyone! I'm glad all of you could make it on this beautiful day. What we're going to do is go through the basics of the company, and get everyone started on their own computers."

This was a surprise to a few in the group and they made some soft sounds of approval.

"The name of the company is TheLoveliestPlaceAround.com. The name doesn't quite give a hint as to what the company is, but that's exactly why we're called that. In this way, we can fly under the radar, so to speak, and reach more clients."

Clyde wasn't sure of this theory, nor did he think that everyone understood what he was talking about, but he kept going (the boss was supposed to be a little confusing anyway).

"TheLoveliestPlaceAround.com is dedicated to satisfying the needs of it's clients. That is our number one goal. We are here for them, we are here to serve them, we are here to satisfy them and all their dreams." Clyde paused a moment. "Is anyone lost yet?"

Thankfully, no one said yes. Clyde resumed, hoping to make his whole speech coherent. "In a little bit, I will teach everyone how to use their computer, but right now I'll explain what you'll be doing. All of you will be on the website under a working name. That is, you will come up with a new name. There are two reasons for this. One, because you don't want to give out real information about yourself, and two, this is a fantasy site; a real name would mean reality, not fantasy. Is this making sense?"

Mumbles of agreement.

"Now you can use any name you want. Have fun with it, come up with something cool."

Someone in the group spoke up (Clyde thought her name was Lisa). "Can we use our middle name?"

Clyde paused for a second. "No. The reason being is that it's one of your real names. This leads us to *who* your new name actually is. You are to come up with a new you: new birthday, new favorite ice cream, new hobbies. You are all going to do this and show me what you come up with. Again, the reason for this is to keep it all in the fantasy world. Your clients are not to know anything about the real you, not one little thing. Is this understood?"

Mumbles of agreement.

"Now, once you start communicating with your clients, which I'm going to show you how to do soon, not only will you be sexy on the screen, but every session will be recorded so you can save information on every client. This may be a bit confusing, I know. Does anyone know why?"

Mumbles of uncertainty.

"Because the more we know about our clients, the better their experience will be. You'll review your sessions and will take notes on each and every client that visits you. Every little thing they share with you: what their names are, what they do for a living, how old their kids are, their favorite food. Anything and everything, okay? That way, if so-and-so client visits 'Clarice,' for example, and had done so a month before and 'Clarice' had taken down notes, then 'Clarice' can look up so-and-so client in her files and already know something about so-and-so client, which will make so-and-so client feel really good."

Clyde caught his breath for a moment, allowing this information to sink into the group's consciousness.

"Another reason, which might be a part of the same reason, is that another so-and-so client recently visited 'Rebecca,' and 'Rebecca' was so hospitable that so-and-so client can't stop thinking about the experience and has told the world how wonderful it was. Now 'Rebecca' pleases many clients every day, so she can't realistically remember everything about every client, now can she? So that's why she takes notes!"

"Ahh's" of understanding.

"And imagine 'Rebecca's' so-and-so client visiting her again because it was the greatest experience of so-and-so's life, and 'Rebecca' doesn't remember him. How is so-and-so client gonna feel? That's why we take notes." Clyde caught his breath again, hoping he conveyed this policy clearly. "Now when the clients come to TheLoveliestPlaceAround.com, they'll have a choice of operators… that is, all of you. All they have to do is click on your name and they can visit you. Now, if they've already been with you before, chances are they'll go to you again. One of our biggest goals is to get people to come back. That's what'll keep this business running."

"What if I'm in the shower?" someone asked. Clyde couldn't tell who, though.

"Okay! That's a good question. What if you're in the shower? Or what if you're out shopping, or what if you're just not home with your computer? In that case, then your name on the website will be turned off. It will still be there, but it won't be lit up, so no one can click on it." Clyde stopped again to gauge the crowd; they seemed to be on the verge of becoming frazzled. He kept going to try to bypass the confusion. "And each of you, through your own computers, which I'll show you how to do soon, can turn your name on and off by yourselves. So if you have to run out for some groceries or you want to get soup dumplings or whatever, you can easily just log into the website and turn your name off. And then, when you want to work again, you can just as easily turn your name back on."

"Ooh's" of amazement.

"You will each earn about a dollar for every minute you work, just as long as you work a minimum amount of time every week, which I'll get into more later. And if and when things start to get going, I'll eventually get a medical plan together and some benefits for everyone." Clyde took in all the faces staring back at him. They seemed to be a bit overwhelmed, but pleased at the same time. "Is everyone with me?"

Nods of approval.

That was over five years ago. Clyde was now a hundred employees, a thousand women, and millions of dollars past that day. At TheLoveliestPlaceAround.com, he had set out to do one simple thing; to satisfy his clients. This simple idea with a simple computer and a simple group of employees had grown into a powerhouse.

But now, Clyde only wished that finding a girlfriend could be so "simple." He was the father of all players but he'd never had a girlfriend. Sure, he filled his time with other pleasurable activities, but now he wanted to know what it was like to have that one person. Someone you could talk to about anything, someone you could hang out with anytime, someone you could have wild jungle sex with, or if you'd prefer, you could just make love to.

Chapter Fifteen

CLYDE'S CELL phone started ringing again, waking him from another daydream. He had to scramble to find it even though it was right on his desk. It was Lulu Nice (at least that's what she called herself), a woman he'd slept with weeks before. After a series of "Hmm's" and "Uh-huh's," Clyde finally said, "Sorry, no can do tonight," and hung up. Although he was hung-over and tired, crazy upside-down sex was quite tempting. Clyde was really trying to do the right thing, though, for himself and for his new, "I want a girl-friend, not a sassy-ass sexpot," philosophy.

Secretary Marge scurried back into the office and handed him the usual piece of white copy paper upon which she had outlined his day. Like a helpful counselor, Marge always read it to him out loud so that everything made sense. "At one, you have lunch at Crimson's with Denise, Missy, Alison and Steve. At four, you have a conference call with Jimmy Seachin from Rising Productions. And at seven, you have class with Mr. Sebastian."

Marge finished and waited, just to make sure he understood; she knew that running such a large company was all encompassing, and that the little things could slip through his mind. Clyde stared blankly back at her.

"So why am I here now?" he asked, but more to himself.

Clyde spun his chair back around and faced the window again. He just sat there for a while, dozing in and out of daydreams, feeling relaxed but perhaps a bit lonely. His romantic life was different than most. When he thought about it, Clyde saw himself as a rock star and a professional basketball player and the President of the United States all wrapped up into one. The only thing that separated Clyde from them was that he felt he hadn't accomplished anything spectacular (like selling out every arena in the country).

Clyde had slept with more women than he ever could've dreamed of. For a stretch, when TheLoveliestPlaceAround was building momentum, Clyde was with someone new every morning and every night. He used to say that he was "on fire," and that "fire" still hadn't cooled down. The only thing that had changed was him. He was becoming more and more disinterested in that lifestyle. Sure, it was amazing having sex with some of these women (in fact, amazing wasn't a strong enough word), and when Clyde thought about it, he could never get past that point because it truly was amazing. But when he did manage to get past the comma to the "but" part, he was able to see a bigger picture, a picture where he was with just one of these women, and he was with her for a long time, and they were standing in front of a cute little white clapboard house surrounded by trees and grass and tweeting birds, and he was nodding with a sly grin that said, "That's right, baby. Don't cha know it?"

Unfortunately, that dream required one thing: A girlfriend. There'd been more than one occasion when Clyde went on dates with women who, he thought, had solid relationship potential. He curbed his sexual appetite so he could actually *try* to get to know them and he avoided the more sketchy spots where he'd normally take "other" dates. Not only did he get so bored that he found himself alone at the restaurant bar more than at the table, but he also had sex with them on the first night. It was after a few of these so-called "legit" dates when Clyde realized he was not like the average (internet Porn King worth over 30 million dollars) guy. Clyde figured that most of the women he dated weren't really interested in "this cool new technology that was coming out which will make the company run almost twice as efficiently" or that when he was eleven years old he had a pet rat. No, they were interested in other things. He had figured out that he was no longer human to a lot of people, that he no longer had hair, flesh, and bones. To them he was made of something else; something as light as air, and something as shiny as gold.

Clyde knew, though, that he was half the problem. He realized that he would have to drop his "Bad Ass" persona, let his porno-tycoon guard down and lose his "Who's Your Daddy?" attitude. He would have to be himself. That's not to say that he wasn't comfortable with being himself. He knew he was when he was at home, when he was talking to Marge, and many, many other times. But when potential women were sashaying about Clyde would turn up the attitude to full power. It was a natural instinct. But Clyde knew that as long as he did that, he'd still be getting more sex than a small country, but no one would really be able to get to know him and therefore love him for who he really was.

This evening's class was an afterthought action to meet new women, and perhaps a better way to make his country-home dreams a reality. Clyde was certain that his past "legit" dates had failed, at least emotionally, because of who he was; because of his celebrity status. At a random class in the city, Clyde deduced, he could meet women outside his circle of sex. The day after his last "legit" date (which was with a corporate lawyer named Eva who "dragged" him into the shower at the end of the night and kept him there until she'd emptied a jar of apricot preserves all over him), Clyde had asked Marge to find a good and proper class that he could take. She came back with five options; "These all seem to be very popular, Mr. Casino." He looked at the list with one question in mind: Upon which day do I want to meet my future wife? For reasons unknown, his gut answered, "Tuesday." That narrowed the list down to one.

To fill up his morning, Clyde tried to avoid the dreamer's trance and to keep busy with external stimuli. He read the paper cover to cover, surprising himself (and Marge), and learned something worldly. He checked out the sports section to see how the New York teams were faring. (He hadn't followed sports since his company's inception because there was not enough time, but being a season-ticket holder for every team, Clyde thought it was worth getting up to date.) He even tried to do the crossword (but he couldn't so he threw the paper across the room). A few more ladies called his cell phone; Lori Lovesweet, Julie Smoothie, Rachel Cones, Stephanie Licks, Gwenneth Garterbelt, DeeDee Delicious. They were all women Clyde had slept with weeks before. After a series of "Hmm's" and "Uh-huh's" and an occasional "Whoa," Clyde finally said to all of them, "Sorry, no can do tonight." And finally, after denying Tricia Tricksta a date, he turned the ringer off.

Marge knocked on the door at 12:30 and came into the office carrying a button-down shirt on a hanger. Clyde was finishing another random thought as he looked up.

"Your car is here," Marge began, "and you might want to wear this shirt." She paused for a second. "I think it'll go well with your jeans."

Clyde realized that Crimson's, his luncheon destination, was a rather elegant eatery and that a ripped-up 70's concert shirt probably wouldn't go over well with the maitre d' (even if Clyde *was* the President of the United States).

"Thanks, Marge. I'll try it on," he said, taking the shirt from her. Clyde kept some clothes in the office for just this reason, although he didn't know where Marge put them, nor did he buy any of them himself, nor did he really know what he had.

Chapter Sixteen

MANIACAL LIMO Driver dropped Clyde off at Crimson's. Clyde wasn't sure if the guy was trying to impress the Porn King or if he was just trying to frighten him. Reckless driving wasn't a new world to Clyde; he'd had his share of unorthodox car maneuvers, but he'd grown out of that stage by age seventeen. These guys who took him for hell rides were in their 50's (a bit old to have that youthful auto-angst). Clyde wondered if these guys still went to keg parties. Maybe they still liked to rumble.

"Mr. Casino, your party is waiting for you," the maitre d' announced as Clyde walked in. Denise, Missy, Alison and Steve, like happy workers, had all arrived early. Clyde joined the table, scanned the menu, and as best as he could, ordered lunch for everyone: steak au poivre, medaillons d'agneau, saumon au foie gras, et bien sur, pommes frites pour cinq. As the not-so-amused French waiter left for the kitchen, Clyde turned back to his guests and began the "Client List" dialogue.

The "Client List" was how Clyde always started out meetings with his workers and everyone knew it, which meant that most everyone was prepared to answer the question. When hiring someone new, Clyde stressed the importance of the "Client List," explaining how it was the cash cow of the company. The list didn't include every client that logged in. Rather, Clyde had developed a system in which the client couldn't be considered for the list until they had logged in three times with the same operator (if they logged in three or more times with different operators, they were considered to be company clients). It was the repeat customers that drove the company's revenue and Clyde let everyone know that (perhaps to a fault).

Denise was quietly eating her lunch amidst all the others' stories, waiting for her turn to speak. With so many employees, Clyde couldn't keep up with everyone's progress, but he knew that Denise had been doing rather well. In person, she wasn't quite the knock-out. But online, she let it all hang out. There weren't many operators whom Clyde would turn to for the occasional "fling," but Denise was one of them.

When the company was in its infancy, Clyde had never thought to indulge himself in his own creation. But as the company starting growing, the idea finally popped into his head. He was reluctant to cross that ethical line (nor was he hurting in the sex department), but after a wild night out celebrating the hiring of his 50th operator, he was home alone and feeling a bit randy. He booted up his computer and logged onto TheLoveliestPlaceAround for no other reason than to goof around. At that hour, only about a quarter of the operators were working (and he made a quick note to himself: More should be working during these tempting hours). Clyde monitored some of the operators and became enveloped by the voice and ass of Mona, who was working from her apartment somewhere in Denver. Her language was captivating, her energy was awesome, her rump was divine. She strung along some guy for almost thirty minutes before he disconnected. In the business, that was an extraordinary length of time to hold someone. It may have been a whim, or a primal urge, or the alcohol in his brain, but that was the night Clyde deviated from his path of righteousness.

Using passwords and tricks that only he knew of, he clicked on the name Mona, bypassed the 'approximate fifteen-minute wait' and went right into her room. The masses would have laughed at how inexperienced the founder and CEO of TheLoveliestPlaceAround was at his own game. Wearing red-lace lingerie, she began the dialogue, introducing herself and starting the small talk (which all the operators were trained to do). Clyde was proud that she was doing her job well, but he also had some serious anxiety; he didn't know what to do. It was both strange and embarrassing when it occurred to Clyde that the leader of the best online brothel, who'd had sex with a thousand beautiful women, was still an e-virgin.

He finally relaxed and started responding to Mona's questions; he was from New York, he was in his twenties, he didn't have a girlfriend, he was wearing jeans and a T-shirt. He also admitted that he'd never done this before. Clyde was consumed by the experience, and it hadn't even become racy yet. The small talk was a turn-on. He couldn't believe how much of a thrill it was. Without realizing it, he'd even become physically excited.

Word by word, Mona took him by the hand and walked him through the hottest fantasy he'd ever had. While quietly describing her turn-ons, she slowly slid off her clothes. She demanded that he touch her entire body, and let him know how good it felt once he did. She touched and played with herself, telling him how good it felt, working herself to a shivering orgasm.

When she settled back down, she announced that it was his turn. After telling him how she was going to please him in every way imaginable, she proceeded to. The level of passion moving through Clyde was unbelievable. He never thought that online sex could feel like this. Although he was half naked in front of his computer with the scent of sex abundant, he didn't care at all. He'd just had the best sex of his life. When he finally logged off, he'd been on for almost forty-five minutes.

Since then, Clyde realized that he could easily become addicted to that habit and it would somehow lead to the demise of TheLoveliestPlaceAround.com. That's when he decided that a little self-indulgence was acceptable, but that he'd also have to limit his interaction. The simple solution was that he'd have only one online mate at a time. That way, he wouldn't allow himself to visit all of his operators (which was shamelessly tempting). He determined that he'd stick with one operator for at least a week before being permitted to move on to someone else.

That was a few years ago, but Clyde had since lost his lustful obsession and had therefore dropped all of his personal restrictions. Now, only on a rare late evening would he check out the scene. A few months earlier he'd "hooked up" with Denise and she was quite good. Clyde had only been with her twice in that format, but she had made a lasting impression. Clyde always wondered if the operators knew of his delving, and ultimately came to the conclusion that they must assume he did. Looking across the table at Denise, his instincts were telling him that she was totally aware that she'd had sex with her boss.

Maniacal Limo Driver was waiting for him outside. Clyde reluctantly got in the car as it sped off and almost hit a bus. There were a couple of operators milling about the office when he returned and they laughed when he ripped off his button-down shirt. He sat back in his comfortable chair and immediately spun around toward the window. It was almost time for his conference call with Rising Productions, a company that owned a nationwide circuit of strip clubs. Clyde had agreed to talk to them to explore the idea of sponsoring some events for promotional purposes. Their clubs catered to some of the same markets, so a deal between them could be mutually beneficial. Today's call was to be just a 'break the ice' conversation.

"Good afternoon, Mr. Casino," Marge said as she wobbled into his office, again waking him from a daydream. "Mr. Jimmy Seachin from Rising Productions is on line four."

Marge didn't wait for a response as she exited his office. He looked at the phone while reaching inside to find his "Tough Guy" attitude.

"Jimmy Seachin? Clyde Casino! How the hell are ya? Ya there?" Clyde hollered into the phone.

"Yeah, yeah, yeah... I'm here, yeah... Jimmy Seachin here. How ya doing, Mr. Casino?"

"Call me Clyde, please. So what's goin' on? How's business?"

"I tell ya, it's fantastic. Our girls are the best. From Boston to L.A., we got the market to ourselves. You gotta come down sometime. New York's one of our best clubs."

"Sure thing, would love to."

"Just let me know and we'll take care of you. You'll get the royal treatment, I guarantee it."

"So what's up?" Clyde asked, as if he had some place to go.

Jimmy paused for a moment, nervous to talk real business. "Well, I'll tell ya, we think we have a lot in common, but in different places, and some in the same places, if you know what I mean. So we thought, hey, maybe we should, ya know, do some gigs together."

"Could do," Clyde said, "Could do."

Jimmy continued. "So we could probably do some crazy things together, ya know, if we talk about it some. One idea is to do a pretend computer sex-webcam thing, kinda like what you guys do. Our girls'll be on stage pretending to talk to some guy and her voice, ya know, will be coming through the sound system, right? The whole place will feel it, see? We think that'd make a good show, people'll like it. That's just one idea, but I think the possibilities are endless, ya know?"

"Doesn't sound so bad, Jimmy." Clyde thought about it for a moment and felt there was some potential. "Tell you what, give me a call in couple weeks and maybe we'll set up a face-to-face and we can start putting these ideas on paper. 'Kay?"

"Sure, sounds great," Jimmy said, privately ecstatic that the porn king might be interested. "Sounds, great. So I'll call you in a few weeks, and we can set something up."

"That's right," said Clyde. "Talk to you then." Clyde hung up and sat back in his leather swivel chair.

Clyde finished up his last daydream of the day and decided to go home for a while before class. He said goodbye to Marge and the operators who were still there and walked back to his apartment. The remnants of his epic night remained on the floor: cans and bottles, bong, bowl of double-fudge brownie mix. He cleaned up so the smell of alcohol would lessen and then plopped down on the couch. Checking his cell phone, he saw that he had fifteen messages from local and international females, but he knew what each one said and therefore didn't listen to them. He was tired of it all.

He enjoyed the class he was taking because no one knew who he was; he was just another student. When asked what he did, he'd say, "I work for an internet company," and they'd say, "Ooh, that's great," and that was it. For Clyde, this was ideal. And in his opinion, the potential dates he'd met in class were worth a hundred times the enrollment fee. He hadn't made any "moves" yet, but he thought he might soon. However, much to his surprise, and equally as much to his dismay, he had contemplated not propositioning anyone at all. Clyde realized that these ordinary people played by different rules and that he'd have to do the same if he wanted this to work. For him, this was intimidating. Clyde weaved in and out of reason trying to explain why this sex-star extraordinaire was getting pushed around by the ways of the layman, but he couldn't come up with an answer. It really didn't matter, though; he already knew what the problem was: The real Clyde Casino was afraid to ask out a girl.

Clyde had been on a most exhilarating sexual adventure, with women surrounding him, willing to do anything he wanted without question or reserve. But now, because he wasn't wearing the mask of a millionaire with a "Bad Ass" attitude, he'd been demoted to being just another "normal" dude. And with that, he feared, came the distinct possibility of rejection. What if he finally mustered up the courage to ask out a girl? She might smile and say, "You're a really nice guy, and I think you're really cute and I'm so flattered and all, but no, no thanks, I'm busy tonight… oh, and yeah, I'm busy tomorrow night, too."

Chapter Seventeen

THE SAME uncomfortable dream woke her again. She couldn't understand it, nor did she really want to. She just wanted it to stop. Maybe it was time for therapy. To clear her mind she turned her head, stared at her clock and wondered why ":00" came after ":59." She already knew the answer but it was a darn good distraction. And why not try to come up with some other possibilities? Her new theory of time would change the world.

Lola Cezanne's job was to analyze numbers all day, and sometimes all night. She figured she would have been one hell of a violinist if she (or her parents) had ever thought of it. Musicians, mathematicians, lawyers; they all use the same side of the brain. Playing a beautiful Mozart piece somewhere in Central Park seemed much more appealing then telling your seniors how this year's numbers compared to last year's, and how "the 'five-year' is looking strong, sir." Her thoughts paused for a moment and then resumed. It was time to get out of bed.

Nope.

She decided to wait another minute. After another minute went by she still couldn't find the motivation to move. Lola gave herself a countdown; she'd get out of bed in twenty seconds. Only she didn't know when to *start* the countdown. This was all a part of the procrastination process, and she was very good at it. Reluctantly, she started counting down. She did, though, without consciously realizing it. It just happened. And once it began there was no stopping it. Even if she changed her thoughts, the voice in the back of her head kept counting. She tried to fight it for twelve seconds, trying to restart it or extend it. It was no use. With eight seconds remaining, she succumbed to the count and readied herself for the morning. Three, two, one... Lola jumped out of bed, avoiding any second thoughts of staying there and ran into the bathroom.

To reward herself for such a dramatic rising, Lola took an extended hot shower. When she got out she was ready for the day. She fixed herself a cup of coffee (well, she called it a cup, but it was really about three cups). As she poured the coffee into the enormous mug, she counted. Her typical count for coffee was eleven, which meant that she would pour until she counted to eleven. Lola had "counts" for many things. Her count for brushing her teeth was forty-five; for making her bed it was thirty-five; for cleaning her glasses it was three per lens. She also counted steps, be it from her bedroom to her bathroom or from the subway to her office. Lola was all about counting. She knew it took nine steps to get to the shower from her bed. She knew that it took a hundred and fifty-seven steps to get from the subway to her office.

Coffee, along with a cigarette, would be her breakfast; a horrible way to start the day, but it sure did feel good. She got into the habit when she started working for a living many moons ago (she couldn't remember the first moon). She knew she would try to change her habits some day soon, but to her benefit, it was very difficult to define 'some day soon.'

While enjoying her breakfast, Lola turned on the television to watch the morning news. Her count for when the television picture was visible was four seconds (the count for the sound was two). Apparently the night before, in a part of town she'd never seen, a man held up a 24-hour diner for it's cheeseburgers. He had walked in, mask over face and machete in hand, and had gone up to the counter and demanded every cheeseburger in the establishment. The frightened clerk quickly obliged, filling up a garbage bag with a reported thirty-three burgers (the gentleman declined the clerk's offer of all the frozen ones). Lola wondered if she had been the clerk, would she have counted the thief's take accurately? The guy was probably under a lot of pressure.

The jolly weatherman told her it was going to be a beautiful day; plenty of sunshine, low humidity. That's wonderful, she agreed. Lola couldn't think when it was humid, especially in New York (she had spent a humid week in the Caribbean and it didn't feel so bad). Humidity had a warping effect on her brain. It tended to speed up her counts, lending to an awkwardly timed day. For example, instead of her standard eleven count for morning coffee, a day with 90% humidity could make it a twenty-four count. She puzzled over why she sped up her count on days like that. Practical thinking led her to believe that the count should be slowed down, but up it went with the temperature. (The opposite would occur when the temperature approached freezing.)

Lola checked herself in the mirror, made sure everything was in the right place, and left for work. The walk to the subway was quick. She was one of the lucky ones; she lived and worked near the same subway line. The train was full, as usual, with a thousand others. She found a snug corner and held on. She wished she was an athlete at times like these. Athletes had amazing balance, and if she had balance like that then she could ride any subway (or stand on any boat, for that matter) and not need to hold on to anything for dear life. But that wasn't her, so she reached out amongst a half-dozen other forearms and found a small stretch of metal to cling to. Unfortunately, she found herself standing face to face with a businessman who kept staring at her breasts. She didn't mind that many men did that, but first thing in the morning on a crowded subway was the wrong time and the wrong place.

She was proud of her breasts and quite fond of them, too. They weren't huge, like the size of a woman's breasts on television. Lola thought they were a notch smaller than that, which was perfect for her. They were large enough to feel confident about, but small enough not to feel self-conscious about. She seldom wore tight shirts because that drew too much attention, which happened at the office from time to time (even if she didn't sport a tight top). There was nothing worse than a co-worker gawking at you. But because of her shapely breasts, Lola found power. She knew, whether it was proper or not (and it really didn't faze her either way), her breasts gave her power over others. It wasn't an everyday sense of relief (the attention was often a burden), but it did make her feel good in many situations. In the event that she did regret having them, which meant that she was having a very bad day (approximately six days a year), her usual coping routine was to continually count them: "One, two. One, two. One, two. One, two."

She hopped off the subway moments before the hard-up businessman grabbed her boobs. About a hundred and fifty-seven steps later she was at her desk. It was just past 9am. Her day's agenda was, for once, something to look forward to. She had some "blah-blah" things to attend to in the morning but for lunch she had a meeting with Captain Cooper's Casino Cruisers, Inc., which could make for an exciting afternoon. When she returned, which could be any time between 4pm and 6pm, she had nothing pertinent to do except go to her cooking class, which was at seven.

The first thing Lola did was check her messages. She marked the ones she had to return, then marked the ones she *felt* like returning, and then erased the ones she wouldn't return. One of her bosses wanted to touch base regarding the casino meeting, one of her co-wor meeting, another boss wanted to make sure that she wouldn't gamble away her life savings (what life savings?), another co-worker wanted to get in her pants, this guy Thomas (ho-hum) wanted to go on another date, and her mother wanted to say, "Hello."

Lola called her bosses first and assured them that she was on top of things and in control. She then called the co-worker and told her that she couldn't go to the meeting but she'd lay down a bet for her if she wanted. This guy Thomas and the other co-worker didn't get their calls returned, and Mom was next.

"Hi, Mom."

"How are you?" her mother asked in her typical slow drawl, taking the typical four seconds.

Lola thought about sharing her odd re-occurring dream but didn't feel her mother was the best person for that. "Fine, having a good day."

"Already?"

"Uh, yeah. Sure."

"Did you meet someone new?"

Of course. Her mother thought she must have had sex last night.

"No, Mother. There's no one new."

"Oh." Her mother feigned surprise.

"Well, actually," Lola paused for three seconds, "I did meet someone last night."

"Ah!"

Her mother loved being right.

"I had such a wonderful time," Lola said, imitating a character from a wholesome family sitcom from the 60's.

"Oh, do tell who it is," her mother said with a little British sophistication.

"Her name is Wanda."

Long pause.

"Mom?" Lola probed, but there was no response. "Mom, I'm just messing with you."

"I know that," her mother snapped back. Lola started laughing.

"But Mom, there's nothing wrong with it."

"Of course there isn't, dear." Lola heard her mother sigh. "I was just surprised to hear you say that, but there really isn't anything wrong with that at all."

"You really think so?" Lola had never had a lesbian talk with her. She wondered if it was a common mother-daughter conversation.

"Absolutely. Just don't tell your father."

Lola laughed. "Does he even know what a lesbian is?"

"I'm not quite sure, dear. But best not educate him right now."

"Okay, I've got to get some work done."

"Kiss?"

"Kiss."

It was certainly unusual discussing lesbianism with her mother. At least if she ever went in that direction, it seemed her mother would be supportive. Lola had experimented with the same sex a few times in her life. The first one was a typical late-night college adventure. A girlfriend had come over one night after a dirty keg party. With classic rock blaring in the background and glasses of white wine in their hands, they plopped down on her couch and started gabbing about the pathetic college boys who called themselves men. Then it happened. It began with an incredibly awkward silence, which drowned out the already loud music. Lola remembered feeling heart-pounding nervousness and couldn't understand what was happening. It was at that precise moment that her friend leaned across the couch and started kissing her. Lola went with it, enjoying the new sensation, but also feeling a bit uncomfortable (like wearing someone else's jeans). They kissed and groped for a while (Lola couldn't recall how long it lasted), and they somehow ended up in her bed the next morning. At a slight loss for words, her friend had quietly put her clothes back on and left with a smile. Lola had remained under the down comforter reflecting on the unique experience. In a small revelation, she realized that most men were horrible kissers.

Chapter Eighteen

HER MOTHER was the most original character she'd ever come across (and that included the clown who rode the seven-foot tricycle around Greenwich Village). Growing up in eastern Long Island, Lola was able to see at an early age that her mom was not like the other moms. Her father supported the family; he was a successful business consultant in Manhattan. This let her mother do anything and everything she wanted (including spending a lot of time alone). From her clothes to her attitude to the way she lived, Lola's mother was different. Her father would say she went through phases; like the hippie phase, when her mother would wear tie-dyes, sandals, long skirts and multiple bracelets and necklaces. She rebounded from that into the strict schoolteacher phase, when she'd wear collared shirts buttoned to the top, dark wool skirts and a matching jacket, and her hair would be back in a pin (Lola wondered if her father had something to do with this). Next was the casual phase, a time during which her mother only seemed to wear sweatpants, sweatshirts, sneakers and a headband. (Which was odd because her mother never exercised.) The casual phase slid into the Gothic phase, when her mother donned mediaeval-witch getups. Lola recalled that her mother even attempted some magic at the time. However, she forgot if the spells worked. ("Your father will come home and he'll be unable to resist me.") Now her mother was deep into the conservative phase, which was close to the strict teacher look but was a little more loose and colorful. It was actually Lola's favorite phase so far (although the witch thing was a hoot).

Her mother went through cooking phases, too. From vegetarian to Italian to continental, back to vegetarian to French (which lasted one night) to Asian (which lasted a week) to Spanish and, finally, to continental with a little vegetarian and Italian sprinkled in. She figured the family could order Chinese take-out and they could go to a fancy French place on special occasions. At least she knew her limitations. Tonight's cooking class had been a bold attempt to expand her culinary horizons, but after some thought she decided it would best suit her daughter. "Lola, darling, you will excel where your wonderful mother could not. And going into Manhattan every week would be too much for me."

What her mother was typically successful at were her hobbies. She'd pick something to learn every season and immerse herself into it. The first hobby Lola could remember was the art of tie dying (coinciding with the hippie phase). Her mother could be found on summer afternoons in the driveway, creating psychedelic patterns on shirts, skirts, bed sheets and tablecloths. (Dad wasn't fond of that.) She actually became quite good at it, making Lola curious as to her whereabouts in the 60's. ("I was with your father, dear.") Then in the winter her mother took on the "decorate the house with her own creations" hobby, turning the Cezanne household into an arts and crafts fair. Her mother mastered the art of taking what appeared to be insignificant objects and transforming them into aesthetic decor (like the famous three-dimensional shoe collage). Gardening was her springtime mission. She studied up on the subject, ordering books from T.V., making daily trips to the local gardening center and buying overalls. She even bought a lawnmower so she could mow the lawn herself (which she did all summer). Lola admired her mother's vigor. When her mother knew what she wanted, she would go out and get it, with no excuses (except for that golf thing).

That was her mother; that was Victoria ("Who on earth likes to be called *Vicki*?"). Lola wondered when she became a mother (if she ever did), would she be just as eccentric? Or would she be quiet and passive like her father? Would she become, for better or for worse, the talk of the town? Would she excel in business and be able to put her kids through college? All her pondering was for naught, though. She supposed that only time would tell. And that might be a lot of time, because so far she hadn't come close to finding a man. Maybe she really was a lesbian.

Lola looked for only one thing in a man, just one thing. She wanted to meet a man who was happy with his life. That was it. She had dated dozens (there was no difficulty in meeting men for her), but half of them talked to her breasts, a third were flat-out jerks, two-thirds were insecure, a quarter were as dumb as dirt, and all of them, less one, were not happy. The one who was happy was a real nice guy but he just wasn't attractive.

There was nothing worse than being in a relationship with someone who was miserable underneath their smile, and that was all she seemed to find. She wanted that guy who was confident and attractive, intelligent and funny, blah, blah, blah, but most of all, content. The gaggle of guys she saw were in love with whining and complaining and there was already enough of that in the world.

But thankfully men never consumed her mind. She didn't stay up all night crying that she didn't have a lover. Lola knew it would happen if it was meant to happen, and when it did she probably wouldn't be ready for it. The idea of marriage, especially at her age, was alluring, but she was headstrong enough to not use that as motivation (like many others she knew). She was certain that one day the right man would come along and sweep her off her feet into an absurdly delightful life. Until then, she determined as she floated back down to her desk, she'd become the gambling queen. She knew she'd have a better chance at winning money than meeting the right guy.

Her phone rang.

"Hey, La! What's up?" It was Stacy; a co-worker and friend who worked on the ninth floor.

"Hey, bitch. What's goin' on?"

"So you're not inviting me to lunch."

"I told you already. You think I changed my mind?"

"Well, maybe." Stacy paused and pouted. "If you were nice."

"You're not supposed to be on the boat. It's not even your department." Lola paused. "Bitch."

"I know. I was just testing the waters. And it seems that the water's full of bitch."

"Yeah, well, someone's got to do it."

"Are you going to gamble?"

"Well, it's not in my job description, but you never know."

"Okay, if you do, bet on fourteen for me."

"Fourteen? What do you mean, 'Bet on fourteen'?"

"It's called roulette, bitch," Stacy said, as if everyone knew.

"Oh, okay. I guess I could do that. But only if you start behaving like a good bitch."

"Fine."

"Good."

Lola hung up the phone and counted to ten for no apparent reason. Perhaps it was residue from counting to ten to calm down, something she used to do during her late-twenties-life crisis. Lola knew of the mid-life crisis, when men bought sports cars and ran off with young floozies and when women submerged themselves into deep medicated funks. But the late-twenties-life crisis was a different kind of beast. Of course, the mid-life crisis would mock the late-twenties-life crisis, knowing the luxury of the latter, but one man's laughter is another man's pain. Lola had many friends who went through it and a few who still hadn't gotten over it. She got past it, though, and believed she'd found a peaceful balance to get her through the next decade of her life.

The late-twenties-life crisis revolves around two things: relationships and careers. The relationship part deals with the fear of being alone for the rest of your life. The other part has to do with careers; that if you don't have a set career then you'll be forever miserable and end up working odd jobs in hellish environments. Both fears have an eerily similar theme; that the person will have no life if a career and lover aren't found by age thirty.

Counting to ten had helped Lola get through it without too many casualties. She had come to accept that her job wasn't so bad and that she'd remain there until something better came along. It certainly wasn't her dream job, but it was good enough. On particularly dreary days, sometimes Lola would think of what her "dream job" would be. As a child, she dreamt of being a "mommy" and having a nice little family. The next dream job she could remember was a schoolteacher. When Lola hit her high school years, a dream job didn't exist (nor did the thought of any job). In college, Lola changed her major to business and dreamed of becoming a high-wheeling CEO. When she graduated, she realized that there was no way she'd instantly be made into a CEO and that perhaps she would have to apply for a lower-tiered position. With the help of her father's connections, she was able to do just that (thereby waiving the "early-twenties what am I going to do with the rest of my life" crisis).

The relationship half of the late-twenties-life crisis was something that Lola couldn't solve; it was something she just had to accept. A part of her, somewhere deep inside, could easily attach to the next man she met and rationalize why this man was perfect for her. She'd have the family she'd wanted since she was a child, she'd go through her mid-life crisis with some real fire, and they'd retire and watch their grandchildren grow. Yes, there was a small voice inside her saying, "Lola, honey, just go out and find *anyone*." But Lola had made a decision: She wasn't going to settle. She wasn't going to let that voice override her conscience. Instead, she accepted that the voice was real, and that it wouldn't go away, but more importantly, that she didn't have to listen to it. It was through her late-twenties-life crisis that Lola taught herself that all crises were derived from fear, and that all fears were conquered by acceptance.

Chapter Nineteen

THE CASINO had solid financials. Lola's job today was rather easy; she just had to meet with them, make sure they were as strong in person as they were on paper, and then tell them her company would invest. Lola supposed she could take Stacy with her but it really wouldn't be appropriate; it'd be obvious she was only there to bet on fourteen. Lola worked with several casinos in Jersey and one in Connecticut but this would be the first one based in New York (though, the ship had to motor out to international waters before gaming could begin). Casinos tended to be well-managed; they had to be with the amount of money changing hands. As long as the casino knew what to do with the money (and not too much was skimmed off the top), they'd be successful.

Lola finished some annoying tasks so she wouldn't have to return to the office. It was almost noon and the car service was on it's way. She was almost out the door when the phone rang.

"This is Lola," she answered in a rush.

"Bitch."

"I'm out the door. The car's waiting."

"Bitch."

"Is there something you want?"

"No."

"Okay, then we'll check your big bitch-ass out tomorrow, 'kay?"

"Whatever, bitch-tits. Remember the number?"

"Yeah, fourteen."

"That's it, bitch-cake."

Lola paused, "What's a bitch-cake?"

"I dunno. Maybe something you get on your bitchday."

"Hmm… nice."

"Can I go?"

"Come on, don't be such a bitch-bag."

"Come on!" Stacy whined. "I can go through the spreads and earnings in half a second."

"Well, then, we'd have to leave early."

"Bitch?"

"Okay, listen, I really don't care if you come along. But by no means is it up to me and you know that. I'm just going to seal the deal and me going isn't even necessary, and you know that, too."

"I'll get the okay," Stacy quickly said.

"Whatever, bitch. Car's leaving in five."

Stacy hung up, presumably to get permission to go. Lola went down to the lobby and waited. A minute later, a black sedan with tinted windows pulled up in front of her. She got in the back and confirmed the destination with the driver, but told him to wait a moment. She wanted to give Stacy at least a small chance to make it. Then she started counting. She wasn't sure if she was counting to a hundred or if she was just counting the seconds until Stacy got there (if she ever did). Lola was at thirty-nine when Stacy came barreling through the lobby. Some people milling about wisely gave her clearance (otherwise they probably would'e gotten knocked down, and maybe even knocked out). Stacy whipped the door open and stood proud.

"What's up, bitch!!?"

"You made it."

"Yeah, I guess I did. Thanks for waiting."

"No problem."

The car took off as Stacy tried to catch her breath. The noon-time drive across midtown Manhattan was unbelievable. Hordes of people flooded the sidewalks and streets, fighting for position, fighting an invisible deadline. Lola usually ordered in lunch, mostly because she didn't have time to go out, but also because she hated the crowds. She hated standing in line at the deli buffet for twenty minutes just to wait longer to find a seat and only to eat something bland and greasy. Ordering in was the only way to go. The perfect lunch consisted of a tuna salad sandwich and a fresh fruit drink delivered from the health food store, a half-hour watching the news in the common room, and then a quick cigarette outside.

"Okay, so what do I need to know?" asked Stacy, much to Lola's surprise.

"I thought you were up to date with it."

"Well, I am. Kind of. Just give me broad strokes."

Stacy was an attractive woman of about the same age (maybe a few years older, Lola thought). She was one of those women who couldn't put on weight. She was tall and thin with short-cropped black hair, and Lola figured that she could be a model if she had a more neutral face. Lola had the opposite look. She had the voluptuous thing going on (which caused Stacy to request that Lola share some of her breasts with her). It was Stacy's personality, however, that defined her. She was a perpetual spark of energy. She was the type who irritated half the people and amused the rest, and nothing pleased her more than gossip.

"Hey, I heard that Mary, you know, marketing Mary? She farted so loud yesterday that not only did everyone hear it, but she might've shit in her pants."

"No way," Lola laughed.

"Yeah, and she was wearing white."

"Oh, no."

"Poor, Mary."

"How do you recover from that?"

"Haircut?"

"Boob job?"

"Promotion?"

"Church?"

"Nothing."

"Yeah, nothing. Not even time."

"It'll be on her permanent record," Stacy concluded.

"Yeah, and on her pants."

They laughed some more, all the while thankful that they'd never done anything like that. The crowds got smaller as they got closer to the piers and Lola wondered if there was some sort of mathematical formula regarding populations and locations.

"Hey," she said to Stacy, but it was directed at her window.

"Hey, what?" Stacy replied to her own window.

"I had a weird dream last night."

"Oh, yeah? What was it?"

Lola didn't know why she was entrusting Stacy with this highly classified information but she supposed she could. "And I've had it a few times, too."

"Well, what was it, baby?"

"Okay… you ready?" Lola held her breath and counted to three.

"Yes, what was it?"

Lola exhaled and spoke. "I dreamt I had a penis."

A mad flurry of laughter was what Lola expected, but Stacy had a different reaction. "Wow."

"Yeah! Isn't that messed up? I don't know what's going on."

"Well, something is," Stacy said with a smirk. "So, what were you doing with your penis?"

"That, I don't remember. I just remember looking down and boom, it was there."

"Hmm. Was it hard"?

"Uh, yeah, it was," Lola exclaimed in a whisper. "It was so weird."

"Was anyone else there?"

"I don't know. I can't remember."

"Where were you?"

"I think I was in a bed or lying down somewhere. Oh, and there was someone maybe in another room, but I just can't remember it that well. Do you think I'm crazy?"

"Hey, look, we're here," Stacy noted with glee. "And, no, I don't think you're crazy."

"Really?"

"Yeah, really. In fact, I think it's kinda cool. In fact, I wish I had dreams like that. Oh, the things I would do."

"So what do you think it means?"

"It probably means," Stacy stopped. "I really have no idea. Let me sleep on it."

Lola felt a great deal better now that she'd told someone, and especially because this someone thought it was cool. She was curious as to what the dream meant and what her mysterious sub-conscious was thinking about, but knew it was out of her control. She supposed that all would be revealed when she was ready to hear it.

They hopped out of the car and stood before the floating vessel. To them, it was massive. Neither had ever been on a cruise ship (notwithstanding the sophomoric booze cruises from the days of old). Lola instinctively started counting all of the little round windows lining the side of the ship. She lost count at around forty-five as they made their way to the entrance. A gentleman was waiting and approached them as they neared.

"Hi, I'm Clark Davis from Captain Cooper's Casino Cruisers," he said cheerfully and without fumbling any of the words.

"Hi, nice to meet you. I'm Lola Cezanne, and this is my associate Stacy Wilson."

"Cezanne? Like the…"

"Yep, exactly," Lola said politely, but firmly.

"Okay, well, welcome to Captain Cooper's Casino Cruisers. Bob Shelly is waiting for you inside."

They started walking up the entrance ramp, excited to experience their first cruise.

"Ever been on a cruise liner?" Clark asked, feigning interest but following protocol.

"Nope," Lola and Stacy responded together.

"Well, we're the best four C's on the seven sea's. You're in for a real treat today."

Stacy gave Lola a look. Who was this guy? Did he have to say things like that? Stacy spoke up with a touch of her little-girl voice.

"Well, that's great, because we love new treats."

Clark gave her a nondescript glance. His gut told him that she was a bitch, but he had to assume that she was being sincere. Man, he hated this part of the job. He tried to sound genuine. "I'm going to take you to the Commodore Dining Room and there you'll meet Mr. Shelly. After lunch, he'll take you on the private tour."

Stacy made the "Ooh" face to Lola, and that was too much. They both started laughing. Clark didn't know how to interpret this behavior. He thought that no one in their right mind would laugh at someone they'd just met en route to a business meeting. He cracked a nervous smile, trying to blend in as best he could, and kept walking with Lola and Stacy in tow.

"Well, here we are," Clark began, "the Commodore Dining Room, home of the best food on the seven seas."

More laughs as they walked in. Clark showed them to a dining table and gestured for them to sit. "Mr. Shelly will be here momentarily. It was wonderful meeting the two of you. Perhaps we'll see you again on a Captain Cooper's Casino Cruiser."

"Thanks, Clar…" was all Lola could manage as he left the dining room. She tried to calm herself for the meeting. Stacy had mellowed out already and was looking for the next adventure. The dining room was almost full, mostly with businessmen eating a power lunch. Lola wasn't sure if the ship was to set sail that afternoon or not.

A waitress came to their table and asked them if they wanted a beverage, to which they both responded that they wanted some water. When the waitress left, they looked at each other.

"A drink wouldn't hurt us right now," Stacy spoke for the both of them.

"No kidding, but let's see what big Bob is swilling first."

"Okay," pouted Stacy.

A terrific horn sounded and Lola glanced at Stacy. After five seconds, right as Lola was about to say something, the horn went off again. They looked at each other and started laughing. Timing the horn, Lola made as if she was going to speak again, only to get cut off. The horn sounded off six times total, and Lola was finally about to say something when she noticed the landscape moving outside the dining room windows. It took a brief moment to realize that the boat was moving, not the pier.

"We're moving," Stacy said, amazed.

"I guess so."

"Maybe we should get those drinks," Stacy suggested.

"Yep," was all Lola could manage, a little hesitant about the ship's departure, "but we'll wait for Bobby first."

The waitress came back with the waters and asked them if they wanted to see a menu.

"We're actually waiting for Bob Shelly."

"Oh!" the waitress said, as if she wanted to shout "Eureka."
"Okay, I'll come back when he gets here."

"Great, thanks."

Lola got up and walked to one of the windows; she wanted to take all of this in. It was surreal: A mass of steel the size of a city block floating down the Hudson River. Lola knew she probably wouldn't do this sort of thing again so she tried to absorb as much as she could. Her thoughts were interrupted, though.

"Ms. Cezanne?"

Lola spun around to find an older man, dressed very nicely (if not too nicely, and with maybe too much jewelry) standing there.

The man continued. "Bob Shelly, great to finally meet you. Sorry to make you wait," he said sincerely.

"Oh, no problem at all. We've been taking in the sights and sounds," Lola said, adding, "Call me Lola. And this is Stacy Wilson, one of my associates."

"Great to meet you Stacy. The more the merrier," Bob said, as if he knew why Stacy was really there.

They went back to the table and took their seats. The waitress promptly returned and again asked if they wanted something to drink. Lola and Stacy nodded that their waters were sufficient, but then Bob spoke up, "Bonnie, can you please get me a double martini."

"Yes, Mr. Shelly," she responded with a grin. Lola and Stacy looked down at the table, but only momentarily. Stacy broke first.

"You know, that sounds really good. Can you make it two?"

"Yes, I can," Bonnie replied and then looked at Lola. "Or shall I make it three?"

Lola nodded and thanked her. The three of them laughed out loud, breaking the tension of land customs.

"We do things differently out here," Bob began and went into what seemed like a practiced monologue. It was quite interesting, though, and Lola and Stacy listened while sipping their martinis. Bob reminded Lola of a grandfather. He was like a wise old man who'd sailed around the world with stories from every port. After they ordered lunch (which he did for them), they started talking business. Bonnie soon returned with three Caesar salads and a giant platter of fresh seafood. It seemed every edible aquatic creature was represented on the ice-covered tray, from shrimp to clams to crab to lobster. They were barely halfway done when Bonnie came back out with a hot platter filled with seared tuna, grilled calamari, sautéed conch and onions, and finally, Captain Cooper's World Famous Shrimp Scampi. By the time lunch was over, Lola had consumed three martinis, two dozen assorted pieces of seafood, and had full confidence in Captain Cooper's Casino Cruisers.

"Okay!" Bob bellowed. "How about the tour?"

"Yes!" Lola and Stacy chirped.

"Great! Then follow me," Bob commanded, perhaps a bit tipsy. That'd be good, Lola thought. At least the three of them would be on even ground. Bob took them everywhere on the ship. They spent some time (about a drink's worth) on the upper deck, which had a huge pool, an outdoor bar, hundreds of lounge chairs and what appeared to be a dance floor. They also went to the ballroom, which was enormous and filled with tables and chairs and a dance floor the size of two tennis courts. Bob told them that they also had entertainers perform there (for which they'd bring in a stage). Bob showed them the different types of cabins, from the luxury suites to the tiny economy rooms to the crew's quarters. It was such a different way of life, Lola kept thinking. Finally, Bob led them to the action-filled game rooms. The rest of the ship had been deserted (Lola thought it'd been a slow day), but the casino was packed. Everywhere she looked there were players and onlookers. The casino had just opened five minutes before (when the ship had reached international waters) and already the scene was ablaze. Lola was thankful she had a few drinks in her; it soothed some of the intensity.

"So here we are," announced Bob, "Captain Cooper's Casino. We have dice, cards, slots. You name it, we got it and people love it."

That was the dumbest thing Bob had said all afternoon, but Lola let it slide. She was still in awe of what was before her. They walked in and toured the room. No narration was needed. Only after a full lap around did Bob speak again. "So would you like to play some games?"

Stacy was the first to speak up. "Definitely!" she said, with maybe too much enthusiasm.

"Well, then. I'll leave you two to have some fun. I'll check up on you later, see how well you're doing. And if you have any more questions, just ask an employee and they'll get me."

Sailor Bob walked away and disappeared around the corner, leaving Lola and Stacy at the casino entrance.

"Ready?" Lola asked.

"Ready."

They made their way into the crowds and looked at all the games. Lola knew how to play blackjack and roulette, but the other games were a mystery. Stacy seemed to have the same mindset as she maneuvered to one of the roulette tables. There were no seats available, but it was a good to watch for a while to see how people bet, how much they won, and how much more they lost. Out of the eight seats Lola counted, six of them had people who looked like professional gamblers. They were very serious and didn't seem to be having any fun. The other two seats were occupied by a couple of folks who were obviously out for a good time. They were laughing and drinking and moaning and cheering (often to the dismay of the pros) and soon lost all their money. They politely dismissed themselves, a bit dejected that they'd lost, but with smiles that said they really enjoyed losing. That gave Lola and Stacy an opportunity to sit down and play. Lola wasn't sure if she was ready, but determined she might not ever be ready. They sat down and cashed in twenty dollars each. Lola received blue chips and Stacy got green ones. Counting them, Lola figured out that each chip was worth a quarter. There was a $2.50 minimum bet, so that meant ten chips. Lola kindly made note of this to Stacy, who wagered almost everything she had.

"Stace, maybe you should take it easy," Lola suggested.

"Whatever, bitch."

Stacy had the eyes of a lunatic (a drunk one at that). As soon as that thought came and went, a waitress brought over two martinis, compliments of the house ("and by the way," the waitress added, "all drinks were compliments of the house"). This is going to be a long afternoon, thought Lola. She hoped she didn't show up to class too drunk.

"Final bets," declared the roulette dealer. "Final bets."

Lola had failed to make one, perhaps a bit too concerned with Stacy's fifteen-dollar bet and five-martini buzz. The little ball spun around and around the wheel, eventually landing on the number thirty-nine. Stacy lost everything and knocked her drink over.

Chapter Twenty

LOLA BLINKED when she looked at her watch (which required resting her forearm on the blackjack table to keep it steady). It was half past 10. She was in disbelief as she tried to recall how many drinks she'd had and how much money she'd lost. When her count kept growing, she stopped. It was dizzying. Stacy looked as though she'd gone to bed and woken up four times. We're not in good shape, thought Lola. A waitress came by with another round (what an evil woman) and Lola asked what time it was. After the waitress glanced at Lola's watch, she answered that it was just past 10:30pm. Trying to look serious and sober, like a woman of decent stature, Lola inquired as to when the ship would return to "the port side." The amused waitress replied that they'd return at 8 in the morning. Lola turned toward Stacy in surprise but Stacy had her eyes glued to the dealer's cards.

"Super," Lola said back to the waitress, pretending she already knew that. The waitress then told her that she could pick up their cabin keys at the main desk on the B deck.

What happened? That was all Lola could think of. No one had ever mentioned an overnight cruise. Maybe the ship changed its schedule? Maybe she misread the memo? Unbelievable. Well, so much for tonight's class, she thought. She nudged Stacy, competing for her attention. That didn't work, so she wound up and punched her.

"What, bitch?" Stacy demanded, waking up from her gambling coma.

"Know what time it is?"

"I'm not ready to go yet."

"Do you know what time it is?" Lola repeated, enunciating every word with a slight slur.

"Oh!" Stacy understood as she checked her own watch. "Uh, it's ten-thir..."

Lola smirked.

"Wow!" exclaimed Stacy. "That's crazy! This place is amazing!"

"You know what time we get back?"

"Ah, midnight?" guessed Stacy.

"No, eight," Lola said flatly.

It took a moment for that to register. "Oh."

"Yeah," Lola responded, nodding her head.

Stacy pondered this for a while and then seemed to solve some equation in her head. "They give us a room?"

"Yeah."

Stacy didn't say a word. Though they'd had enough drinks for ten people, Stacy, at that exact moment, seemed perfectly sober. She smiled at Lola, but not the usual "I'm a little devil" full-smile, and not the "I'm kind of bored" half-smile, but rather, the dangerous "This could get very interesting" quarter-smile.

Lola, who was still using the blackjack table as support, thought she understood the message but wasn't sure. She was swimming in a pool of vodka.

"Cool," Stacy finally said, breaking Lola's trance.

"Yeah, I guess," said Lola, not yet sure if it was.

"Whatcha mean, you guess? That's great!" Stacy declared, scaring some of the awkwardness away. "We're gonna have a great night!"

"It was just a bit surprising. I'd no idea."

"Yeah, but it's a great surprise."

Lola paused. "Can you see straight?"

"Nope."

"Me neither."

"Let's get some snacks or something, and I need to find that ATM again."

Food wasn't such a bad idea. Lola figured that all the booze could use some company. As far as going to the ATM, though... that could be trouble. The last thing she wanted to do was blow four hundred bucks on a boat. But then again, her id reasoned, what else are you going to do?

Lola and Stacy bounced and swayed up and down the boat, looking for a place to eat. After twenty minutes of wrong turns they finally found the Captain Cooper Landlubber's Cafe and inhaled some cheeseburgers. "Mmm, this is the best cheeseburger I've ever had." From there, they continued their helpless drunken quest to find an ATM. They stumbled past old couples donning evening gowns and suits, they giggled at guys sporting muscle shirts and high-top sneakers, and they became self-conscious and quiet as they passed others who appeared to be equally intoxicated. The ship was a four-level maze. Lola had completely lost her sense of direction and used her blind instincts to maneuver. She started counting the amount of steps she was taking to keep her mind off the idea that they were utterly lost within a finite space. They walked in circles and into dead-ends for what felt like an hour. At one point, they somehow reached the outside deck at the front of the ship. It was quiet and dimly lit, and no one else was there. They decided to rest for a while and take in the ocean breeze.

"Where are we?" asked Stacy, who was slowly coming down from her buzz. There was no land in sight and no lights on the horizon.

"I think we're out on the Atlantic," replied Lola, figuring it was the only logical solution.

They enjoyed the ocean's tranquility in relative silence. The cool saltwater wind was soothing and a lost amount of time had passed before Lola realized that Stacy was standing behind her and massaging her shoulders. Relaxed as she was, Lola tensed up. What is she doing? How long has she been touching me? *Why* is she touching me? Lola felt a wave of anxiety falling over her. She couldn't move. She couldn't remember anything and she didn't know what to do. As Stacy turned her around to face her, Lola instinctively started counting to five as fast as she could, over and over again. She braved a look up at the taller Stacy, who was again sporting that dangerous quarter-smile. Lola tried to return it, but their lips met before she could.

Lola let the sensation flow through her and it energized her entire body. As their kiss deepened, their figures pushed into each other, searching for the perfect place to rest. Once they found it, they locked their arms around each other and held on. Lola's fear had mysteriously vanished and a soft comfort settled in. Somehow, in the middle of the Atlantic Ocean, she was at peace.

When the surge of passion finally drifted, their embrace slightly loosened and their kissing became gentle and forgiving. Stacy looked down and, braving it once again, Lola slowly looked up. Their lazy eyes connected and they shared a silent moment together, though it was eventually interrupted by some shy little grins. It was then when Lola noticed that her counting had stopped.

"Let's go," Stacy suggested.

"Okay," Lola responded in a daze. They were both ready to crash.

The elusive cabin was small and cute and smelly. There were two extra-slim single beds and a port-a-john-style bathroom in the corner. The bedroom amenities didn't matter at all, though. They were both post-drunk and rapidly approaching painful hangovers and anything resembling a place to sleep looked luxurious. They plopped down and gave up on the night. Lola could hear the ocean waves smashing into the side of the ship which, at that point, wasn't comforting at all. She started counting again. When she reached forty, she started over. She did this for what felt like hours, but it was only about ten minutes. The next thing she remembered was waking up to a deafening knock at the door and someone yelling, "All passengers must depart! All passengers must depart!"

They'd finally returned. It was 8:30am and Lola felt like a pile of bricks. She wreaked of alcohol and smoke and couldn't see straight. Stacy had somehow ended up on the same bed with half her clothes off, but that was the one thing that Lola felt good about. What a night.

Stacy was out cold. Lola did her best to wake her up, but no amount of shaking and badgering seemed to work. As a last resort, she went with the soft sensual kiss on the lips. Upon impact, Stacy shimmied closer to Lola then carefully opened her eyes and smiled.

"I had this crazy dream," she whispered.

The two of them made their way off the vessel and into the humid New York City morning. Their hangovers, coupled with the heat, prevented any communication until they reached 10th Avenue, where they could finally find a cab. Lola got the first one. "See you later," she mumbled, not knowing when "later" would be, but hoped it'd be soon. Stacy responded with what sounded like a grunt.

Chapter Twenty-One

PERPETUALLY EXHAUSTED in the morning, Will Canter was used to it. His boss thought he was on drugs, his family thought he was on drugs, his fiancée, Ginny, thought he was on drugs. In return, Will thought his boss could use a bong-hit, his family could use some pain killers, and if his fiancée did coke, it would speed her up even more, so maybe a bong-hit for her, too. He and Ginny would wake up at the same time. Sometimes they'd make love (rather, she would get on top of him). She always got out of bed first, got ready first and left first. Will would be just sitting up in bed when the door closed. He wasn't concerned, though; a five-minute shower, throw on some clothes, walk a few blocks to work. No big deal.

He was an assistant editor at an entertainment rag and his schedule was rather lax. This provided him with plenty of time to sleep, which he appreciated and took full advantage of. Ginny, on the other hand, was in the party-planning business. She had started a firm with a couple of girlfriends and knew just about every hip spot and person in the city. Her schedule was packed and she'd often come home late (and a little buzzed on something), and by then Will would usually be half-asleep. Despite living together, they really didn't see each other much during the week. Tonight, though, was the one night when they'd actually do something together. Will took a mental note of this; cooking class at 7pm.

His eyes popped open again when he heard the door slam in the distance. It was the perfect alarm clock (as long as she left on time). He used every muscle in his body to pull himself out of bed. As per usual, he took a quick shower, threw on some clothes, and walked a few blocks to work. He'd been working at *The Celebrity Poll* for two years now, and wasn't quite sure why he was still there. The work was mundane, at times hectically mundane, and the only subject discussed was entertainment gossip. He found copy editing to be a rather simple job and that was presumably why he stayed there. Copy editing and thinking of headlines were almost second nature to him. Because the final product was solely for entertainment junkies, quality was not as important as quantity, and that made things even easier. Will had worked as a freelance editor and writer for a handful of blogs and dailies, but *The Celebrity Poll*, unlike his previous employers, gave him a steady paycheck.

Will settled into his desk area with his favorite breakfast: a pastrami, egg and cheese sandwich on a roll with a large coffee. While sipping and chomping he perused the internet, mostly looking for entertainment blurbs (although he preferred international news). It was the responsibility of everyone at *'The Poll'* to stay caught up with any and every piece of celebrity gossip. For Will, this was a chore. For most of the others, it was satisfying. Will knew that he probably excelled at his job only because he didn't care. The "Gazers" (the obsessed ones) provided a level of job security for him because they cared too much.

Will realized that it was a strange phenomenon that existed in all arenas of life; the less you care about something, the better you are at it. If you don't worry about hitting a golf ball and just walk up to it and hit it, then you're more likely to be a better player. What Will did enjoy at the office was egging on all the Gazers into what was secretly called a "Frenzy." It was a bit cruel, but it was fun. When these people became excited with celebrity news, their eyes lit up, their heart rates increased and they looked like they might piss in their pants. Will knew that as long as he could evoke these kinds of reactions, then he'd shine brighter and brighter to upper management.

Tara came by his desk to say hello. Her desk was in a different zone but their job titles were the same. She handled more of the television stories and he handled more of the film stories, but often their work crossed. Tara was a plump redhead who, like himself, couldn't stand the celebrity hoopla and excelled at her work because of it. Tara also enjoyed instigating "Frenzies," getting the Gazers in a tizzy because she'd heard that Lisa Roxy of the chick-band Dish had been seen with Mackie Maroon on the corner of 1st and 1st. News like that would lead to hours of Gazer speculation and plans to go to that street corner, all of which made an editor's job a whole lot easier.

"Morning, Canter," Tara greeted. "You're looking kind of burnt."

Will smirked. "Good morning to you, Cardinal."

Tara always referred to him as "Burner Boy" or "Ol' Smoke-A-Lot" or something similar. He always referred to her as something red, be it a cardinal, tomato, or stop sign.

"Whatever, Smoke Nuts."

"Anything good going on?" he asked, referring to celebrity news.

"Well, Wesley West might get his own sitcom this fall with Susie Rich, but only if he stops working on 'Bullets and Bones' with Jenny Penny. That's just in today."

Wesley West was married to Jenny Penny but had been allegedly having an affair with Susie Rich. They were supposedly seen in Venice together.

"Is it public?" Will asked, referring to whether the Gazers were privy to the information.

Tara slyly looked around the office then back at Will. "Nope," she answered with a grin.

"Nice." Will was glad at least one of them had some ammunition.

Tara went back to her desk and Will began to review the day's agenda. The morning was filled with headline duty and the afternoon mostly depended upon what the rest of the office did (hopefully that would be when Tara dropped "the bomb").

When it came down to Will's favorite thing to do at work, 'nothing' was usually the go-to answer. But if someone was dangling a ten-thousand pound air conditioner over his head, demanding that he choose his favorite task, then he'd have to say creating headlines.

After an article or interview was edited there needed to be a few headlines to sell it to the reader. The writers sometimes tried their own headlines but they were rarely usable. It was one of Will's jobs to come up with something more appropriate to show to the managing editor, who more often than not changed the headline, or at least adjusted it. Will liked the work because it didn't require scrutinizing five hundred words. It only entailed understanding what the five hundred words meant. Will wasn't the best headline writer at *The Celebrity Poll* and most of the time his ideas were dismissed, but on rare occasion he'd have a breakthrough. A few months earlier, there had been a heartfelt article written about Stanley Fitzgatto, the famous stage actor. The story concerned how he left a huge Broadway production to prove he could work in Hollywood. But after a disappointing debut as a leading man all he could land were small, one-liner roles. Will's headline, FITZ QUITS RITZ FOR BITS, went to print. Not the proudest moment of his career, but it was better than staying at home and planning a wedding.

Ginny absolutely loved her job. She never thought that life could be this good. Six years ago, Ginny foresaw that she'd one day be working a crappy job while being married to a chump loser. But now she was working at her own company *and* she was marrying a rather cool guy. She never stopped for too long to think how it all happened. She was afraid that if she did, then it'd all go away.

At Bash, Ginny worked with her two closest friends, Beth and Julie. After a blurry college experience and a few years of exploring the New York City party circuit, the three of them had decided that there was nothing in the world they wanted to do more than party. Then at brunch one Sunday, while nursing their hangovers with unlimited Bloody Mary's, they came up with the idea of starting a party planning business. At the time it sounded amazing, but it was realistically just a buzzed-brunch mind-settler.

A few weeks later, though, Beth received a phone call from an old sorority sister living in Texas who wanted to throw a huge celebration for her husband's 30th birthday. She asked Beth to help her as a favor since she'd only been to New York once and "didn't know the difference between Madison and Lexington." Beth, with famously clever poise, told her that her new company planned events just like that. The sister, excited that she wouldn't have to deal with "all those catering and club folk," quickly agreed. Beth jotted down everything the sister wanted; type of food, entertainment, number of guests, dress attire. She wanted it to be the "party of the year" and had said that "price is of no concern." Beth hung up the phone, giddy as a little girl, and immediately called Ginny and Julie. That night they celebrated and got wasted on fruity vodka drinks. The next morning they woke up, grabbed some coffee, and got to work. That was day one of Bash. They initially called themselves The Party Girls, but soon changed it to Bender because they received too many calls requesting escorts. Eventually, Bender turned into Bash, a more accessible name for the older set.

The three of them, whose only job titles had been professional socialite, finally had something to do. They talked and talked and talked, brainstorming and bouncing ideas off one another, taking into account that money was no object, and ended up planning one of the best celebrations Texas had ever seen. They threw the party downtown in a swanky club space with three-story ceilings. They had a DJ spinning house music and made part of the dance floor weave through the tables. They had caterers spit-roast a hog on one of the balconies and all the fixings were routinely stocked at every table; cornbread, slaw, collared greens, sweet potato mash. They had two bars strategically set up at either end of the room, as well as a roving bar (Julie's idea) which wheeled its way past all the tables. They hired random circus-type characters, donning sexy eclectic costumes, to perform about the room. They hired a photographer to take candid photos, and even invited some members of the gossip press to witness the evening. Finally, in a mostly networking move, they invited several "important" friends just to show them what they could do.

When it was all over, this party for an unknown Texan rancher caused vibrations from Southampton to Fairfield County to deep in the heart of Texas. Bash was the talk of the town (actually, the party was the talk of the town, but those on the inside knew that Bash had planned it). The next morning, or rather afternoon, the three of them woke up and smiled (despite each of them sporting wicked hangovers). They knew they were on to something good. That felt like a long time ago to Ginny because they'd come so far since. Bash was now a full-time party machine, planning every event one could think of, from birthdays to "We just want to celebrate the shortest day of the year."

That first party was planned from Beth's cushy living room but they'd since moved to their own chic office space (which they decorated like a living room). They compiled the most complete who's-who list of venues, decorators, caterers, and entertainers, and bought a vacation home in the Caribbean. Their clients included an array of celebrities, from actors to agents to producers, to politicians and alleged criminals, to athletes and rock stars. They had to turn down business because they had so much coming in. They were also able to jack up their fee so they could live comfortably planning just one event a month, even though they took on upwards of a dozen. Julie had stopped drinking during the day, they'd all ditched most of their drug habits, and they all took yoga together. For Ginny Lasher, growing into adulthood was the best time she'd ever had (and she thought it'd never get better than college).

Chapter Twenty-Two

GINNY HAD met Will a year after Bash's inception. Bash had already established itself and Ginny was in a constant state of planning and partying (which was great, but it was wearing her out). The business was successful and Ginny knew that it would keep growing and prosper but she was craving a time-out. Since the Texas rancher birthday, Bash hadn't taken a day off, and a day off was the only thing on Ginny's mind. August was approaching and Ginny decided to get out of town for a week. It was all right with Beth and Julie, who took it upon themselves to plan their own vacations when Ginny returned. Ginny wanted to disappear for a while. She didn't want to see anyone and she didn't want to do anything. In August, the city seemed to lose half it's population, so she knew she could just stay in Manhattan, but that wouldn't feel like "getting away." Ginny figured an escape to the end of Long Island would do the trick. Maybe the Hamptons, maybe Montauk, maybe somewhere in between. She didn't care, just as long as there weren't too many people. But work was so busy that she didn't even plan out her trip. When the time came, one of the top party-planners from the greatest city on Earth just got in her car and drove without a single reservation, without a single map, and without her phone.

In the middle of the night, after hours of dizzying traffic, Ginny stumbled upon a dark, quaint inn far from the main road. She managed to get a room, which was small, yet comfortable, and proceeded to collapse on the bed. When she awoke the next morning she'd forgotten where she was and how she got there, but when she peered out the window, she saw the beach, the ocean, and what appeared to be only one person enjoying it. Ginny knew she'd found what she was looking for. After some coffee and a fresh blueberry muffin (which were provided by an adorable old lady named Eleanor), she slowly walked out to the beach with a chair and towel. She didn't bother asking Eleanor where she was; she didn't want to know. There were only a few folks staying at the inn and Eleanor cooked every meal for them. That was all the information Ginny needed. The beach was instantly relaxing. She set up her "zone," stripped down to her bikini, sank into her chair and listened to the waves. Then she giggled; she'd been waiting for this moment for a long time.

"How's it going?"

Ginny heard a voice but didn't open her eyes. The voice was soft and peaceful. She'd been resting, if not sleeping, for a couple of hours and didn't want it to end. But then she figured it might be awkward if she didn't respond. With her eyes still shut, she made sure her bikini was on properly, took in a deep breath and replied just as peacefully, "Wonderful." She paused, enjoying this mysterious moment. "You?"

"Perfect," the voice responded in that slow, soft tone. There wasn't any doubt in his reply and it made Ginny think that maybe she was in some heavenly place where everything was, indeed, perfect and wonderful and this guy was some sort of angel. Still, she refused to open her eyes, savoring the experience for all that it was worth. Nor did she say anything else. She felt his presence leave but even then she didn't open her eyes. She was content.

The wind and the water relaxed Ginny more than she could've imagined. All of her non-stop phone calls, meetings and cocktail parties came to a therapeutic halt. Her first day of doing absolutely nothing was a culture shock but by day two she couldn't picture doing anything else. The beach remained quiet and empty aside from the waves crashing down. On the second day, at what felt like 2 o'clock in the afternoon, the same soft voice spoke.

"How's it going?" the voice asked again in that serene, peaceful manner.

Ginny knew this angelic voice was not part of the inn's amenities but she thought it'd be great to incorporate it into a vacation getaway. Just have someone with a tranquil voice walking around and asking folks how they're doing. In the meanwhile, she had the prototype floating before her and she thought she should answer soon or else he'd fly away. "Wonderful," she said at last. "You?"

"Perfect," the voice said, this time with more of a smile. It seemed that her angel understood the joke, too. And then somehow, and Ginny couldn't quite figure out the logic of it, she knew he was going to walk away again and come back the next day. Maybe then she'd take a look.

The next day, Ginny was again lying on the beach, taking in the sun and listening to the waves. It was amazing how the relaxing calm of the ocean simplified her life. She felt that the ocean was teaching her how to think a little more clearly, how to see things in their purest form, how to be patient with her every move. Ginny wished there was a portable beach she could take back with her to the mad city. If only she had that, then she could easily recall all the lessons the ocean had taught her and maybe her hectic life would slow down just a bit.

"How's it going?"

The voice was back. Was she going to look and see who this person was? She was absorbed in the mystery of the whole thing and checking out the face behind the voice would surely be disappointing. Ginny didn't know if she wanted to risk that. But then again, she was very single and hadn't had much romance in her life since Bash began, unless she counted tipsy make-out sessions with random guys (which she didn't). It was just safer for all involved if she kept her eyes closed. If this guy was anywhere near cute, she might not be able to control herself.

"Wonderful," she replied, but she could sense dilemma in her own voice. She wondered if he had heard it too. "You?" she asked weakly. Damn, she was letting her guard down. She really hoped he couldn't feel it.

"Not so bad," he said, surprising Ginny. He went from "perfect" to "not so bad."

She speculated about what that actually meant. Was it because she wouldn't look at him? Ginny stopped her ego right there and spoke again. "Not perfect?" she asked, still with her eyes shut, still absorbing the radiant sunlight on her face.

He didn't respond for a while and she was getting curious as to what he would say (and hoping he wouldn't leave). She had a comfortable feeling about him, whoever he was, and didn't mind that he was just standing there. Ginny's intuition was telling her that this peaceful stranger was just staring out towards the ocean (and not ogling her barely covered body) and "not so bad" only meant that he was fine. Her anxiety started retreating and she separated herself from the worry of opening her eyes.

"Not yet," he finally said in that soft tone.

"Oh," Ginny said, not knowing what else to say.

"But maybe later," the voice continued with another smile.

"There's always time," she said, playing along.

"Perfection comes through patience."

"Did the ocean tell you that?" Ginny asked, wondering if this angel had learned the same insights that she had. The warm sunlight hid behind a cloud, dropping the temperature a few degrees. Ginny instinctively opened her eyes, completely forgetting her mystery game, and noticed that the passing cloud was actually kind of cute.

That was the day Ginny met her future husband.

Ginny and Will spent the remainder of the week together lounging on the sand, going for an occasional swim, and talking when there was something to say. They ate dinner every evening and strolled along the beach every night. Will was the opposite of her world back in Manhattan. Like his voice, he was mellow and free of stress and was never in a rush. This was all new to her and she only hoped that it would last. Fortunately, Will also lived in Manhattan, so perhaps they could continue this little thing they started. He was like no one she'd ever met (or at least no one she'd ever socialized with). She was entirely too used to the dappers of the East Side and the model boys who were too pretty for their own good. Will was just a humble guy who seemed to have his priorities in order. She could definitely get used to this.

By the end of the week, Ginny and Will had bonded in the way only lovers can, and on the last night they shared the same bed (and Ginny was even more sure that he could be the one). Will shortened his stay and they took Ginny's car back to Manhattan. They dropped off the car at her garage and said their good-byes. She knew he was special, but she didn't want to go too fast. That usually ended in some kind of natural disaster and this was too important to her. Thankfully, Will's patient personality stretched out into the realm of relationships and he was comfortable with anything Ginny wanted to do. As it were, they were living together within a month. I'll move as slow as a turtle next time, Ginny swore, but knowing full well there might not be a next time. She wanted this feeling to last and she had a notion it would. In some twisted sense of logic, Ginny knew she had just found her portable beach, and she smiled every time she thought about it.

Chapter Twenty-Three

THE EDITING process was never-ending. Everything created could be edited down to nothing, and that was how Will Canter approached his job. The hierarchy at *The Celebrity Poll* was simple: The writers would write the story, the assistant editors would make it compact and tight, the head editors would finish it, then millions of people around the world would read it (and often write *The Poll* if they saw any mistakes).

Will's morning agenda consisted of four stories to be edited, as well as creating some headlines for them. Being an editor, or even an assistant editor, was somewhat empowering. Will was the shepherd and the second-rate writers were his flock. It may have sounded like a small God complex, but Will didn't have that attitude. It just felt good when he did his job. The few times he did feel above the rest came when his own pieces were untouched by the head editors; when his work went straight to print. But then again, everyone in the office felt immortal when their work was read by the masses.

The Big Hooka was releasing a new, controversial album that week; an album that had received excellent reviews, but was banned by chain stores across the country and was immediately put on the "PERKY" (Parent's Who Really Care About Youth) boycott list. Georgia Dunelle, aka *The Big Hooka*, was a white female rap artist who, with her name alone, had the ability to shake up the establishment. Which establishment that was, Will wasn't sure, but the woman was creating rifts everywhere. Her new album, *Ass Avenue*, had a picture of her on the cover standing on a busy street with her back (and full ass) facing the camera. She was wearing her usual garb (tight black leather pants, tight leopard-skin top, heavy-product blond hair), with a cloud of smoke surrounding her. She had spoken to *The Celebrity Poll* in an exclusive phone interview, venting her disgust with those who would ban her album without even listening to it. She also noted that the chain stores that had banned it were acting on the reviews and not their own discretion. She claimed that the worst thing she rapped about was how much fun it was getting high with her crew, then added, "You know what, honey? I ain't the first and I ain't the last who's gonna tell it like it is."

The fifth installment of the *Man on the Move* film series was premiering in New York and Los Angeles. *Morgan Speed*, played by Donny "Ladies Man" Binger, faced a whole new set of obstacles in his endless quest to capture *The Chameleon*, his arch-enemy whom he'd never seen. As far as Will was concerned, the second film was the only decent one because Al Aston, a Hollywood pro, was brought in to pen the screenplay. This latest *Man on the Move* might be good as well because Aston had returned to write it. In an interview conducted by *The Poll*, Aston discussed the story line and how he'd used the film's formula to its advantage, as he'd done for the second film.

Carla Lotta, the glamorously aged model who now lived abroad, posed nude for an Eastern European adult website. Predictably, it caused quite a stir in the fashion industry as it did in the rest of the entertainment world. No one knew why she did it, but there was speculation that she had blown all her savings on manservants, drugs and international horse racing. Some thought she did it to prove that she still "had it." Unfortunately, her liberal pictorial proved otherwise. "It is a sad day for our industry," reported an entertainment news show. Ms. Lotta wasn't available for interviews, let alone a comment. In fact, the former *"Ms. Delicious"* lacked even a spokesperson. Will thought this could be an effective strategy, though, because by being silent you could raise public curiosity, and then BAM!!! You're back in business, doing your own talk show, and making millions again.

The final piece Will had to edit was a column called "Celebrity Spit." This was where *The Poll* reported celebrity rivalries and battles. The latest "Spit" was between two well-known magicians. One of them, *Fantasma*, claimed that the other, *Marcus FireBreather*, stole his climactic trick for his upcoming tour. He maintained that *FireBreather* had spies invade his private rehearsal space and swipe all the blueprints for what *Fantasma* called *"The Eruptor,"* a volcano-like structure that he had to escape from or else be doomed. *FireBreather* fully admitted in a press conference that he had added a trick to his show called the *"Volcano of Peril,"* but added that he had conjured up the idea a year before while mud-bathing in the Alps. He also said that *Fantasma* was making the whole thing up and actually stole the idea from him after showing up incognito to one of his shows in Luxembourg. *FireBreather* concluded by calling *Fantasma* a "fat wussy."

Now that he was done editing, it was time to come up with some headlines. At *The Celebrity Poll*, headlines were routinely changed by the head editors, so Will had learned not to exert too much energy into it. (Occasionally someone would throw a tizzy when theirs weren't used, but it was usually a new employee or this one knothead named Craig.) Thinking of headlines was a process for which Will could just ease back in his chair, tune out the office noise, and relax. He thought that perhaps during one of these times (when his eyes were closed and he was in somewhat of a trance), when someone noticed his meditative aura and thought he was stoned. Maybe that was how his reputation as a pot smoker began. It did not, however, explain why his own family thought he was burnt.

For Carla Lotta, the fashion queen gone nude, the headline, *A LOTTA THIS, A LOTTA THAT,* repeated itself inside Will's mind. It was a decent headline that the head editors might like but there was something about it that made him uneasy. His concern, and the probable cause for the stubborn repetition, was that he wasn't sure if he was thinking about the story or about his upcoming marriage.

Doubt is common, Will reasoned, as common as corn. Ginny was wonderful, but did he want to spend the rest of his life and then all of eternity with her? He didn't know the answer to that, and because the word "yes" didn't instantly pop up he'd been frantically trying to come up with a solution. Editing down a relationship was an unusual activity and probably more suitable for a philosopher, but Will couldn't help it. He wanted to know if what he had was real or only ideal. He wanted to sweep out all of the glitz and see what was left. Since their engagement, Will couldn't stop asking himself one question: Was he in love or had he just become used to someone? Where this came from, he didn't know. But it wouldn't go away.

The Gazers were beginning to distract Will from his head-line-turned-therapist state. Even with his eyes closed he could feel their stares. They all knew what he was doing as he'd been using this technique for quite some time. Their unfeigned curiosity meant only one thing: It was almost time for lunch.

The Gazer's behavior was predictable. Every day, close to the lunch hour, they suddenly became bored with whatever they were doing and snooped around like a dog looking for a treat. The stares were blank, and Will was convinced that these people had no recollection of this part of the day. If they were asked that evening what they were doing at 11:30am, they'd say, "I'm not sure. I think I was working on a story." When the clock struck noon, the whole herd would file out to the elevators. Approximately one hour later they'd all return in the same fashion (which was when Will took his lunch, thereby reducing the amount of time he had to endure their company).

Will tried to focus on entertainment headlines but he was caught inside another subject. The fact was that he wasn't sure. He'd always say that everything can be edited down to nothing, but after many sessions of deep thought he had concluded that a healthy relationship (and marriage for that matter) can be edited down to one thing: Love. About seven weeks before, while tooling around Central Park and munching on a vendor's pretzel, Will had determined that if he honestly edited down his and Ginny's relationship, the only thing left would be sex. Sex was the savior of their love. At least it was for him. Or at least it seemed to be. He couldn't help but think there was something better for him out there, something beyond a sexual dream. Yes, he enjoyed her company. Yes, he cared about her. Yes, he could probably spend the rest of his life with her. But was it because of sex? Was it because he was used to her? Both? Neither? Or was this love?

CONFUSION topped Will's personal headlines.

The Gazers formed their line and proceeded toward the elevators. Will avoided making eye contact, slouching down as low as he could in his chair. When the last Gazer was gone Will let out a deep breath. The office was silent and Will envisioned it always being that way.

After lunch, Will would organize all the headlines with the appropriate articles and hand them in upstairs. He could finish them now but had no real urge to. He picked up his phone for the first time that day and called Ginny.

"Hey, Babe! Good morning!" Ginny was Ms. Energy, which was one of the things that Will liked about her.

"Hey, Hon, it's not morning anymore," Will observed.

"I know," Ginny replied in a tone that really meant, "Hey, Will, maybe we should speak before noon once in a while."

Will understood. "Oh, yeah, I know. So how's your day going?" he said, rushing to avoid the "Can't we talk in the morning?" conversation. It was not as though he didn't want to talk in the morning but he was so used to their current pattern that he just didn't want to change it. She sometimes called him Old Man Willy.

"Oh, fine. We're still planning Baroot's 50th b-day, but they keep calling, wanting to have it here or there or some alley downtown, and I try to tell them, 'Listen, this is our specialty. Hello? Like, we're gonna take care of you so stop calling, you idiots.' But they keep calling, but whatever. How's it over there?"

"Ah, it's all right. Did some edits. Maybe I can get out of here early or something."

"Yeah, and maybe plan some of your own wedding," Ginny said with a whole lot of sarcasm, implying that he'd been noticeably absent from the process. Will, in return, rationalized that it's tough to plan something that you're just not excited about. He wondered if Ginny had ever picked up on this or if she maybe felt the same. He had trouble believing that he was all alone in his doubt.

"It's your wedding, too," Will answered back weakly. He couldn't compete with Ginny when it came to the spoken word. (The written word, however, was a different story. Too bad they didn't communicate with memos.)

"Hey, why don't we grab some lunch? And then we could actually talk about our wedding for once." She emphasized the words "our" and "once," and Will knew that she was right. Though still uncertain, perhaps it was time to help out. His original strategy was to let Ginny, the premier party planner, plan their wedding weekend (and he'd just nod in approval of everything she'd recommend). But he didn't anticipate her mother getting so wrapped up in the process, trying to out-plan her daughter. Nor did he expect his own mother to go mildly berzerk about her own little wedding-wants. Ginny had remained in the center of the 'Wrath of Mom' while Will had casually stepped a few hundred feet away.

"Sure, yeah. When can you get out of there?" Will asked without enough enthusiasm.

"Now, Baby! Let's do it!" she ordered with her authoritative voice, the same voice that would keep their kids in line.

Chapter Twenty-Four

THE CHESTER BURGER was one of the best in the city. Always cooked medium-rare with a slice of American cheese, the "Burg" was all one needed to consume in a day. On weekends, you couldn't eat there because of the tourist factor (Chester's was on every "Must Do in New York" list), but the middle-of-the-week lunch usually allowed you to get quick take-out or even the coveted table. Ginny Lasher, of course, knew the owner (it was her job to know these people), but even so, it was difficult to get preferential treatment when the restaurant was slammed. Will and Ginny tried to have lunch together a couple times a week, but it evolved into once every other week and Chester's had become their go-to place.

Surprising himself, Will arrived first. Even more to his surprise, the coveted table was available (perhaps a reward for his motivated timing). The table was near the others but was in its own nook and out of sight from them. The coveted table allowed for a private, if not intimate, Chester Burger lunch. Maybe getting there first would show Ginny that he was fully receptive to wedding planning.

The lanky waiter followed Ginny to the table and took their order as she sat down. Knowing what to order was not a challenging task. The only variable was whether or not to order French fries (which they did). Will leaned across the table to give Ginny a kiss, to which she turned her head just enough so that they both kissed burger-broiled air. In a quick sexual flashback, Will remembered that they used to kiss because they wanted to. Now it seemed they kissed because they had to, because it was required behavior for couples. Maybe she was having doubts, too.

Will playfully started the wedding dialogue with a wild west accent, "So I hear there's a wedding in need the empty noise between bites, he started talking about their class that evening but Ginny mumbled that she probably wouldn't make it. Unfortunately, the Chester Burgers weren't working their magic.

Ginny and her mother had been engaged in guerrilla warfare since the day Will proposed. (Actually, her mother allowed a five-day grace period before putting on her camouflage.) With his fiancée so preoccupied with psychological family tactics, Will was left alone to question his marrying desires. Ginny seemed to have picked up on that today, though Will had no idea how. Maybe it was that female intuition thing. Will wondered if The Queen's drillings had finally broken down Ginny's morale; there hadn't been a recent day when he and Ginny hadn't had a spat. The cooking class that evening was really a covert operation. It was designed to get them together and do something other than wedding plan or wedding argue. However, up until this point the mission was a failure. Ginny had only made it there once (the first day).

Will deduced that Ginny's successful business was the reason for the decline of her and her mother's relationship. The Queen had a different, and perhaps outdated, mentality. Her 'little Ginny had a social responsibility to keep herself abreast of the forever-dynamic infrastructure of the upper-upper class... Ginny Lasher was not meant to work with the masses.' (The Queen, however, had been overheard at a black-tie fund-raiser for the museum saying how excited she was about her daughter's "entrepreneurial adventures.") The real issue, though, was that her mother only wanted to share a part of herself; she wanted Ginny to let her be a mother, to have respect for her and to have admiration for her. Will speculated this as the subtext, but kept his thoughts to himself. He didn't have much respect for The Queen nor did he like her. The more he envisioned her as his mother-in-law, the more he wanted to move to Tahiti and marry a topless girl on the beach.

An improperly planned wedding had the potential to ruin the closest of relationships and Ginny and The Queen were illustrating that. "Why should there even be a discussion of what flowers are on the damn table?" Ginny would demand. "It's not her wedding! Bitch..." After a moment of guilt passed for calling her mother a bitch (during which Will would reach for a 'beyond his years' level of wisdom and stay silent and still), she'd slouch and frown, "I'm so tired of this."

The rehearsal dinner was an easier ordeal to plan. If it'd been too complicated and frustrating, Will was sure that he would've already bailed out and gone into hiding. The guests were limited to members of the wedding party, the immediate families and a select amount of close friends. His parents had merely made reservations at a restaurant (Alumnus, the "Best Steakhouse on Campus"), which only required some family influence (cold cash) to reserve the Homecoming Room. The reservation was for one hundred guests, which was more than enough. So not only was the evening planned, but they had room for any over-inviting slip-ups.

After the burgers vanished they went out to the sidewalk and Ginny smoked a "just once in a while" cigarette. Little had been said since Ginny's question, "Do you even care?", which was fine with Will because he was afraid of getting into that kind of discussion. He knew he'd have to talk about it soon, but he had to think it through first. They politely kissed and Ginny hopped into a cab. Will strolled back to the office, taking his time, and wondered if others had been in his place and what they had done. He paused for a moment, let out a Chester Burger belch, and regained his stride.

Chapter Twenty-Five

"DO YOU even care?"

The Gazers had gone into a "Frenzy" and Will didn't even notice. Tara "Red House Over Yonder" passed by his desk sporting a smile, letting him know that she was responsible. Will tried to return the smile but couldn't figure out which muscles to use. It's odd, he thought, when something that was once so important (like setting up a "Frenzy") loses its significance. The question Ginny had posed during lunch was now rattling him, and all the activity at the office was just a mild distraction.

"Do you even care?"

Will imagined Tough Teddy Mason, one of the larger employees at *The Celebrity Poll*, coming over and punching him in the face. It didn't hurt at all. He felt like he was on super-drugs. Everything around him was moving in slow-motion. Great, Will thought, now even *I* think I'm on drugs. Knowing he'd have to address Ginny's question soon had immobilized him. She'd probably forgotten about it and had just said it sarcastically but he was taking it very seriously. It had, in many ways, summed up all the questions floating around his mind. He found himself in an anxiety-driven daydream in which he and Ginny broke up, got back together, broke up again, then got back together. When he finally realized what he was doing, they had just broken up again.

"Do you even care?"

The thought of ending their relationship was terrifying. Picturing a life without Ginny was nauseating. Yet thinking that marriage could be the worst mistake of his life was nauseating, too. What the hell was going on here? Will wasn't sure if it would take more courage to face the consequences of breaking up, or to hang in there and commit to something that he didn't have much confidence in. Will recalled the old expression, "Courage comes after the fight," but it wasn't uplifting whatsoever. This was the wrong time for a session of malaise. The Gazers were pre-occupied and this could've been a wonderful, easy-going afternoon at *The Poll*. But now, instead of writing headlines for *The Big Hooka*, Will was obsessed with something he couldn't understand.

"Ginny?"

"Yeah, Babe?"

"Hon, we gotta talk."

"I know that."

"No, not about the wedding. I mean, yes, about the wedding… but there's something else."

"Will, I know there's something else going on, but I don't know what it is."

"I know."

"You're just being so distant and detached. I have no idea what you're thinking and I feel like I can't do anything right."

"I'm sorry you feel that way. That's not what I want."

"I feel like I'm walking on egg shells around you. I don't want to do anything to piss you off, and I've never had to walk on eggshells for anyone… that's just not my thing. So I'm going to ask you this once, and you're going to answer me once, and that'll be it. And just to let you know, when I asked you today if you cared, I was also flat-out telling you that I don't. At least not anymore."

"I do care."

"Yeah, well, whatever. That's not the question. The question is whether you want this or not. Yes or no. Do-you-want-this? Are you in or are you out?

"What do you mean?"

"You know what I mean, and I'm tired of all this. Just give me a yes or a no, and we'll take it from there. Either way, it's fine with me. I just need to know. I just need to hear it from you right now."

I DON'T KNOW!!! was Will's newest personal headline.

He eventually had to call her. There was no way to avoid that. They had to talk about this, or at least figure out what "this" was.

At the moment, "this" was ruining Will's day. If he could get some cooperation from his father regarding the wedding list, then that would perhaps ease the tension in his and Ginny's discussion. But knowing that The Queen was going to hurl grenades when confronted about her own wedding list, Will figured that Ginny wouldn't be in the mood for constructive chatter anyway. Just then, he wondered if *The Big Hooka* was good in bed.

"William Canter's office. How can I help you?"

"Hi, uh, this is his son," Will said so weakly that he doubted the receptionist believed him.

"His son?" she asked in a tone of surprise rather than disbelief.

"Yeah, it's Will Canter... the fourth," Will replied, as if that would prove who he was.

"I realize that," she began, "Let me see if he's available, okay?"

Will was thankful that he'd made it this far. How he went from hanging out with *The Big Hooka* in a hot tub to being on hold for his father was beyond his recollection. He wished he could confide in his dad; ask him what to do, ask him what *he* would do. Maybe he'd gone through the same range of emotions and doubt. Or maybe not. Maybe it wasn't a favorable topic to bring up six months before the big day. After about three minutes (which felt like twenty), the classical music was interrupted.

"William!?" His father had one of those deep booming voices (the kind you liked to have on your side). Will had never been "Will" to his father, he'd always been "William."

"Hey, Dad," Will said. "It's me."

"Everything copacetic!? Are you all right!?" his father boomed.

"Oh yeah, everything's fine."

His father assumed that there was something amiss. "That's wonderful, son! You don't call often when I'm at work!" he said in a semi-questioning tone.

"Yeah, well, I had something to ask you... to run by you," Will began, not sure where he was going with this, "and I thought that I should do it sooner than later, you know?"

"What's on your mind!?" his father asked.

Will wanted to say, "Well, Dad, I'm having doubts. I don't know if I'm in love anymore. I don't know if I want to marry Ginny."

"Well, it's about the wedding," Will said, going slow, trying to maintain some poise.

"Ah! The wedding! You know, your mother and I are really looking forward to it. We're very proud of you, son!"

Was that just a piece of positive reinforcement? Was that his father saying, "I know how you're feeling and that's perfectly normal. You know, I wasn't sure either, and neither was your mother." Will wondered if his dad had a strong enough intuition to read his thoughts. The ideal answer was yes, but the real answer was no. His father was clueless.

"Yeah, it'll be great," agreed Will, without much assertion. Mustering his strength, he debated whether or not he should reach out for some help. "But I need to talk to you about the guest list." Nope.

"Ah! The ol' guest list! What, does Lasher want more faces in the crowd!?"

"Actually, there's not enough spaces for all the faces," answered Will, realizing he'd just come up with a decent headline. He suddenly felt a shade more at ease, a little closer to his normal self, closer to how he felt before lunch.

His father paused before speaking, seeming to analyze that last statement. "Oh…" he responded without the boom. Will didn't have a follow-up sentence, so he waited until his father spoke again. "I see," he continued and paused for a while more. But then he regained his old composure. "Weddings can be quite a burden, can't they, son!?"

"Yeah, Dad, they sure can," Will answered softly. If you only knew.

"All right, son!" his father started. "Since you're telling me about this, I assume that your mother and I have to adjust our guest list!"

Well, half of that was true, Will thought. Maybe they could work it out between the two of them. Maybe Will didn't have to bring up the Barrow Club folk. "Well, yeah, kind of," Will replied, not knowing the best way to respond.

"So what you're saying is get the list down to one-fifty."

"Yep," Will confirmed.

"I see," his father said, again in that rare non-booming voice. "Looks like I'll have to make some modifications on my side." After a lengthy pause, he finally came booming back. "No problem! Son, I'm looking at our list right now! I'll take care of it, all right!?"

His tone was friendly, and Will felt a little more pressure alleviated from his tense shoulders. "Thanks, Dad, that'll help out a lot."

"Son, I know how it is! Way back when, your grandpa Stu was a real hard-ass about your mother's and my wedding! No need to explain. I'll just take care of it!"

"Great. Thanks a lot, Dad, I'm really glad you understand."

"Absolutely! So how's everything else!? You need anything!?" he asked, as he usually did.

Yes, Dad, I need to know how I really feel. A brief wave of panic returned and zipped through Will's body. "No, Dad, everything's fine. Just trying to work on the wedding."

"Well, I know you and Ginny will have it all worked out! Your mother and I really look forward to it!"

Was that positive reinforcement again? Maybe he had underestimated his father. "Okay, Dad," Will said as lively as he could.

The "Frenzy" was beginning to subside and Will could sense random eyes studying his every move. The uncomfortable aura around him was probably visible enough for the Gazers to notice and, subsequently, be curious about. Will wished he was on a different floor. Tara walked by his desk again and asked if he was all right. Will barely nodded in return and waved her off. He mumbled, "Yeah, I'm fine," and then added "Good job," referring to the "Frenzy." Maybe you can help me organize my mind, Madame Rouge.

Did getting used to someone mean that you were in love with them? The feeling of relief Will had after talking to his father started disappearing and the anxiety started coming back. Unanswered questions were smothering him. Despite the mental pandemonium, Will knew he should have some sort of "go-to" phrase handy for when he talked to Ginny. If he had that, then he could at least fall back on something if he got frazzled. Unfortunately, the effectiveness of "What can I do?" had just expired.

"I don't know if this is working out."

"I just think we've lost our spark."

"I don't know if I'm ready for this."

"Our relationship is just about sex."

"Are you sure you want to go through with this?"

His editorial talents were failing him and panic continued to peck at him. He had to call Ginny soon because he didn't want to feel like this all afternoon, especially with the Gazers creeping about. Out of self-created desperation, he grabbed a pen and paper and began writing furiously. When he was finished, he picked up the phone and dialed Tara's extension.

"Hey, Cardinal, I need a favor. Can you fly by for a sec?"

Tara, who could tell that something was irking Will, agreed without comment. She came by right away and dragged over a chair.

"What's up, Smoke Nuts?" she asked.

"Listen, I'm in a little funk and I don't know what to do and I thought of one thing that might help and you're the only one I can trust here."

"Go on."

Will handed her the scribbled-on piece of paper. "I need you to ask me these questions."

Tara scanned the list and then looked at him sideways. "Have you graduated from the cannabis?"

"No, listen, I'm just in a weird spot right now and I'm trying everything I can do to get out of it."

"To get out of your wedding?" Tara asked as she glanced at the piece of paper.

Will paused, not wanting to reveal anything he shouldn't. "No, just out of this weird spot." He took a deep breath. "Okay. Let's start."

"All right, Doobie Boy. Ready?"

"Yes."

"Okay, here we go." Though excited about this personal life infiltration, Tara kept her emotions to herself. She didn't want the Gazers to vulture where they didn't belong. "Are you happy?"

"Yes."

"Are you in love?"

"Yes."

"Are you sure?"

"I think so."

"Hmm. Are you getting married?"

"Yes."

"Is this what you want?"

"I don't know."

"Do you even care?"

"How can I not?" Will took the sheet of paper away from Tara and tore it up into thin strips. The great experiment didn't work.

"You just answered a question with a question," she noted.

"Yeah, so?"

"Good luck with this," Tara said as she stood up. "Between you and me, you should toke up and try meditating on this."

Tara of the Red Hairs walked away, leaving Will to contemplate yet again what the hell "this" was. She had used the word twice in her parting statement, confirming in his mind that it was a vital part of the mystery. Will knew that if he could define it, then it would be a tremendous help in his struggle.

"This" could be love, he thought. That was the easiest solution. "This" could also be his relationship, which was probably a more accurate definition. Or, maybe, "this" was his true feelings, the ones he was afraid to reveal. All the answers were realistic and all the answers were part of the truth, but as Will privately cheered that he may have solved the riddle, he realized that it didn't make him feel any better.

Will dreamed of a perfect life, with a perfect woman, living in a perfect house, with perfect kids running around and cleaning up their toys when they were done playing. Ginny, however, wasn't the dream woman. But to her credit, Will acknowledged, that dream woman only existed in his dreams. Is there a time when you give up the dream and just go with what you got? In perhaps the deepest thinking day he'd had since age seventeen, Will concluded that the answer was yes.

Unfortunately, the philosopher wasn't finished. Will asked himself if he could get closer to the dream than he was now? It took less time and thought to come up with another yes.

"Hey." Will wanted to remain neutral in tone and attitude.

"Hey," echoed Ginny with a similar amount of enthusiasm.

"Talked to my dad and everything's cool." Hopefully good news would soften things up. "He's going to take care of it."

"Great," was Ginny's response but it sounded more like a "whatever."

"Talk to your mother?"

"Yeah, we talked."

"How'd it go?" asked Will, who was obviously the one pushing the conversation.

"She called me a princess."

Will didn't say anything for a while. The overwhelming fears he'd been having all day had temporarily vanished as soon as Ginny had picked up the phone. Will didn't understand what that meant but he realized he should've started talking about this a long time ago. Across the telephone line he could see Ginny staring at a wall and, perhaps, about to run into it head first. They both knew that The Queen wasn't going to be receptive to their request, but Will also knew that this was now a number two priority. With this knowledge as his guide, Will prayed for wisdom as he formulated his next sentence.

"Ginny, I think we need to talk."

"Oh, really," Ginny quickly replied.

Avoiding the sarcastic bait, Will continued. "I think that there are a lot of things going on, and we just need to talk about them. You know, just to get them out of our system. Just to get on the same page."

Ginny was silent, but Will didn't want to add to his statement so he patiently waited. When Ginny finally spoke, she used the famous frosty Lasher monotone.

"Will, I really don't know what you're talking about. What I do know, though, is that something is going on with you and I don't know what it is. So if that's what you want to talk about, then fine. I think we need to, too. But just do me a favor and leave me out of it, okay? All I've done is fall in love with you, gotten engaged to you, and done all the planning for this damn wedding."

Will could hear her tears. He instinctively wanted to tell her that there was nothing wrong and that everything was going to work out, but he didn't. There actually *was* something wrong and Will didn't want to go any further until he knew how he felt. Right now, he felt like the evil one.

"You know, you're right. It's me. I'm just saying that maybe we can talk about it tonight," Will humbly offered, but then corrected himself. "No, you're right. Maybe *I* can talk about it tonight. You've been taking care of everything and, I don't know, I guess I've been in my own world. I think I just need to talk a little, to vent a little. I guess I've been a little confused lately, or something like that."

The truth felt good, especially when expressed so diplomatically. He didn't say that everything was going to be fine, nor did he adopt the evil one's persona. He just politely told the truth.

After a lengthy pause, Ginny mumbled, "Fine." Then added, "But, you know what? Nothing I'm going to say is going to solve anything in your head. So maybe you should figure it out on your own, and then we'll talk."

"Listen, Ginny, we're a team and we have to do these things together. We're not going to solve anything tonight, at least we're probably not going to, but at least we can… sorry, I mean at least *I* can get some things off my chest." Will caught his breath and added, "If this is going to work, then I need your help."

Ginny snapped back, "Well, PB, I really don't know what I can do to help, but if that's the way you feel, then fine. We'll talk about it later."

Click.

Whoops. Maybe the "I need your help" line was a boo-boo. Will drifted down, using his arms as a pillow and his desk as the mattress. Until now, Ginny had called him "PB" at random times of affection. It stood for "Portable Beach." She'd once told him that he reminded her of the beach where they had met, that he was a comforting symbol of tranquility, that he taught her how to relax. Will appreciated the nickname, was touched by the sentiment, and even shed a tear when she told him the story. But now, thinking back, while she was seeing her peaceful savior on a sunny beach in the Hampton's, he'd forgotten if he had seen the woman of his dreams, or just another hot chick in a bikini.

Chapter Twenty-Six

SHELTER WAS a necessity, and Paulson Neilson never realized it. He just sold real estate. He loved his job, every day, all day long. He enjoyed waking up at 10am, he enjoyed seeing apartments, and he *loved* getting his commissions. His main haunts were Chelsea and the Village, where he'd been since he moved to the city seven years before.

He got out of bed and smiled at the new sun. His lover looked at him with sleepy eyes, grinned, and fell back asleep. They had met in the local supermarket. Paulson was having a most interesting thought in the dairy section when James came strolling by with his shopping cart full of organic whatnot. He was definitely cute, and Paulson had a thing for healthy older men, so why not. Today was going to be full; five appointments, a new showing, contracts to sign, cooking class at 7pm.

Chelsea was a far cry from North Dakota. His whole life had been an uncomfortable passage until he'd found New York. Being gay in a town of three hundred just didn't sit well with the other two hundred and ninety-nine. But this he understood. He'd been home four times in the last seven years and, thankfully, the town's nerves seemed to have relaxed. During his last visit, he was actually met with open arms by the same people who had once berated him. Paulson assumed that his town had somehow become "proud" to have a gay alumnus. Perhaps his mother, he thought, had done some serious spinning, changing the mental foundation (which was difficult to do). So now when he came home, he was treated like a celebrity.

Paulson realized he was gay when he first became aware of sex, when he just couldn't get aroused by the cowgirl porno mags that his best friend, Billy, used to peruse. At first, he didn't quite know what was going on but eventually he had a very good idea, though he kept his secret hidden until after high school graduation. The schools he attended were a couple of towns over and it seemed that every girl had flirted with him at least once. Paulson had reluctantly done some light dating but never got fully involved with anyone. Holly Goods was his senior prom date. She was one of the more attractive gals in school and had essentially chosen Paulson to be her date. At the end of the night, when all the couples drifted off into their own seclusion, Holly stripped off her clothes and jumped him. When he didn't accept her advances she stormed off crying. The next day the town was talking.

Paulson pointed to that night as the moment he sent out invitations to his "coming out" party. After a semester of community college, Paulson knew it was time to leave. The town was not in his favor and the pressure was building for him to make a move. (His mother said she'd always known.) His first stop was Miami. There, for the first time in his life, he felt like he belonged.

As comfortable as Miami was, the atmosphere became stale. Paulson couldn't believe it but he was tired of having fun all the time (which was all that seemed to go on down there). He was raised to wake up, work, and come home. He certainly didn't mind a mild workday and staying out dancing and drinking until 6am, but like with the cowgirl porn, it just wasn't right for him. That's when he decided to come to the center of the world (or so he was told): New York City.

Through some seasonal friends in Miami, Paulson found a place to stay in Chelsea. When he arrived he was overwhelmed. The hustle and bustle of Miami didn't come close to Manhattan, and it took a few months of exploring and socializing before Paulson became acclimated. From that moment on, though, he knew he'd found his new home.

Then it was time to find a job, something beyond temp work at accounting firms. He also wanted to stay away from the club scene (he'd had his fill in Florida). After learning how much commission a real estate broker made, he knew he had found a career. This was something that really appealed to him. He loved seeing charming little apartments, as well as extravagant penthouses, and he knew he could sell, too, having done so for over eighteen years in North Dakota.

After getting his real estate license, he easily found work with Proud Properties; he already knew the targeted neighborhoods (he'd been exploring the terrain since he'd arrived) and he had a friendly personality. Paulson calculated that he could live comfortably with two rental commissions a month, and two a month didn't seem unrealistic. As it turned out, it wasn't. It was all about patience (which was very difficult for some brokers). People unfamiliar with the city didn't know what was worth what and usually had to make a mistake before they learned. With this in mind, Paulson didn't take the "Virgins" too seriously. He would timidly show them place after place, and oddly enough, his success rate grew substantially. If he acted passively, the people would want the place. If he tried to sell it, they would find some excuse why it wasn't right.

The job was growing on him. The more he learned about it and the city, the more proficient he became. About a year later Paulson crossed over into sales. He maintained some presence in rentals but sales was where the real action was at. A few sales a year could keep your tummy full. It was extra pleasing to Paulson that his selling strategy applied to sales as well. For all the first-time buyers, he'd behave nonchalantly; for the old pros, he'd give all the attention in the world.

New York had abundant activities: clubs, bars, restaurants, shopping, museums, parks. But Paulson had his own personal favorite: bowling. It took his new friends a while to understand his passion, but once they did they, too, embraced the sport. Paulson didn't know where his love for the game came from but his feelings were strong, and the more time he spent away from it, the more he yearned for it. There was a bowling alley in a neighboring town in North Dakota that he'd visited maybe three times, but that was it. Those were the only times he'd ever played in his life.

It started one day when he was walking around the Village with some friends and happened upon one of Manhattan's few bowling alleys. The group decided to check it out for a lark. By four in the afternoon, they were drunk off of cheap pitchers of beer and having the greatest day of their lives. Their scores were low but it didn't matter. For Paulson there was something wonderful about picking up an eight-pound rock and hurling it down towards ten unknowing, yet elusive pins. In the games they played that day he averaged close to a hundred; the best of the bunch. That night, while curing his hangover, he had the realization that bowling was the greatest sport ever invented. He soon became a regular at the alley, befriending the manager and the staff, and honed his game. Wednesday night was bowling night and everyone at Proud Properties knew it. After a few months of constant playing and studious tournament watching on television, Paulson's love for the game became an obsession and he bought his own bowling ball.

Paulson figured that everyone had their own "thing." Some folks, for example, liked to fish. Some liked to knit. *He* liked to bowl. His average score rose to about one hundred and sixty, which was acceptable for a while, but soon it just wasn't good enough. He wanted more. Unfortunately, more never came. He had remained at the same level since, occasionally getting close to two hundred but never breaking it. After some time, Paulson decided to give his bowling wrist a rest. He returned to a healthier bowling schedule of once a week and tried not to burn out his passion. The Wednesday night game dissolved and his co-workers and friends had all but forgotten about the days when bowling was the fad. Paulson didn't stop playing (he went every Monday), he just stopped talking about it. He was good at keeping secrets, so no one ever knew what he was doing on the first night of the week.

It had been a year or so since he'd gone into hiding, only sharing once in a while when necessary. He was of a dying breed, he thought. When bowling made its comeback (which he assumed was a given because so many fads came back from the grave), then he'd be ready.

In the meanwhile, he'd sharpen his skills and maybe look into what else the city had to offer. Being proficient in real estate lent itself to a lot of free time if you wanted it, and Paulson did. He used the time to stay in shape and to explore the city's interior. He tried to broaden his North Dakotan horizons by teaching himself about art and wine and even dog grooming (though that didn't survive his curiosity). He also started treating himself to different classes in the evening to further his knowledge base. The class he was taking now, and meeting with tonight, was just another way for him to get closer to something he couldn't quite explain. He just needed stimuli. From a town where almost none existed, he loved that there was enough for the whole western hemisphere in New York.

By 10:30am, Paulson was ready for the day. He had an 11am showing down on Perry Street. James had already left, which was quite typical. Paulson tended to wake up first, brew some coffee, make some waffles in his cherished waffle-maker, and then look through yesterday's mail. James would be off to work by the time the coffee was done, usually taking a cup to go. Their age difference didn't hamper their relationship (Paulson thought it actually added some spice), but Paulson's "Appetite For Affection" (as he privately called it) absolutely did.

The security and stability were there, and even the love was, too. What more does one need in a healthy relationship? Paulson had his own answer to that: sex, sex, sex. It only took a few weeks of serious dating before Paulson grew tired of James' sensual offerings. James wasn't a great lover nor did enjoy all the naughty things that Paulson did. James wanted a warm fire, a mug of herbal tea, some classical music, and long talks about little things.

Unfortunately, this criteria led Paulson to stray. Though he was emotionally committed to James, Paulson's affairs started soon after their first kiss. He knew it wasn't right but he had needs that were being ignored and he needed to satisfy them. Lately though, Paulson was trying a new experiment. Instead of fooling around with anyone cute enough or interested enough, Paulson was using the "Slap Method" to satisfy his uncommon libido. Since Sunday, when he had begun the experiment, he had "Slapped It" six times; twice on Sunday, three times on Monday, and once that morning (in the kitchen). Paulson wasn't sure why he was going through with the new plan. He knew it wasn't a guilt issue; there was no time for that. So he reasoned it might've had more to do with his fear of not being able to have a healthy relationship because of his sex addiction. There'd been plenty of temptations since he started "Slapping," but now, instead of pursuing the opportunity he would run to the bathroom. So far, so good. He firmly believed that neither the "Slap Method" nor his affairs were personal attacks on James. Rather, they were for his own benefit. Paulson could get his fix on his own, and then easily give James what he wanted; no sex and a lot of snuggling.

Chapter Twenty-Seven

IT WAS time to get to Perry Street. Paulson had an exclusive apartment for sale and some lunchtime shoppers coming by from 11am to 1pm. He wanted to get there to make sure the owner was gone and that he'd left the place in selling condition. Paulson walked downtown, passing the hip little restaurants and shops, all of which were mostly empty since the area wasn't busy in the morning. He soon found himself in the tranquil West Village, which didn't even feel like the city. Paulson was ahead of schedule, and Perry Street wasn't too far away, so he grabbed some coffee and a glazed donut from a local bakery. This place is celebrity central, thought Paulson. It seemed that every time he was in the neighborhood, he'd see an actor of name or there'd be some sort of movie being shot or he'd see someone who just had to be someone but couldn't remember who they were but was quite sure they were someone he should know.

The apartment was surprisingly presentable. Paulson did a quick walk-through and made some minor adjustments to make it more "sellable." He opened all the shades and curtains, letting the late-morning sunshine fill in the corners. The majority of apartments he'd seen were not sunlit places so he had to try to make them look as if they were. There was something about sunlight that helped a buyer say yes. The few windows in the apartment were already clean, which was good considering they were a part of the whole sunlight deal. After organizing some random piles of clutter, the apartment was ready to show. Prospective buyers would start showing up at around 11:15am. Paulson placed a customary sign-up sheet as well as a floor plan on the coffee table. He still had about twenty minutes unless, of course, there were any early birds.

The early birds were the one's who showed up before the scheduled time, and they always had a scavenger's look in their eyes. They were the true hunters of real estate. At least they had a passion, Paulson figured. With that thought, the apartment's buzzer sounded: An early bird had arrived.

Paulson buzzed them in and waited. A minute later there was a knock at the door. Paulson managed a cheerful smile and opened the door. It was 10:55am.

"Hi, how are you? I'm Paulson Neilson and you're the first person to see this fabulous apartment."

"Hi." (Or was that a harrumph?)

"If you would just sign in and take a floor plan, I'll give you the tour."

She signed the piece of paper, "Donna Bomba," and didn't bother taking a floor plan. Paulson had a good read on her: She wasn't there to buy. He could tell from the moment she walked in. She was probably hoping for a thousand square feet and a servant. What she saw was four hundred square feet and maybe a hair more depressing than where she already lived.

She walked slowly from room to room, stopping frequently to take in something (but nothing that Paulson could see). He followed her, keeping silent; he didn't want to waste his breath. The showing, which she paced, lasted for fifteen minutes. During that time she never changed her expression or made a sound beyond a faint "Hmm." She didn't ask any questions or comment on the nice wood floors. She took it all in and left. But she did say 'thank you' afterwards. Not the ordinary scavenger, thought Paulson. Typically, they'd go through and analyze every nook and cranny, boasting their knowledge about apartment quality. Donna must have been a rare breed, the quiet type, but always ready to strike if need be. Paulson put her personality in the client psychology files in his head. The more minds he knew, the better.

Paulson buzzed in the second client of the day. He opened the door with a smile and had them sign in. Paula and Pervis were looking for a charming one-bedroom to begin their lives together. Knowing this apartment fit that description, Paulson thought of how he should approach them.

"Do you currently own or are you renting?" Paulson asked without sounding patronizing.

Paula responded, "We're renting now, but we think its time for our own place."

"Great," Paulson began. "Sometimes it makes more sense to buy."

He left it at that. He didn't want to say, "It's better to buy" or "It's really the way to go" or anything too opinionated. Paulson let them know that he understood how they felt and that there was no pressure. (Of course, that's not how he felt. He wanted them to buy, buy, buy!)

Paulson concealed his enthusiasm and let Paula and Pervis think freely. He casually pointed out some of the apartment's highlights, like the nice wood floors (the apartment didn't have much else). But these types of clients needed privacy so Paulson walked out to the living room while they remained in the bedroom, talking just above a whisper about finances and furnishings. They didn't ask too many questions, which was a good sign. Clients who asked a lot of questions (and often the same questions over and over) inevitably never bought or even bid.

Paula and Pervis thanked Paulson and grabbed a floor plan as they left. Paulson thought they looked optimistic and could very well make an offer. As they opened the door they nearly walked over a startled man who was slipping a menu under the door. Time stood still as everyone gathered themselves and summed up the situation (it's not every day that you see Menu Man). Paula apologized and scurried off with Pervis, leaving Menu Man face to face with Paulson.

If there was one thing that Paulson hated, it was Menu Man. Why, why, why? Paulson would demand. This particular Menu Man slowly crept away, pretending to leave the building but merely walking down to the floor below. The old "If you can't see him, then he's not there" technique, mused Paulson. That's so overused.

The buzzer sounded again and Paulson gathered himself for the next visitor. He slid the "Spicy 700" menu under the neighbor's door and waited. The next arrival was a young gentleman in a suit, most likely sacrificing his lunch hour to find his first apartment. He had a preppy way about him and was visibly uncomfortable with Paulson's disposition.

"Hi!" Paulson said, a bit more than friendly. Though he was trying the "Slap Method," there was no harm in flirting with this little lamb chop.

"Uh, hi," the poor soul responded, avoiding Paulson's sparkling eyes.

"I'm Paulson, and I can't wait to show you this place. You're going to absolutely love it. What's your name, sweetie?"

"Uh, John."

"Well, John, are you renting now?"

"Uh, yeah."

"And have you looked at many places yet?"

"Uh, not really. A few."

"Well, John," Paulson began, as if John was a very special name, "this place is absolutely divine. Why don't you sign in, sweetie?"

John scribbled his name down on the sign-in sheet, trying to keep his hand from shaking.

"You're just gonna love this apartment. It's in a fabulous neighborhood. I have so many friends down here, so I know. And the apartment is perfect for the eligible bachelor. Are you with anyone now?"

"Uh, no." He was starting to sweat.

"Interesting," Paulson said as he reached out and held John's tie. "This is a fantastic tie! And the colors are so you!" That may have been too much.

"Thanks," John slowly responded, not sure of how to react.

"Okay!" Paulson bellowed, breaking the purposeful silence. "Let me show you around."

After a brief tour, Shy John had had enough of Paulson's flirting and had abruptly left. It was enough time, however, to get Paulson aroused. The couch would do, he concluded, as he got comfortable and kicked his feet onto the glass coffee table. While he was "Mid-Slap," the buzzer rang but Paulson ignored it. He figured that one lost client wouldn't be so bad.

A few other folks came by to see the apartment but no one seemed too serious about buying. Paulson finally locked up and left. It was 12:45pm and Paulson was getting hunger pangs. Paulson walked east, looking for some appealing cafe or bistro. All he could think of was food. He eventually found a little sandwich shop and walked in.

"What's good?" he politely asked Short Man behind the counter.

"Everything good," bragged Short Man.

"I'll have some of that then," Paulson smiled.

"For here or to go?"

"For here, please. And can you put it on whole wheat?"

"That we can do."

"Great."

"And to drink?"

"Water's good."

"Very good. Sit," Short Man commanded and got to work on some kind of sandwich on whole wheat.

He sat down at a small wooden table and waited. He was still trying to figure out the theme of the place when Short Man brought out a sandwich and some bottled water.

"Thank you very much," Paulson said.

"You're welcome very much," Short Man retorted, which wasn't impressive at all.

Paulson studied his sandwich for a while, not wanting to bite into anything undesirable.

"What's in here!?" he finally yelled.

Short Man, however, was finished with their game and ignored the question.

Chapter Twenty-Eight

PAULSON DID some more exploring after enjoying a tasty "everything" sandwich (which turned out to have ham, turkey, lettuce, tomato, and blue cheese dressing). He had walked these streets countless times but there was always something new to see. All that remained on his day's agenda was a 4pm appointment with a rental-shopper and class at 7pm. That gave him about two hours of recess. He continued walking east towards Broadway, noticing the quirky little shops that sold colored wigs. He wondered how many they sold and how long the buyers kept them. Probably one night, he thought. Paulson veered up and down some quiet streets, avoiding the loud sounds of the main drives, and before he realized it he had walked right into his favorite bowling alley. He feigned surprise but knew that he'd been walking in that direction all along. Trying to play it off, he casually opened the door and slipped inside.

Growing up, Paulson had a few favorite sounds; the sound of a motorcycle in the distance coming closer and then passing by; a dog barking in the next valley; autumn leaves sifting on the ground before a storm. But now, as a city slicker, he deemed his favorite sound to be the crash of bowling pins falling mercilessly out of sight, and the sound of a strike was the greatest of them all. Nothing else on the planet sounded like that. After playing the sport as much as he did, Paulson was able to guess how many pins (within one) went down just by listening. It was a beautiful sound and that's precisely what he heard when he walked in. It was comforting beyond explanation. Maybe that's why he played so much. He walked past the hi-tech video games (which is what non-bowlers did) and the main counter, but kept his eyes focused on the alleys.

"Hey Paulie! What's goin' on?" Robby was the daytime manager and occasionally worked the evenings. Paulson knew everyone on the staff; they hadn't seen someone so obsessed with the sport in their lives.

"Rob, my darling, I was just walking by. Decided to stop in and see what's happening."

"Just walking by, eh?" He knew him too well.

"Okay, you got me. I just can't stay away, I guess."

"How'd ya do last night?" Everyone there knew his schedule.

"Same old, same old."

"Well, that's not so bad. Gonna play now?"

"Maybe a couple of frames, I suppose." Is that what he really wanted? Of course it was; he had two hours to kill.

Robby looked him up and down, noticing that he didn't have his bowling apparati. "Where's your gear?"

"I'll have to play like the common man today," Paulson said, disappointed that he'd have to rent shoes.

"Well, then get over here and we'll set you up nice."

Paulson walked over to the desk, took off his shoes and handed them over. He felt like a silly dope and hoped no one was watching. He put on the rental shoes and tried to smile but couldn't.

"You got lane twenty-two all to yourself," Robby announced as Paulson walked away in search of a bowling ball. He quickly found one as there were many options during the less crowded daytime hours. The ball he picked was mediocre at best, but he knew he'd be wasting his time trying to find something better. His walking accelerated as he approached lane twenty-two with childish excitement. He sat down in the scorer's chair and gazed at the overhead digital scoreboard. An amazing invention, he thought. The machine could tell how many pins you knocked down and handle all the intricacies of scoring. It even knew that you had three shots at the end of your game. If Paulson ever moved back home, he would try to bring one of these. He then typed in the name, "Fierce."

Paulson stood up, dried his hand on the mini bowler's fan, lifted the bowling ball, set his feet to position one, brought the ball up to his right cheek, breathed out, stepped forward, swung the ball behind him, took another step, started swinging the ball, took another step as he brought the ball forward, released it, and finally slid his right foot past his left, ending with perfect form. The ball rolled down the alley with considerable speed straight towards the gutter. But as soon as it looked like the ball was going to roll in, it defied physics and changed direction, moving back towards the middle of the alley. As it was reaching the middle it collided with ten helpless bowling pins. Nine. Nine went down. Paulson accepted it, but didn't understand. He felt the ball had the proper momentum, accuracy, and angle, but only nine went down. "A game of inches," is what old Dougie would say.

Paulson finished off the spare with relative ease; he'd become proficient at hitting the corners. Halfway through the game, Robby brought him a Virgin Colada (Paulson's drink of choice when he wasn't bowling socially). Paulson finished with a score of one fifty-two. Not bad, he thought, considering it was daytime and he was wearing clown shoes. He took a break, got himself another colada and mentally prepped for the next game. The strategy of the game was simple: Aim for the pins and knock them down. Paulson was almost certain that the best preparation one could do was to become confident to the point of cockiness. Confidence came and went with Paulson. He thought he might be crazy, but it seemed that he had the most confidence at 9 o'clock at night. That's when he bowled his best scores. He didn't go out and tell the world this little-known fact, but he believed it to be true. And when he pushed his mind to think back, he recalled that in North Dakota, 9pm was often a very peaceful time. The sun would've just disappeared and that dog would start barking in the next valley.

Paulson's reminiscing gave him a glaze in his eyes, making the bowling somewhat surreal. He felt he was in some kind of bowling heaven. He was all over the alley, even rolling a few gutter balls, but he didn't care. Maybe Robby was spiking the coladas. He was still somewhere in the clouds when he finished up. Glancing up at the scoreboard, Paulson wondered who "Fierce" was.

But then he remembered. "Fierce" was the brave philanderer, the dashing urban sex-junkie, the resilient seeker of carnal completion. At least that's who he imagined "Fierce" being.

After any particular affair, Paulson never felt satisfied. Sure, there were the mental and physical thrills, but the feelings would always diminish as soon as the session was over. Paulson just wanted it to last. Going into these scandalous scenarios he really was "Fierce," king of the Alpha Wolves. Yet coming out of them, he was just another Omega named "Ordinary." He didn't want to give up, though. He didn't want to quit until he could fill this sexual void. The "Slap Method" had kept him under control for the last three days, but Paulson knew that it was just a matter of time before the truth would override his will. And the truth was that his relationship with James lacked something, and the wolf named "Fierce" was on a perpetual hunt to find it.

Chapter Twenty-Nine

PAULSON'S VIRGIN Colada-high dismantled as soon as he stepped foot into the Proud Properties office. All the broker-gabbing and shuffling of papers and dangling of keys was enough to break the deepest of trances. The sounds were ugly compared to the sweet tune of bowling pins. Avoiding a minor breakdown, Paulson gathered some keys and left. His client was interested in studio apartments, mostly because of price. He had called a week before hoping to find a place in the Village or Chelsea. Paulson had done his best (at least that's what he'd told him) to scout out something suitable, but there really weren't too many places within his price range (Paulson had only found one, and it was a dump), so today he'd be seeing some things a bit out of his budget.

That's the way the rental market typically went. A client will say that they want to spend X amount, but in the end they'll always spend Y. Amending that thought, Paulson added that they'd spend Y amount plus Z, which was his exorbitant non-negotiable fee. The best way to find an apartment in Manhattan was through networking with everyone you knew. Folks who moved there who didn't know a soul were the ones who paid the most. Of course, as a broker, Paulson had some pretty good feelers out in the marketplace as well as loads of personal acquaintances. This meant he usually knew of an available apartment that was reasonably priced with no broker's fee. He saved this type of knowledge for good friends.

Paulson was meeting his client on 18th Street and 7th Avenue at 4pm. It was only a few blocks from the office, so he just walked over. The building was a pre-war structure with mostly studios inside. Paulson had an "in" at the building, which gave him the privilege of being the exclusive broker. He had rented almost fifteen units there and was more than comfortable showing them. Paulson didn't delve much into rentals any longer, being sales broker "Number One" (in his own mind), but the building's owner called him at least once a month to rent an apartment. They either trusted him or thought he was good luck. Since it was a simple sell, Paulson always obliged them. He considered it his own rent money.

At 4:15pm his client arrived. He was an attractive young man wearing a dark business suit and nice shoes. Always on the prowl for a fling (but now on the prowl for "Slap Material") Paulson instinctively wondered if he was gay. Paulson's "Gay-dar" was exceptional, but those particular senses were somehow failing him now. Some of his other senses, though, were becoming quite aroused. He would just have to wait for Mystery Man to reveal himself. In the meanwhile, he knew it was almost "Slap Time" again.

On the elevator up Paulson recited some details of the apartment; rent, square footage, laundry, other tenants. Paulson had not been to this specific apartment but most of the building's units had the same layout, so he knew what the space would be like. He didn't know how the tenant left it, but luckily the place was empty and clean. It could be tough to sell a place containing someone else's furniture (especially if the apartment was poorly decorated). On the other hand, if an apartment was brilliantly decorated then it could be a much easier sell. Regardless, empty and clean was a good starting point.

Paulson allowed for the traditional moment of silence, letting Mystery Man take it all in. Paulson had to keep an eye on him, though, and make sure his thoughts were positive. If he looked unhappy, Paulson would cut the moment of silence off and go in for the sell. Mystery Man seemed to admire the apartment's look. He walked around a bit, disappearing behind the L-shaped wall then reappearing again. He went into the kitchen, studied the appliances and the water pressure and looked out the window. Paulson was tempted to say, "Nice view, right?" but held his tongue, not wanting to break Mystery Man's concentration.

Paulson was desperately trying to figure out Mystery Man's sexuality. He determined that his style was impeccable and he seemed to be in excellent physical shape, but his demeanor was right in the middle of the spectrum. Paulson could usually tell right away but this guy had him stumped.

Mystery Man opened, studied, and closed all three of the closets, then walked into the bathroom and tested the water pressure as well as opening and closing the medicine cabinet. When he was done, he just stood in the foyer area, taking in one last look. Then it was time for Paulson to speak.

If a client was wavering you always, without exception, told them that the property would be snatched up soon. That worked 99% of the time. It didn't bother Paulson that the studio cost more than what Mystery Man wanted to spend, nor did it bother him that there was a DJ living next door who blasted acid-jazz techno. Paulson knew he'd take the studio. If he didn't bite right away then Paulson would take him to some lesser apartments. It wasn't wise to confuse a "sold client" with better options. What he really wanted, though, was to spend more quality time with him.

Paulson had met his boyfriend, James, six months before and they'd been dating ever since. Paulson still had his own apartment but they spent most nights together at James' place. James was a dentist in Chelsea and Paulson liked to call him his "Dear DDS." Paulson thought a broker and a dentist were quite compatible. Who could complain with a nice set of teeth and a beautiful apartment? As far as the future was concerned, Paulson had a pretty good idea what might happen. He loved James but didn't know if he was "in love" with him, and every time it came up in conversation he'd change the subject. He knew his avoidance of the issue probably meant that he wasn't ready to give it serious consideration.

Paulson was new to the long-term relationship scene. James was his first. All the other men Paulson had been with were gone within three weeks, and that was the way Paulson liked it. The tension in their relationship started about a month before when James brought up the idea of moving in together. This took Paulson by surprise and his reaction showed it. The time had finally come to confront how he truly felt, and when he did he was convinced that moving in together wasn't the best option. As expected, that didn't sit well with James. It was similar to the feeling you get when you ask someone to marry you and they say that they're not sure, which tends to mean that the answer will eventually be "no." But fortunately, Paulson had somehow managed to bury the issue, selling James on the fact that there was still plenty of time to plan for that day.

Paulson had cheated on James about twenty times. Committing to one person wasn't very appealing and Paulson thought maybe this "Slapping" experiment was a test to see if he could do it. But he knew he had some more exploring to do and would occasionally laugh at how understated that statement was. Paulson kept these thoughts to himself, though. What is one to do, he wondered? He couldn't just go up to James and say, "You know, James, you're a lousy lover and I need a lot more than you're giving." That would only make James feel incompetent and inadequate, and Paulson didn't want to do that to him. So how do you politely tell someone, "I'm really horny and you're not doing it for me?" Was sex something you had to give up for love? Paulson had no clue. There were only two things that Paulson was sure of. One, that he wanted to live in Manhattan, and two, that he wanted to be a real estate broker. Relationships weren't even close to making the list. Still, he was trying to enjoy his relationship with James for what it was. The day when James insisted on something more might be the day they break up.

Chapter Thirty

PAULSON AND Mystery Man reached the second apartment in about ten minutes. On the way, Paulson had pointed out places of interest in the neighborhood (not even for selling purposes; he just liked being a tour guide). They passed by his favorite donut shop, his favorite diner, a funky dive bar with tinted windows, and a huge multiplex movie theater. Despite the extended conversation and time spent, Paulson still couldn't read Mystery Man's "Sex-o-Meter."

The next apartment was on a busier street and in a shabbier building (all in accordance with Paulson's selling strategy). They walked up four flights to unit #4B. Paulson fumbled with the keys for a while, trying to figure out which key went where, and after a couple of minutes the door finally swung open. (Paulson thought he saw a mouse scurry away, though it might've been a giant roach).

The floor was as dirty as dirt; there looked to be a thin layer of tar smeared across it. Mystery Man seemed a bit frightened as they walked into the middle of the room. The windows were closed and there was no ventilation. It felt like a sauna.

"Well, here it is," Paulson said glumly. "It's more in line with your price range, so I guess that's a positive."

Mystery Man didn't say anything, but this time Paulson knew it wasn't because he liked the place.

"It's not as nice as the other place," Paulson said matter-of-factly.

"No, no, you're right. It's not as nice," Mystery Man replied, trailing off the last few words.

"It *is* closer to all the action, but I'm not sure if that's what you want."

"Yeah, I don't know."

"Well, let's take a look in the kitchen," Paulson suggested, knowing that Mystery Man wasn't going to move on his own. The kitchen was disgusting. Dirty dishes, flies, rotten leftovers, decaying aluminum cabinets and something that looked like a mound of dark chocolate on the floor.

"Hmmm, not so good, eh?"

Mystery Man grunted some kind of response, but it was definitely in agreement.

"Why don't we check out the next place?" Paulson suggested. (Or maybe you want to fall into my arms, my sweet Mystery Man...)

Of the two places left, Paulson knew that one was a dump (though not as bad as the one they just saw) and the other was decent (but, still, nowhere near the quality of the first apartment). He decided to take his dashing client to the nicer of the remaining studios (and who said he had no mercy?). Location-wise, this studio was the best, nestled on a mellow street close to all the local festivities. Condition-wise, however, it was not pristine.

It's difficult in Manhattan to find a home on the right street *and* in the right condition. That just didn't happen a lot. Given the two options, one always had to go with location. You could always change your apartment with paint, but you couldn't change the community. Within every neighborhood in New York there were both good and bad sections, safe and dangerous sections, loud and quiet sections, sparse and crowded sections, clean and trashy sections, and bad-smelling and good-smelling sections. Paulson figured that as long as the good stuff outweighed the bad stuff then you were doing all right. Being the talented broker he was, Paulson could usually find a place with all the goodness the city had to offer: safe, quiet, sparse, clean, and good-smelling.

There was some indecipherable graffiti on the building but nothing that appeared to be too menacing. The entranceway was dark and dingy but it was surprisingly clean and almost comfortable. There was an old-fashioned elevator that had some more graffiti, but the antiqueness of it outshone Sugar Daddy's scribble. They rode the elevator in a somewhat awkward silence to the sixth floor. Paulson didn't understand what the silence meant but hoped it wasn't because Mystery Man was bored by the apartment hunting process. They found apartment #3R and, again, Paulson fumbled with the keys.

The studio was small (or charming, as they'd say in the industry) and the dark wood floors made it feel even smaller. It was clean, though. Not sparkling, but livable. The apartment consisted of one main room that was square-shaped and a Pullman kitchen on the southern wall. There were two closets right by the front door and a bathroom on the other side of the kitchen. The highlight of the apartment was the huge window that cast a massive stream of light into the middle of the room. It was actually a bit uplifting in a spiritual sense, Paulson thought. As they walked into the apartment, Mystery Man looked around expecting the worst, yet appeared pleasantly surprised. Paulson was somewhat taken aback by his reaction (he was almost certain he wouldn't like it) but the apartment did have some character.

"Wow," Mystery Man said in amazement.

"You like?" Paulson asked, rather unsure as to how he should sell the place or if he had to at all.

"Yeah."

"Well, let's look around," offered Paulson with a slight nervous crack in his voice.

"I think I just did," Mystery Man said while flipping the front door closed. Was that aggressive on his part or was he making a joke? Paulson wondered as his heart began to beat like a drum and a great feeling of uncertainty started choking his circulation. It was an awkward silence times ten.

Mystery Man walked into the middle of the room and placed himself in the center of the huge ray of sunshine beaming in through the window. The light surrounded him, filling the shadows of his dark suit, and sending Paulson into a trance. Paulson put his "Slap Method" on hold and took a step forward. The sun was blinding as it rushed through the giant window and Paulson was somehow knocked down by it but then was effortlessly lifted up. Heat scorched his face as he flew into the explosion, racing by birds and trees and particles of golden dust. The room began to vibrate, softly at first, but then rising violently as the subway trampled below. The rumble was intense, shaking everything within sight, and Paulson held on as tight as he could, desperate not to fall. Then all became still, or as still as could be, and the train disappeared, leaving behind a calm, cool breeze and a flickering trail of electricity.

"Nice light," Mystery Man noted.

For the first time in recent memory, Paulson kept his mouth shut. He was unable to formulate any words let alone string them together to make a sentence. Mystery Man stood there for what felt like an hour, taking an occasional step to the right or left to check the kitchen area and the bathroom.

"So what do you think?" Paulson finally squeaked, ending his own personal record for staying quiet.

Mystery Man spoke more than he had all afternoon. "I like it. Is it the same price as the first place we saw?"

"A couple hundred less," Paulson spit out an octave above his normal voice. He was now sporting a nervous smile, the kind that could frighten people. He couldn't help it, though.

"Not bad."

"No, not so bad," Paulson repeated while trying to remove his disturbing smiley face.

"I like the view."

"You're right," Paulson blurted. "It's fabulous."

The apartment looked over a quaint garden wedged in between the building and the building next door. You could also see some of the Midtown skyline.

"Okay, I'm ready," Mystery Man said as he walked to the door. Paulson, who was in no position to make any decisions, appreciated someone taking charge. As soon as Paulson locked the door behind them, his nervousness calmed down considerably.

Back on the sidewalk, the outdoor air gave Paulson an essential energy boost and helped him find his old personality. They stood outside the building and talked about the procedure for securing the apartment: Mystery Man would have to bring by a bunch of checks and sign some papers, meet with the landlord (and maybe the building's board), provide a few references, and if he didn't have a high enough income then he'd have to find someone to co-sign the lease. "Just a few things," Paulson kept saying. It seemed like a lot, but it really wasn't. Then they said their good-byes and walked away in opposite directions. The feeling was unusual but the timing was good. Paulson had an hour before his cooking class started, just enough time to drop off the keys at the office and go home for a bit.

It didn't occur to him until he was chomping on one of his favorite donuts and walking to class that he had, once again, cheated on his partner. Way to go Paulson, he mock scolded himself. Well done. He then began to reflect upon the quantity and quality of his previous affairs and how this last one obliterated them all in every measurable way; from First Look to First Touch to Release. "Wow," he murmured through a mouthful of donut dough.

That he'd only lasted two and a half days utilizing the "Slap Method" didn't bother him. It was actually a point of pride. Professional bowlers, he reasoned, didn't start their careers with ten strikes in a row. Real estate agents don't sell brownstones on their first day of work. Learning something new always takes time. Therefore, Paulson concluded that two and a half days was a commendable amount of time to withhold from his lustful maneuvers, and now he could try to build on that; he could now try to break his own two and a half day record. Maybe he could double it.

Chapter Thirty-One

AT 10:45am, Dana McDougel's phone started making sci-fi laser gun sounds. Maybe she should change to sweet fairy whispers, she thought as she slumped out of bed. She made some coffee and a large bowl of cereal with sliced bananas. Recently she'd elevated bananas to her all-time favorite food after she realizing it was the perfect creation; a healthy food with its own protective shell. Bananas were now her best friend. When she was finished with her cereal, she poured the leftover milk into her coffee, a technique she'd invented years before. Dana felt comfortable and strong and imagined herself in a national commercial. Taking advantage of that feeling, she went through her monologue a few times in her head.

The truth of the acting world revealed itself to her long ago but she was so un-amazed that she'd forgotten what it was. Despite that, she'd still enjoyed limited success in New York; an obscure off-off Broadway play, a couple industrials, a commercial for a local car dealer. She knew that her big break would come, though. It might take fifteen years, but what the hell, she had nothing else to do. Her audition today was at 4pm, conveniently sandwiched between her lunch shift and her cooking class. The role was small but the show was big and unlike most parts she'd tried out for, this one had the potential to lead to better things. At worst, it would give her credibility on her home turf and, at best, it could spark a championship career.

After enjoying her cereal-scented coffee, Dana jumped in the shower to wash off the morning grime. It was shower number one. By day's end she probably will have taken at least three. She couldn't remember the last day she had only showered once. Even two-shower days were rare. It was either a powerful, uncontrollable addiction or a constant feeling of being dirty. She no longer thought about it, though. She just got clean.

Dana went through her monologue a couple of times in the shower. It was beneficial to practice it in as many places as possible. By doing so, she reasoned, she'd feel comfortable reciting it any-where. She figured she'd already mastered it in the kitchen, at her little dining table, in the bedroom, and in her building's stairwell. She wasn't, however, pleased with her shower performances. If she could feel confident there, then she knew she could do it anywhere. Maybe being naked deterred her abilities. Maybe the shower was sacred to her so she felt she was betraying her own secrets. Whatever it was, she knew they were all excuses. She had to conquer.

"I was never a happy girl, nor was I a sad girl; I was a block of wood, or perhaps a cumbersome stone. My memories are cloudy and somewhat faded, like a flame in the far distance. I cannot recall who I was back then, but I know that I was of a solid nature. Was there a puppy dog? I cannot recall. Was there a canopy bed? I cannot recall. Were there dolls and toys and sweets to eat? Again, I cannot recall. Was I just Daddy's little girl?"

Dana knew the words; she could echo them on top of each other while dancing on a bar. It was the delivery in the shower that she was having trouble with. She tended to overact in the shower, empha-sizing the wrong words in her delivery. She knew she shouldn't be emphasizing the *"I cannot recalls,"* but she kept doing it. She should be emphasizing the questions, not the answers, the way she could do it everywhere else. She was very hesitant to audition material that didn't pass the shower test, but the one thought that comforted her was that she'd have another shower before the audition. Then maybe she would nail it.

Dana grew up in the entertainment business, always watching and learning, becoming familiar with the different personalities and all the hardship. Her mother was one of the lucky ones; her foot-modeling career took off after her first job and she was able to support the family because of it. Dana knew that after her own big break came, she'd never have to worry about work (or personal self-worth) ever again, too. At least, that's what she believed, and that's what motivated her. Dana also knew that being a model was nothing like being an actor (even though some producers disagreed). A model only had to look good; an actor had to look good *and* act accordingly.

Her father was a veteran "B" movie director. He'd never had a great payday but he was always a good dad. Dana learned that you had to be careful when your father was a "B" movie director; it's not something you announce at parties. When she'd tell people that her father was a Hollywood director, they'd perk up, get giddy, prepare their head shots and ask what he'd made. But when she'd tell them that his body of work included *Big Bad Blondes For Sale* and *One, Two, Three… You're Mine,* the conversation would lose some momentum. Dana usually kept the family secrets to herself, only giving inquirers just enough information to keep them satisfied: "My mom's a model and my dad's a director."

The worst situations were when someone had actually heard of her father and was a huge fan. Then it was time to leave the party. Dana wasn't ashamed of her father's work. However, she couldn't sit through one of his films. He had always offered her parts, saying that she could pick and choose whatever character she wanted, but Dana couldn't go there. Early on the temptation was strong, knowing that she'd be the star. But she also knew that by doing so, she'd outcast herself from the "A" industry. With that to help her decide, Dana tried to stay clear of McDougel Productions. That's not to say she never took a role, though. When she was eighteen, she actually did accept one so that she could get her union card (which meant that she was a legitimate actor). For this, she was thankful. Having that card opened doors, and sometimes it could take years to get. After that role, she successfully avoided the "B" circuit with only one exception. But sometimes she let herself wonder… what if she had taken all those roles that her father offered? Would she now be the "B" movie queen of Hollywood?

Given that she was waiting tables for smug businessmen, that wasn't such a dreadful thought. Of course, she'd never earn any respectable awards, nor would she be admired by her peers, nor would she ever inspire anyone, nor would she be living in a lush mansion… the list kept growing in her head. She had to remind herself she was doing the right thing because that temptation was always there (even if that meant her fans would be weirdo's). Some thought her to be crazy for not accepting the "B" roles. Friends would say, "Play the hand you were dealt" or "It's better to be the "B" movie queen than a small-time player." This made sense but she felt that there were better things waiting for her and she wanted to get there on her own. Besides, she reasoned (and this was always the final motivating factor), she didn't want to take her shirt off in front of dad.

The house she grew up in was decorated with photos of her mother's feet and movie posters of scantily clad women with forced looks of terror. The house was also full of her father's film memorabilia (which were mostly old props that he just couldn't throw away). Dana remembered going for drives with him, stopping at tag sales, then watching the silly glee in his eyes when he saw something he absolutely needed in his next picture. He'd even add scenes to his films just to use a particular prop. Early one Sunday morning, they'd pulled up to a yard sale and found a giant cigar (measuring seven feet long with the diameter of a basketball). The next year he wrote and directed a movie called *Don't Mess With Mama Tall,* a film that incorporated a large cigar for the extra-large lead character (all accomplished with "trick" photography).

When Dana started seeing the world as an adult (at age fifteen, when she stopped playing "House" and started playing "Doctor"), she felt the need to explore the area beyond the L.A. desert. With the help of her mother and her high school guidance counselor (who really wasn't too helpful), Dana surveyed some colleges that she could get into. Her mother didn't realize until it was too late that all the schools Dana had applied to were on the east coast. At that point she'd asked, "Honey, all these schools are so far away. Isn't there something closer that appeals to you?" Dana had just shrugged in response. "But what about your acting?" Dana quickly said that many of the schools had fine drama departments (although she wasn't sure). And to that, she remembered, her mother just shrugged.

Dana was accepted into a small liberal arts college in Maine. Half of her felt empowered; years of planning were blooming with beautiful results. The other half (a half she didn't anticipate having) was mortified to leave the comfort of home and all those foot photos. Going to the east coast made Dana the subject of many neighborhood discussions. It was taboo for someone to venture so far (and to actually want to do it). She would get the occasional stare in town and often heard amplified whispers directed at her. Dana liked the attention, though. People were talking about her. Even though their words were probably not complimentary, it made her feel important (and perhaps like a star).

Woodward College was hidden within a few hundred acres of forest in northern Maine. Dana was surprised, if not pleased, that she was the only Californian in her class (which gave her some status). The other students were curious about her; they watched her, looking for clues as to how the West Coast culture behaved. It took a few weeks before Dana realized this (until then she'd just thought everyone was shy), but then she took full advantage of it. For four straight years, Dana was on a stage (playing herself, of course), and she loved it.

The drama department was quite good and Dana was somewhat disappointed when she saw there were other amazing (and perhaps more talented) actors. She eventually settled into an elite social crowd of dramatists, the ones who lived and died for the art. Dana relished the fact that she was from a different background; her uniqueness allowed her a comfortable spot in the clique. Everyone else was from more of the gloomy Northeastern actor mold, absorbed in the darkness that the art can drape over you. Dana had never seen this before. She only knew of the sprite-like "acting is fun" personality.

What she learned at Woodward, be it through the Gloomy Dudes or through her insane instructors, was that there was a lot more to this acting thing than she'd ever imagined (she wondered if her Dad knew about this). She dedicated herself to learning as much as she could, expanding her abilities and making herself more complete. She had difficulty excelling in these new, unfamiliar areas, though. The acting technique she brought with her was simple: Study your lines and say 'em like you mean 'em. This method didn't seem to be effective at Woodward and when Dana performed she felt one-dimensional and too self-conscious. Her other classmates, however, when doing a performance (or even a reading) had so much of the character inside of them it was scary. They overflowed with their characters and appeared oblivious of themselves. This passionate style was something that Dana aspired to (especially since she starting feeling like the "B" actress her father always wanted her to be).

The one thing that Dana didn't like about Woodward was that it seemed like everyone had seen her father's films. Initially, Dana thought it was a joke (an East Coast vs. West Coast prank), but the more she talked to the ones who claimed to be fans, the more she realized their sincerity. Apparently, her father's films were in regular rotation on late-night cable. Some of her classmates knew the movies so well that they could recite the dialogue. Dana tried to avoid them (she called them "The Freak Boys," which also happened to be the name of one of her father's films). When the shock of the situation dissipated, and when Dana realized that everyone was not messing with her, she embraced her position; the first-born daughter of "King" McDougel. (Most of the Gloomy Dudes, however, were unimpressed. Dana never knew it, though, for they were talented at their craft.)

After four years of intensive drama training, Dana had an underlying feeling that she hadn't learned a thing. There were no tears at graduation; she hadn't become close with too many classmates. She felt that they never let her into the "Northeastern Circle." She walked into Woodward as that Southern California girl and left as that Southern California girl. Dana knew that home would be her first stop on her post-collegiate tour but she also knew that it wouldn't be her last.

After making a quick pit stop at her parents' place, Dana found a small apartment in Santa Monica. Her plan was to stay there for one year. Three years later she was still there. No big roles came her way and Dana was on the verge of accepting Dad's offer to star in *Where's Me Mummy?* It was at that time when her agent called with a commercial audition. It was for a soap company and the slot would be national, meaning that she'd make a lot of money and her face would become instantly recognizable (especially to casting directors). When Dana arrived, she wasn't the least bit nervous and was ready to read (she'd done this many times). It took a while before her name was called but in that time she'd been mentally preparing. She was brought into a private office and given a one-page script. After a moment of polite introductions she was asked to read.

"It makes me feel… good!"

Dana thought she gave the *"good!"* a respectable level of enthusiasm and the *"It makes me feel"* part enough certainty, and that's all she could've done. The auditioner thanked her and told her she'd done a good job. Dana had learned that it didn't matter what they said to you; it usually wasn't them who made the casting decisions. All these people did was weed out the amateurs. Someone else would choose the most appropriate candidates and have them come in for a callback, which Dana felt that she had earned. What she wasn't sure about was if she had the right look (which could make or break any audition). It was time to wait for the phone call.

The call never came and it was no big whoop. It happened time and time again. If an actor couldn't handle it, then they shouldn't be acting. It was then when Dana had one of those dreams you have when you're not actually sleeping, but when you're trying to sleep. She saw herself in a skimpy, furry tank-top holding a spear, shouting out orders to a tribe of tail-tucked men wearing caveman suits, and then slaying what appeared to be a medium-sized dinosaur (although it looked like a college mascot).

She promised herself she would only do this once. She called her father and subtly inquired about his next project. Dad knew from the start why Dana was calling but he let her maneuver towards the big question. She couldn't see it, nor could she feel it, but he was grinning wide. His baby had finally come to him for help. They began talking about his new action film, *Kikoo Hiya!!!*, which was the story of an ancient female ninja warrior who falls asleep and wakes up in modern day L.A. He was so excited, and she was so hesitant, that he nearly broke down and begged her to play the lead. But he resisted the temptation, shaking in anticipation of the glorious moment. Sure enough, after about an hour of chatter, Dana popped the question.

"So, I don't know, I've been thinking about doing some new things. Do you think there's a role in it for me?"

Elation.

At that precise moment in time, on some higher cosmic level, his entire career (and perhaps his life) had become justified and vindicated. He swore to himself that this picture would be his opus, it would be his greatest work yet.

The movie was a flop and it damaged Dana's career, but its commercial success didn't matter much to her dad. It would've been a nice bonus, but that wasn't his motivation. Now and forever, on his sacred shelf of films, *Kikoo Hiya!!!* would always be at the top.

Dana was bummed out that the film never did anything (it barely made video) and somewhat regretted her decision, but she absolutely loved the experience; day in and day out being on the set with some rogue crew following the barking orders of her father, memorizing her lines in the trailer, fighting for the last muffin at the breakfast table, not having to take her shirt off. Although she didn't learn too much about acting, she learned firsthand how a film was made from conception to completion.

Starring in her father's film had its benefits, but the setbacks soon became apparent as Dana's acting opportunities vanished (offers from the L.A. sewers didn't count), and within weeks she'd re-found her locational angst. It was time to move. She realized she'd been there for five years, which was much longer than she had originally planned. She thought she owed it to herself to make good on a prehistoric promise, and she had a good idea of where she wanted to go: New York City. It made sense; she was an actor, actors live in L.A., where most of the work resides, or in New York, where it's tough to get any kind of work whatsoever. Dana figured that she couldn't get anything in L.A. anyway, so she wouldn't be at such a disadvantage. Mom loved the idea (she really didn't want her little Dana to hone her "B" acting skills), and Dad thought it'd be best as well (although he didn't want to admit it).

Within a month's time, she headed off to the Big Apple. She had a place to stay (friends of the family) and knew a couple of old classmates from Woodward. Her agent (who was livid that she had accepted a role in *Kikoo Hiya!!!*) generously gave her the names of a few agents in New York who might take her on. Smiling on the plane, Dana realized she was getting closer by the second to what she really wanted: a new home, a new agent, a new life.

Chapter Thirty-Two

LUNCH AT Brgst was particularly slow during the week. Business picked up towards the weekend, though, when hordes of tourists flocked to the restaurant with no vowels. At first, Dana thought the name was cute but soon became quite fed up with it after having to explain it's origin to thousands of diners. She had even petitioned the manager to create placemats with all the necessary literature printed on them, but he had said no. Brgst was a small, bistro-like eatery that would be charming, comfortable and quiet if it were not for the fifty tables. On busy days, the sound was deafening. Dana tried earplugs once but couldn't hear the customers order.

If Dana ever opened up her own restaurant, which was a little dream she had, then she'd want it to be similar to Brgst. They would serve American and anti-American bistro fare but with maybe half the tables. Her cooking class tonight was like a pinhole between her and that dream; a chance for her to see how realistic it could be if the acting thing didn't pan out. However, despite this class and others she'd taken, and despite browsing through several best-selling cookbooks, she still couldn't cook that well. She conceded that her business skills were deplorable, too. One thing she was sure of, though, was that she was a good people person. Making customers feel at ease was something she *could* do. She knew her restaurant couldn't survive on just Dana the Friendly Maitre D. But what if she became a movie star? Then she knew it could.

"I was never a happy girl, nor was I a sad girl; I was a block of wood, or perhaps a cumbersome stone. My memories are cloudy and somewhat faded, like a flame in the far distance. I cannot recall who I was back then, but I know that I was of a solid nature. Was there a puppy dog? I cannot recall. Was there a canopy bed? I cannot recall. Were there dolls and toys and sweets to eat? Again, I cannot recall. Was I just Daddy's little girl?"

Reciting the dialogue while marching down Second Avenue and holding a banana was empowering. The words felt bigger than a bus as they churned out of her. She kept her eyes focused straight ahead, never letting herself get distracted. When she needed an energy boost, there was a banana bite available in her left hand. There was something about the daytime-walking-public performances that was easy for Dana. Auditioning for one of the productions in the park crossed her mind every time she rehearsed on the streets. But every time she was sure that it might be her destiny, she'd realize that an outdoor amphitheater didn't have enough walking room, so she'd probably lose all the fire she channeled from the avenues. Right now, her confidence was peaking. The pressure of her upcoming audition had temporarily diminished and she was ready to take her career to the next level.

Effectively reciting her monologue gave her confidence despite wearing her work clothes: a vibrant orange short-sleeve collared shirt with "Brgst" printed on the left breast, and matching orange slacks with "Brgst" printed on the right buttock. On most days it made her feel like a carrot. Dana had once attempted to change the dress code but Albert, the strange manager, completely disagreed, thinking her to be a silly little girl and said something like, "The colors are the catalyst." And then once, out of sport more than spite, Dana arranged a dress code coup with the other waitstaff. She had everyone (four others) wear jeans, white button-down shirts and blue visors (which she had provided). The coup failed. Not miserably, but badly enough. When Albert had ordered everyone home to change it didn't seem like he cared at all. He merely had a slight look of confusion on his face, reacting as though this had happened before or it was just another flaw of American youth.

"My favorite actress! Good morning, my dear," Albert greeted.

"Good morning, Bert," Dana teased.

Albert paused, "Yes, good morning," Albert managed, trying not to appear displeased.

"Yes, good morning," Dana echoed.

Albert wasn't in the mood for the young American copycat game, so he tried to make his next sentence a bit more complex. "Maggie will be late, yes? She telephoned before and said so. And we have big party of ten for lunch at twelve."

"Ten for lunch at twelve?" She hoped that perhaps she could wait on the party.

Albert, again, took note of the copy play but deemed it unintentional. "Yes, there is. You are first, so you can do this if you like."

"Sure, yes, definitely," Dana quickly responded.

"Good, good. Three yes's," Albert mused, impressed by his own observation and wit.

Dana didn't understand his reply and went in back to get some water and relax before the rush. Diners wouldn't start showing up for about half an hour. In that time, Dana made sure that all the tables were set, the dishes and utensils were clean, the iced tea supply was full, and that her hair looked good.

Marc, Bill and Lucy showed up one by one. No one who worked there wanted to be there, but Lucy was the only one who made it known. Once, when Albert was away, Lucy had ignored all of her tables. She walked by them and they'd try to get her attention but she pretended they weren't there. Then she made some phone calls from behind the bar, forcing the patrons to come to her for service. But even then, she held up an "I'll be with you soon" finger. All of her tables ended up at the bar to order their food and drinks. Lucy thought she had invented a new form of restaurant hospitality, but Dana had pointed out that she may have had too much fast-food experience.

"Wazzup, girl?" Lucy greeted Dana. "You ready for me or do you need some time?"

"Bring it on, Big Tits," Dana replied, using her friendly nickname for Lucy.

"Ooh, you're good! That's the way I like it!"

"Well, I got more for you... if you behave." Dana was playing the dominating role.

"I can be good," Lucy assured her with a smile.

Sometimes they'd pretend they were lesbians, sometimes they'd pretend they were French, and occasionally they'd communicate only using abstract non-vowel words (an homage to their employer). Dana thought that Lucy would make a great actress; she had confidence, independence, attitude and smarts. Lucy had told her, though, that she tried it once (she had earned the leading role in a high school play). She said the experience depressed her, that it was an everyday bore, and that the other actors were all "Quality" (which meant she couldn't relate to them on a social level). The director wanted her to reach inside for something that she didn't have and didn't feel like finding. "It's just not for me," she'd told Dana. "I don't like being someone else, especially when they're an ugly, sobbing, alcoholic wench."

"Perhaps we'll do some licking this evening," Lucy said seductively (or as seductively as one could say it).

"No can do, my tempting slut. I already have a date with many others."

"All the better," Lucy whispered. "I like crowds."

"Do you like classrooms?"

Lucy paused, not prepared for that last question, and came out of her sexual tone. "A classroom? What are you doing?" Just then she remembered. Dana didn't need to explain.

"It's my Tuesday class."

"I know, I know, I know. You're so lame. I give up."

"Maybe tomorrow night?" Dana offered.

Customers started filing in, angling for the best tables. The lunch turnout, as expected, was small. Dana only had four tables (which wasn't many for her) and Lucy only had three (which was too many for her). The table of ten turned into a table of eight and then into a table of five and Albert ended up giving it to Marc. Albert sat all the patrons down, strategically placing them so that all the waitstaff would have some. After that, he didn't have much to do except read some foreign newspaper.

Dana's tables were pretty mellow except for one guy who kept demanding more water. Dana ignored him for a while after giving him his fourth glass. She wished they had pitchers so she could just leave one on the table. Just when 'Can I Have Some More Water? Man' looked as though he was going to throw a temper tantrum, Dana mercifully brought him a fifth glass. For this he was grateful, and looked guilty for behaving like such a child.

Chapter Thirty-Three

TOWARDS THE end of her shift, Dana was getting hungry. One of the golden rules in the restaurant was to never eat in front of customers. If you wanted to eat, you had to do it in back. Surprising herself, Dana agreed. She understood that the server should appear pure and virginal, clean and comforting, safe and kind. The server was a part of the dining experience and if he or she had dirty hands or a runny nose or was stuffing a chicken empanada in their face, then the customer probably wouldn't enjoy their food as much.

When she was hungry, Dana would get a bowl of soup and hide it by the doorway in back. She would then take small pieces of bread and dip them in while walking in and out of the door. By the time she reached her tables she'd be done swallowing. This was clearly against the rules, but Dana didn't think it was too noticeable and Albert usually didn't see the exiled bowl of Lobster Bisque when he made his military rounds. When he did, he'd confiscate the bowl and storm out (as much as Albert could storm) and stare down the waitstaff. This did not instill fear into anyone. If anything, it made them laugh. "What, Albert?" they'd ask. "Why are you looking at me like that?" This, in return, would make him uncomfortable and he'd forget about the incident until all the customers had left. He'd then demand to know whose bowl of Lobster Bisque it was. Of course, no one would respond. They'd all just look back and forth at each other. They were all guilty of this menacing crime and not a one had ever confessed (or ratted out another). It was the code. Not that it was a serious violation in terms of punishment anyway. Albert would just desperately say "You can't no longer break the rules!" If anyone admitted guilt, then Albert would win. Keeping it a mystery tortured him.

Dana determined that she'd only have time for a banana after her shift, which was too bad because free food was one of the perks of working at a restaurant. She always enjoyed a free meal, especially when someone knew how to cook. The only negative was that after a while all the food started tasting the same. Whether it was the soups or the salads or the gourmet sandwiches, a restaurant's flavors tended to be consistent. In time, the French Onion Soup will taste exactly like the Waldorf Salad.

"Whatcha doing, sweetie?" Lucy asked as they were clearing the tables.

"I gotta go soon. I have an audition at four."

"Classes, auditions, hot steamy sex... you're a mad, mad woman."

"Hah! You're kind of funny."

"What's the audition?" Lucy asked as if she didn't have any interest.

"Porno," Dana replied as she peeled her banana and walked away.

"Wait, wait, wait a second! You're not auditioning for a porno. Seriously, what's it for?"

"Like I told you," Dana said before taking a healthy banana bite. The majority of their time was spent discussing Lucy things, so Dana wanted to soak in the spotlight for a while.

"No," Lucy said in disbelief.

"Yeah."

"Whatever." Lucy ended with a challenge, waiting for Dana to say, "All right, you got me." But Dana held her ground. The longer she did, the better it felt and the more Lucy glared at her from a distance. The tables were mostly cleared and cleaned and they were free to go. Lucy and the other two waiters, Marc and Bill, put in their food orders and milled about.

Dana gathered her things and walked up to Albert. "When do you need me next?"

"I will see now," answered Albert while he opened up the book. "Dinner tomorrow. Dinner tomorrow? Yes, that is good?"

"Yes, that is good," Dana said, smirking ever so slightly. Albert picked up on it but didn't appear to mind the echo this time (probably because the answer made sense and he thought it to be clever).

"Good then, tomorrow dinner... Miss Dana," he said while jotting it down in his book.

"Tip me out?" Dana asked with a mouthful of banana. Most of her tips were on credit card and Albert had to deal with that. But he gave her one of his "I'm so busy and it'll take some time to do that" looks.

"Tomorrow is good?" he asked.

"Of course, gorgeous," Dana teased. "Just don't spend it all on the ladies!"

Albert almost laughed but then caught himself, not knowing whether it was a compliment or a tease. Lucy, who was still glaring at Dana, sat alone at a table, waiting for her lunch.

"Dana, what are you *auditioning* for?" she begged.

"You working dinner tomorrow?" Dana asked with a smile.

"Yeah," Lucy replied sourly.

"Cool. Well, I'll see you then," Dana said and turned to leave, but halted. She looked at Lucy and shrugged. She really didn't want to tell Lucy the truth. This audition was way too important. It could potentially ignite her career. She knew she had to carefully protect her confidence from Lucy's probable off-hand comments, and that meant keeping it a secret. This improv was a good experience. too. "It's a hot, sexy porno called *Green Thumb Gardeners*."

"Stop messing around!" Lucy yelled without realizing it. Dana couldn't tell if Lucy was actually losing this battle or using a more complex strategy. She had to assume the latter; Lucy was too good at these things.

"Okay, whatever, so it's not an all-nude role and there's no sex involved. I would never do that. But there is sex in it. And it is a porno. I'm auditioning for the part of the lady who's the neighbor."

"What?"

Either Lucy didn't believe it at all or she was absorbed in this story. Again, Dana went with the latter then continued to hone her acting skills. "Yeah, the neighbor. I'm pretty sure she watches all the action from her bedroom window and, you know, gets a little excited. I'll probably, if I get the role, just have to show my boobs… and they'll imply everything else my character is doing. *If* I get this role," Dana re-iterated while crossing her fingers.

Lucy was silent and Dana was still unsure if she was buying the lie. "You're full of it," was the response, which meant that Lucy was close to believing the whole thing.

"It'll pay well," Dana justified and took another banana bite.

"Come on."

"Whatever. I gotta go. I'm late as it is."

Victorious in the verbal war of Brgst, having slain a most formidable opponent, Dana confidently headed towards the door. Five words, however, stopped her before she could leave.

"Was I Daddy's little girl?"

Dana spun around and stared at Lucy like a confused Labrador.

"Oh, sorry. I meant 'Was I *just* Daddy's little girl?'" Lucy snickered.

Dana was more shocked than surprised as she finished off her banana. "How do *you* know that?" Just then she remembered. Lucy didn't have to explain. Lucy had helped her with the monologue a month before for some weirdo's performance art project. It was just shocking that she had remembered it. Too dumbfounded to hurl back a witty response, Dana turned towards the door again but stopped when Lucy continued her mimicking rant.

In this lifetime, Dana had learned years earlier at a Malibu community bake-off, there was always someone better than you and there was always someone worse. Her mother, for example, didn't have the prettiest feet in all the land, but there were a lot more ugly ones out there. Likewise, there were a lot of filmmakers out there who were better than her father, but he certainly wasn't the worst. Though she never looked away from the backwards Brgst painted on the glass door, Dana had heard the whole thing. When Lucy finished, Dana let out a sigh and left the restaurant. Lucy had, without a doubt, just recited the monologue better than Dana ever could. And it was in the middle of a restaurant.

Dana let that sink in as she returned to her apartment. Every line and every breath of Lucy's performance was dead on. She didn't miss a thing. She *was* "Daddy's Little Girl." Dana kept going through it in her head, taking notes on how Lucy approached, or rather, attacked it. She wanted to be able to do it just like that. Dana stripped down and marched straight into the bathroom. If there was a more appropriate time for a shower, then Dana didn't know when. She cleaned off all of the restaurant grime while attempting her monologue. The shower, as usual, lent itself to another emotionless performance.

She was going to be a little late to the audition but Dana didn't care. Lucy the Terrible had successfully damaged her spirits and had plagued her with doubt. And again, like many times before, just when Dana thought she had Lucy on the verge of surrender, Lucy had busted out the heavy artillery and sailed home waving the victory flag. In a strange twist of karma, however, Lucy had also calmed Dana down (information which Dana would withhold in future conversations). Dana reasoned that a considerable amount of pressure dissolves when you know, for a fact, that someone is better than you. Knowing you're not the best is humbling, Dana theorized, and it allows you to stay true to your ability. She now had a "nothing to lose and everything to gain" mentality.

Chapter Thirty-Four

IT ALWAYS occurred to Dana before auditions: What if she had become a "B" movie queen? She certainly wouldn't be waiting tables. And she would certainly be able to choose any "B" movie role she wanted. There was also a strong chance that she'd be able to write her own dialogue and, perhaps, her own screenplays. If she ever did write for herself, Dana knew she'd write respectable stuff. She wouldn't delve into science fiction or horror or the "mostly sex" genre. She'd write something that people could relate to. Dana just didn't believe that people could relate to *Kikoo Hiya!!!* and had an uncomfortable feeling that it only appealed to bored men who wanted a quick tit fix. Her own "B" movie would be about real relationships, and how difficult it is to survive, and how beautiful the sunrise could be and things like that. If some comic moments fell into it, so be it.

The one idea she had was a love story. It was about a girl turning into a woman on the beaches of Southern California. She's the manager at an auto repair shop and falls madly in love with the mechanic (who is also a surfer), but he loves engines more than he loves her. She tries everything in her power to win his affection but nothing seems to sway him. Finally, in dire straits, she decides to surf to show that she really cares about him. Unfortunately, she breaks her leg. But he rescues her and rushes to fix the engine of a special truck he'd been working on so he can take her to the hospital. He works with great speed and precision and starts the engine. He puts her in the passenger seat and peels out. On the way to the doctor he finally realizes that he's in love with her... fade to black.

Dana didn't know who would be the male lead but she, of course, would play the star. She was waiting for the right moment to tell her father about it (he'd help with the screenplay and then direct it). But Dana knew that she'd probably never tell him (she was praying she'd find success on her own). She'd share the story with him years from now, when they were reminiscing about the olden days. She'd tell him and he'd be proud of her. His little girl was always thinking.

But so much for "B" movie queen fantasies, she had an audition (and a respectable career to start).

The waiting room was full when Dana arrived. She was fifteen minutes late but it looked as though she hadn't missed a thing. She checked in with the receptionist, who gave her some forms to fill out and told her to take a seat until her name was called. Judging by the amount of people there, the wait looked long (Dana was upset that she'd forgotten some reading material). The receptionist didn't know which part the audition was for, or so she claimed, but she probably did. She just didn't feel like chatting with a hundred actresses.

When an agent gets a role description they try to match it as best as they can with their clients. Dana was now accustomed to seeing a room full of girls who looked like her, but it had taken a while.

The first time Dana remembered this phenomenon was in high school when she went out for a commercial. All the other girls there looked like her, dressed like her and seemed to behave like her, too. But back then, Dana didn't notice how odd it was; she just thought that everyone must've been cool. The first time she felt uncomfortable with it was when she was living in Santa Monica. The audition was for a fast-food commercial. Her agent had told her they were looking for a natural look (to show that fast food could appeal to healthy eaters). Dana came in with faded jeans, disheveled hair and no make-up. When she walked in the waiting room, she saw that every other girl had the exact same look. It was like looking into a fifty-way mirror. Dana felt insignificant, which will happen if you thought you were somewhat original and stumble upon an entire village of you.

Instead of focusing on bettering her acting skills, Dana decided to make herself so unique that there'd be only one of her. How she was going to accomplish this, she had no idea. She started simply because she knew that was always a good place to start. The first thing she came up with was her goal and an official name for it, a battle cry of sorts. She called it "Ultimate Uniqueness," or "U-U."

Her first change towards "U-U" was to dress the same for every audition. This meant picking an outfit that made her feel courageous. She came up with tight stretchy black pants, a loose blouse, sneakers and just-out-of-bed hair in a ponytail. When she dressed like this normally it made her feel good, so she knew that this outfit would serve her purpose. Next, she developed the appropriate disposition; the best way to behave going into the audition. She decided to play everything low-key, as if the audition didn't matter much to her. Those were actually the only two things she did to achieve her state of "U-U," but after one try it seemed to have worked wonders.

When she showed up at the audition (for a small part in a sitcom), she was the only Dana there. She remembered how she felt and it gave her an incredible confidence boost. The other girls were dressed in plaid skirts and knee socks while she was in black stretchy pants. They couldn't touch her. The audition only got better. When she went in to do the reading, the casting lady looked quite surprised but quickly sat Dana down and had her read. This made Dana feel even more confident; she was getting respect. She finished her reading and the lady told her that she'd done a wonderful job (Dana never got that response from any audition) and she said that they'd call her (they usually just said thank you).

Dana got a call from her agent the next day. She was excited to tell her agent about the great audition and her new approach but her agent cut her off. Her agent said that if she went into another audition like that again, she wouldn't have an agent anymore. Dana took it all in with a disagreeing smile. Her agent had talked to the audition folks, who had asked what was up with the Prima Donna. Apparently, they didn't appreciate Ultimate Uniqueness. Dana wasn't too put out, though. She could easily revert back to what she had been (which was herself).

While patiently nibbling on another banana, Dana went through her monologue in her head to kill some time. She wouldn't have to perform it but she liked to have it handy anyway. One by one, the girls around her were getting called into the room and then leaving the room with a look of relief. Dana could relate to that.

Whether you nailed it or flubbed it, to be done with an audition was utterly relieving.

"Dana McDougel!" yelled a man who just appeared. It woke Dana from a half-nap. The last thing she remembered was staring at the girl across from her and pretending that she was looking into a mirror. That could have been five minutes or half an hour ago. Dana couldn't tell.

"Here!" she yelled back instinctively before the man could yell another name out.

The man tracked her voice from where he was standing. "You're up!"

Dana's mind was full of cliché's: It's do or die; You've been waiting your whole life for this; Put up or shut up; Give it all you got; Go for it. As she scurried towards the room she came to the conclusion that these common blurbs of pep never did a thing to help her. The only thing they seemed to do was divert her attention from what lay ahead. Maybe that's what they were for, she deduced in a rare moment of deep thought.

Dana followed the man into a small office with no windows and he gestured for her to sit down. There was a video camera on a tripod aiming right at her.

"How are you?" he asked, taking a seat behind the desk.

"Great, thanks," she answered, knowing that was the end of the small talk.

He handed her a few pages of a script. "Know the routine?" the man asked, assuming the answer.

"Yep."

"All right, then let's go. Your name is Wendy. You're twenty-four years old and you just started working the phones at an emergency clinic."

"Clinic?" Dana inquired, having learned that she should always ask questions if she didn't understand something.

"Yes, a clinic." The man paused, not ready with a prepared response (which made Dana feel confident). "It's like an emergency room, except that it's nowhere near a hospital."

By the tone of his voice, Dana felt that either the man was frustrated by the question or he was just plain tired. She assumed the latter and used that as motivation.

"Gotcha," she complied.

"You are confronted by a new patient who's either psychologically disturbed or highly intoxicated."

"You mean drunk?" Dana asked. "The guy's either crazy or drunk, right?"

The man paused, closed his eyes and nodded. "Yes. Well put. He's either crazy or drunk."

Dana patted herself on the back. Most casting agents, she thought, appreciated the actor who really understood the characters and the story.

The man continued. "And he needs to see Dr. Campbell. He has to wait but doesn't want to."

"And Dr. Campbell works at the clinic and is, perhaps, pre-occupied with another patient," Dana stated more than probed. She was sure she was racking up points here and she hadn't even started reading.

"Yes," the man continued, "Dr. Campbell is pre-occupied." He stopped for a second, looked at the remote and asked, "Are you ready?"

"Uh, do you mind if I read it to myself first."

Did the man slump an inch? Dana wondered. If so, then she'd better just wing it. She didn't want to upset him. Dana thought fast. "Just kidding, I'm sure you've been getting that all day."

With that, unbeknownst to Dana, she had just done the best performance of her life. The man started laughing. It wasn't one of those fake, cordial type of laughs, but rather one of those "That's a good one" kind of laughs. Dana laughed along with him, pretty sure of why he was amused.

"You would not believe…" the man began before trailing off into more laughter.

Dana thought he must have been doing one of those fake laughs. Either that or this guy had totally lost it. Dana laughed along anyway. She was confused but was kind of enjoying the moment. Then he suddenly stopped laughing and stared blankly at the video camera. Dana promptly followed his lead and stopped laughing as well. But then he started laughing again. And then, so did she (although her laugh had turned into the fake, cordial type of laugh).

"Hah! Okay," the man began, in quite a different mood than he'd been in a few minutes before. "Let's see what you can do."

He pressed a button on the remote and a red light appeared on the camera. Dana had learned at an early age to ignore the red light. Some people get trapped in the red light, paralyzed even. She was at ease with the red light and liked to think of it as the *"Go Light."* When the red light's on, it's time to *go* and perform well, it's time to *go* and show them what she could do, it's time to *go* and ignore the red light.

The man began the dialogue in a monotone voice. "I need to see Doctor Campbell."

Dana took in a deep breath and dove into the character named Wendy. "Okay, just fill out these forms for me first and we'll get you in."

Dana thought she delivered that line rather well.

The man continued, "But I really need to see him now."

Dana tried to imagine the man's character getting frustrated so she used more of a "talking to a toddler" voice. "I'm sorry, but he's with a patient now. If you could just fill out these forms, then he'll see you as soon as possible."

"But I really need to see him now."

"Is this an emergency?" Dana asked, feigning concern.

"I don't know."

"Are you in pain? Are you having trouble breathing? Do you feel faint?" Dana thought she might have sounded like she was reading from the script. (Maybe that was good, as if Wendy had asked these questions a thousand times.)

"I don't know."

"Just please fill out the forms, and we'll get you right in to see the doctor," Dana said without sincerity.

"God dammit! I need to see Doctor Mike Campbell now!" The man had raised his voice, just below a yell. "Now!"

Dana fumbled. These guys weren't supposed to drift from a monotone, That was against the rules. Though she had grown comfortable with auditioning, her head was now suffering from a minor anxiety attack.

"Now!" the man repeated in a bellow.

Dana had to read quickly. She focused on the script and read in her own monotone voice. "I'm sorry, sir, but you'll have to wait until he's finished with his patient. And if you raise your voice like that again, I'll have to call security." Dana knew the monotone thing wasn't proper, but it was all she could come up with.

"Very nice," the man said, back in his normal voice, surprising Dana once again.

There was more to read but the man had heard enough. She supposed that meant she either did really bad or really good. Again, she assumed the latter.

"Thanks, that was fun," she said. He had said, 'Very nice.' No one had ever told her that before (well, that wasn't true, but she was excited) and he seemed genuine about it.

The man walked her out into the waiting room and called for the next actress. He then looked at Dana and said, "Alrighty, you did real good in there. As they say, we'll let you know."

"Great!" Dana replied and walked away, passing all of the others who looked just like her except they hadn't nailed their audition like she had. (Well, they actually haven't auditioned yet, she reminded herself.)

Munching away at the rest of her banana, Dana felt empowered. She felt she could out-audition anyone for any part, anywhere on the planet, including anyone known as Lucy inside any kind of restaurant. She felt that landing this role could be the first step in making Dana McDougel a household name; a name that's loved, a name that's trusted, a name that's held in the highest regard. But most importantly, she felt closer to the person she dreamed of being. And that felt good.

Dana was back at her apartment by 6pm and decided to take a celebration shower. She was in unusually great spirits and that was a perfect time to take one. She washed off all the audition grime while instinctively reciting her monologue. One line kept echoing in her head: "Was I just Daddy's little girl? Was I just Daddy's little girl? Was I just Daddy's little girl?" She thought of her dad, and thought of how proud he would've been of her today.

Dana finished her celebration shower and dressed. Her cooking class was at 7pm and she was looking forward to it. This was her new weekly escape. It was a place she could go where there was no pressure to perform well and no one complained if the service was slow. It was also, perhaps, the perfect way to end a day like today. Dana was feeling so good that by the time she left her apartment she didn't even care if she received a callback from the audition. Okay, that's a lie, she thought. But whatever.

Chapter Thirty-Five

THE MOUND began to move. At first, the movements were small, undetectable to the human eye. But soon they morphed into sweeping blanket-scape alterations. What was once a mound had changed into a starfish and then a horseshoe and then an ocean wave. Then all was still.

An hour later, the ocean wave had become a mound once again. Two human arms found their way out of the blanketed cave and stretched out in opposite directions. Devon Shires peeked his head out, still in a slumberous daze, and pulled the blanket down to his neck. He lay in that position for another half hour, contemplating the day ahead and the night before. The first topic left his thoughts blank, but the second made him smile.

His studio apartment consisted of a king-size bed, an old acoustic guitar, a small table with two chairs, a pad and pen, a coffeepot, two mugs and an ashtray. That was all he needed, or so he reasoned. Devon put on his "funky" sunglasses, pulled up the window shades, and released a flood of daylight into his apartment. The sun was the best alarm clock in the history of alarm clocks. He then took

Francis, his mini-bong, and filled it with a stash he'd just scored. The guy had called it New York White and said it grew in the sewers. Whatever it was, it did what it was supposed to do. Devon then made some coffee and sat at his little table. After a few sips, he lit a cigarette and admired the smoke drifting through the rays of sunshine. Coffee and cigarettes made the perfect breakfast, he thought, and it made him feel like a rock star. It was just after two o'clock in the afternoon.

Devon reviewed his day's schedule. He really didn't have anything to do. It would most likely be another day of songwriting and "Inspo-Seeking," the latter being the justification of why he went out and had fun all the time. With the Inspo-Seeking excuse at his disposal, Devon could stay out all night or eat anywhere or travel the world and then say he was doing it for his art. It was a badge of debauchery, it was a license to live how the others didn't.

His band had played the night before in a dive bar called The Pit. Monday nights at The Pit were pure pandemonium. They had six to seven bands each playing a set, and the house band, *The Liberators*, playing the final slot. More importantly, though, they had drink specials dedicated to each band. Typically a slow night anywhere else, Mondays at The Pit were something of a local must. The bands were usually horrid, the drinks had less taste and the crowd didn't care about a thing. It was a great venue to play rock 'n' roll.

Devon enjoyed playing there because people didn't sit down at tables and quietly watch the loud rock music. In fact, there were no tables or chairs at The Pit so people were forced to stand up, and that was the way Devon thought it should be. There was only one stool at the end of the bar and that belonged to Libby, the three hundred-pound wife of the owner. She was the watchdog of The Pit, making sure there was no trouble with the staff or with the patrons. She also did the bookings for the club so she knew all the bands that went on stage. Libby kept everyone and everything in line. Just looking at her scared off the thought of any Tom Foolery. Devon had once seen her manhandle some guy because he dropped his drink on the floor on purpose and demanded a new one. Even though he was taller she grabbed him by the collar and lifted him up but then lost her balance and they crashed into a wall. The crowd watching exhaled a unanimous, "Whoa." Libby then stood up and peeled the rude man off the floor and hurled him out onto the sidewalk.

Devon's band, *Phase Electric Phase Beer*, had played the 11pm slot, which meant they had started at 11:45pm. Yet they had loaded in their equipment at 7:30pm, as opposed to right before their slot, so they could partake in the night's festivities. With their gear stashed loosely backstage, Devon and his bandmates went to the bar and ordered a round of cheap, nasty draft beer, known to the regulars as Pit Water. They greeted Libby, who was munching away at what appeared to be a burrito, and she responded with a moan. Devon knew two of the other bands because they were Monday night regulars. *Whette Dawguh* was a power trio with some of the ugliest-sounding music Devon had ever heard but their stage presence was so riveting that one could put up with the noise. *Hitch, Bitch & Ditch* was an anti-feminist girl band that played quick, poppy, hard-edged tunes. They sang out of key but Devon, and others, thought they were pretty hot. The other bands on the lineup were not familiar. Devon hoped that they knew the system but secretly hoped they didn't.

What most new acts didn't know about The Pit was that they weren't supposed to bring in a huge crowd. This made Monday nights at The Pit unique from every other venue in the city. There was always a mass of patrons on Monday nights regardless of what bands were playing. If a band promoted themselves and brought in a sizable following then there was going to be trouble. The Monday night regulars (aka The Pitters) didn't like strangers. If the ratio of Pitters to strangers was one-to-three, which was highly unusual, then there'd be a brawl. If the ratio was one-to-two, then there'd be constant screaming matches possibly leading to a fight a notch below a brawl. If the ratio was one-to-one, then all would be peaceful just as long as the strangers didn't act up. Thankfully, the first time Devon ever gigged there, his band, *Dirt*, had no following whatsoever and that made them an instant success with the Pitters.

Devon had been playing music since he was six, when he used to bang on the family piano. By age seven he had destroyed 79 of the 88 keys. While doing so, he'd also had his first three-chord experience. Because of that discovery, he naturally assumed he was destined to become a rock star. After shifting his energy to electric guitar as a teenager, he formed a band with his neighbor who played drums. They focused on playing loud, abstract noise. Even back then, Devon didn't want his band to sound like anyone else. While they were playing, if something familiar sounding started coming from his guitar or from the drummer, they would immediately stop and then start over again after an eight-minute moment of silence. He and his neighbor were so dedicated to their philosophy that they didn't even give themselves a name. Their rationale being that if they did, then they'd be like every other band.

No fortune came their way, nor did any encouragement or compliments from family or friends. After three years of abstraction and not one music lesson taken by either, Devon and his neighbor parted ways with only a CD of their favorite songs, entitled *Greatest Shits*.

At his parents' insistence, Devon went to college. He told them that he didn't need a college education to become an abstract rock star. All he needed was time and a new guitar. His parents made him a deal: If he went to college and earned a degree then they'd buy him a new guitar and amplifier. Devon agreed and went to an artsy college in Pennsylvania for four years. There, he started another abstract band called *Iu* (pronounced "Big I, Little U"). Devon initially wanted *Iu* to have no name at all, but he realized that there'd already been a band by that name (or idea), and so it wouldn't be abstract enough and would go against everything he believed in. *Iu* practiced on and off during Devon's college career. They even managed to play at a few of Bubba Boone's parties, but after every one Bubba would make them promise to learn some real songs. Each time they would agree and then not do it. After the third time they were never invited back.

During Devon's senior year of college, it may have been the oncoming pressure of going out into the real world, or maybe because he was maturing somewhat, or perhaps it was because he stopped using hallucinogenics, but whatever the reason, that was when he wrote his first song (including lyrics). Of course, Devon made sure it still had an abstract sound to it, even going so far as to not naming it, figuring it wasn't copying his first band because that was how he'd referred to the band not their songs.

Whenever *Iu* played it, Devon would yell: "So you want something accessible!? Well, here you go, you idiots! This song is for you! And don't ask what it's called, because it's got no name!"

No one ever heard this introduction except his bandmates because they could no longer get any gigs, but Devon was ready for when they did.

Devon graduated college in four years. His parents were thrilled and he went home for the summer. He had long talks with them about his future; what he wanted to do, what he could do, what he'd be good at. At the end of every discussion, Devon would always think of his music (even though, as his mother pointed out several times, he'd only written one song). The first pact he had made with his parents worked out rather well; he had a beautifully built custom guitar as well as a high-end amplifier (and a college degree). So towards the end of that summer, Devon started negotiations on a new deal.

Devon had the benefit of financing. His parents were well off (his father was close to early retirement) and would give him anything he wanted. Anything, that is, except rock stardom. All they seemed to have wanted was his college degree. Getting a respectable job was not expected of him but they hinted that it'd be nice. Either way, he could probably skip along his path in life for quite awhile without playing one standard song. He had to work on a proposal that would satisfy both parties' demands, but that would still give him exactly what he wanted.

As that summer came to a close, when he couldn't bear to be in the same room as his parents and he consistently ticked them off with his "Lazy Man" schedule, Devon submitted his new deal. He'd move out of their northern Westchester estate and into New York City. He'd get out of their hair and they could both resume their lives. They would pay his rent and give him a small allowance, and he would get a part-time job and focus mainly on his music.

His father scanned the piece of paper over a white wine spritzer, looked up and said, "You got yourself a deal, son. Make us proud."

Rejuvenated and motivated, Devon found a comfortable studio apartment in Gramercy. Since price wasn't an issue, finding a place was easy. When he told his father that he had found something he liked, his father came into the city to look at it himself. The apartment was in a charming area and in a reputable building with good financials. Between the enormous broker fee, the security deposit, the quality of the apartment, and the neighborhood it was in, Devon's father decided to buy the apartment outright.

Devon hired a moving company and brought his arsenal of possessions into the capital of the world. The first living arrangement he had was the opposite of what he would end up with. He had a single bed, set up flush against the wall; he had a couch with its back to the other side of the bed; he had a coffee table and two side tables; he had three ornate lamps; he had a big leather chair and a few Oriental rugs; he had a five-component stereo system with four-foot speakers, a giant screen TV and a computer; he had a full kitchen of dishes, pans, pots and cutlery; he had an electric can opener, a toaster oven, a blender, a food processor and a microwave; and finally, he had his trusty coffeepot which he'd purchased for fifty cents at a yard sale somewhere in the middle of Pennsylvania. Now, almost a decade later, the only original item that remained in his apartment was the coffeepot.

With his parents' bankroll behind him, Devon took a lackadaisical approach to finding part-time work. He held jobs from time to time until he was tired of them and would then spend a few weeks (if not months) on work hiatus. His favorite job was his stint at the local flower shop. The pace was slow and he got free plants; it was just right. Devon's tenure at the flower shop lasted almost six months, surprising him and his parents (and the shop owner). But when he realized one morning how long he'd been there, he immediately quit in fear of damaging his reputation as a free spirit.

Chapter Thirty-Six

DURING HIS New York City residency, Devon had tried working in a coffee shop, a record store, a pet store, a sex shop, a Jewish deli, an art gallery and a multi-media conglomerate, but nothing had really appealed to him. Nasty old rock 'n' roll kept pushing and pulling him to do more. And after five years of abstract acoustic performances (at a bar called The Sensitive Songwriter), Devon finally hooked up with some musicians who were (somewhat) into his sound.

Morris Becker had approached Devon after his set one night. There were four or five people in the bar, all of whom worked there and thought Devon's music was fairly good background ambiance, which was the only reason he was allowed to play there (although it was always a late night slot). Morris, who was friends with one of the bartenders, was the first non-staff person to see him play in over a year.

Morris, drunk-munching a bag of Cheese Chunks, was into Devon's idea. "Hey, dude. Nice set, man."

Devon wasn't sure if this guy was messing with him or not. No one had ever said anything remotely like that and Devon thought he was either being polite or a wise-ass. "Thanks, man," Devon replied nonchalantly.

"No, I'm totally serious," Morris came back a bit defensive. "I think you're on to something."

"Whatever," Devon said, wondering if his music career was reaching it's sad conclusion. What would he do? Become a delivery man?

"I've never heard anything quite like it before," Morris said, trying to sound genuine.

"Yeah, thanks. I guess," Devon answered, feeling more and more down that he'd soon be wearing a fluorescent bib every night.

"Yeah, and if you don't mind me saying, because I know it's your thing and all, but I think if you tweaked out some stuff, then you might have something really good."

Devon stopped packing away his gear and thought about that. He was now listening to whatever this guy was saying. It was one thing to say, "Good job up there" (which was a rarity for Devon unless a friend of his was somehow able to make a show), but it was another thing to give him constructive criticism, which was something he'd never received before (at least not in the city). Maybe this guy really did like his music. Maybe what he was saying was right. But was he suggesting that Devon should succumb to the norm?

"You mean like have specific parts and lyrics and words and chords?" Devon asked with some disdain.

"Well, kind of," Morris replied, just starting to understand what kind of mentality he was dealing with.

Devon didn't speak again for a while. All his life he had devoted himself to abstraction and never budged from his stance. But after ten or so years of remaining faithful to that vision, Devon thought this little fellow might be right. If no one heard the material, how could they appreciate it? Perhaps compromise was in the near future. It would certainly be a better alternative to getting a job.

"Well, I do have lyrics. They're just in my secret language," Devon said, almost wanting this "fan" to prove him wrong.

"You're right," Morris began, "and I think that's somewhat creative. But personally, I don't consider random howls and chirps and moans to be lyrical. But that's just my opinion."

Devon knew this guy had a point and he was probably right. Devon would never tell him that, though. "So what would you suggest?" Devon asked, bypassing the fodder and curious to see if this guy had a solution.

"Well, I'd take your best musical ideas," Morris began but then paused, "if you can remember them, and then structure them into their own songs, maybe using two or three ideas per song. Then maybe add a melody and some words, if not to the whole song then at least to either the verse or the chorus, and then you'd have something. It'd be your sound, custom fit for the masses." Morris stepped back, realizing that perhaps he'd said too much.

But Devon had heard everything, and he hated to admit it, but it was true. "You mean I should make them accessible," Devon said, emphasizing his dislike for the last word.

"Well, yeah. Kind of. I suppose," said Morris, who was starting to wonder how full this guy was of himself.

"That's not my thing," Devon announced defiantly, his stubbornness reborn with fire. He had already tried the accessible approach back in college. He despised it, or so he made everyone believe, including himself. But deep down inside, where only the darkest thoughts lie, he had a small affection for abstract pop.

"You think a little kid would understand your stuff?" Morris asked.

"Probably not would be my guess. But it's not as though I'm writing for them," replied Devon as if this guy was a bit wacko.

"Well, you know, they say that a true genius can explain the most abstract theories to small children," Morris said, perhaps a tad too pretentious.

Morris stopped for a sip of ale and a mouthful of Cheese Chunks before he talked for fifteen more minutes. He talked way too much but Devon kind of liked him (and he definitely knew a lot about music). When Devon finally got up to leave, Morris asked him if he wanted to play music together some time.

"What do you play?" Devon asked, surprised that he hadn't mentioned being a musician.

"I play drums."

"Oh, that's cool," Devon said, thinking that maybe a healthy jam session would be good. "Yeah, let's do that. Why not."

"Great," Morris said, wondering if he sounded more like an excited geek rather than a neo-abstract rocker. They exchanged phone numbers and tentatively planned to play the next week.

Devon said, "Later," and hopped in a cab. Realizing he didn't know this guy's name, he rolled down the window and yelled. "What's your name anyway!?"

"Morris Becker!" Morris replied with his chin up.

When they met up at a midtown rehearsal studio, Devon was more than happy with the way Morris played the drums. He had an abstractness that resounded well with Devon's guitar playing and they played non-stop for two hours until it was time to leave. Devon's gut was telling him that this could be what he'd been preparing for his whole life, that this could be the start of something special. They booked some more time at the studio and got together again. The results were the same and Devon didn't even mind that Morris was slowly forming some of the music into songs (to the point where Morris would say, "Lets play the moody one in A," and Devon would know what he was talking about). After a few jam sessions, and at Morris' insistence, Devon agreed to pen some words for a few songs. At first, Devon's tormented feeling of selling out was quite strong, but into the third song, that attitude began to subside and Devon thought he might be getting hooked on accessibility.

Hate It by Devon Shires (Dirt: Dirt)

I hate it
I hate it tons
I hate it mad
I hate your guts

Hey, hey, hey
Hate, hate, hate
Take a look around
You stupid ass face

I hate it
I hate it all
I hate it more
I hate your mom

Hey, hey, hey
Hate, hate, hate
Take a look around
You stupid ass face

They called themselves *The Dirt*, but soon shortened it to just *Dirt*. When they had compiled six songs from the heap of abstraction, at Morris' insistence, they got a friend of his to play bass guitar. Slimy Ed was an excellent bass player but he couldn't believe or comprehend the music he was hearing. At home, it took him many, many listens to the rehearsal tracks before he could formulate some bass lines. Once the sound clicked in his head, though, Slimy Ed became absorbed with the accessible abstractions of *Dirt* and soon had bass parts for all six songs.

Dirt was beginning to sound like a real rock 'n' roll band. With every practice their songs became more and more coherent (and Devon didn't seem to mind). Devon's singing grew confident and he somehow memorized all the lyrics he had written. It was almost time to start playing live shows and sharing their music with the city, but Morris wasn't ready for that yet.

After one typical midweek practice, Morris spoke up. "I don't know what you guys think, but I'm kind of thinking we could use another instrument, you know, to make our sound complete."

His tone was casual and polite but Devon knew what Morris was getting at. He was basically telling Devon, "Listen, man, you're a really good front man and a damn good songwriter and you're pretty good at guitar, but we need someone else who's really, really, really good at guitar." Slimy Ed quickly concurred, leading Devon to believe that he and Morris had discussed this before.

"I don't want keyboards in this band. That'd be too cliché, and that's not what we're all about," Devon declared, not wanting to give in so easily. He caught Morris glancing at Slimy Ed and that made him feel good.

"I agree. Keyboards aren't what we're looking for," Morris replied, trying to find a way through.

"Yeah. No," Slimy Ed chimed in, almost to himself, but not making much sense. Devon and Morris knew what he meant, though.

"So what'd you have in mind?" Devon asked with a frown. He could have played the cat-and-mouse game for a while but that would just delay the inevitable. Devon was the definitive leader of *Dirt*, but Morris definitely ran the show (sometimes Devon couldn't understand how that had happened).

"Well, I'm thinking we could use another guitar player." Morris braved the words and then smoothly followed them up. "Just someone to hold down the rhythm while you do your thing, you know?"

That was a nice way of saying, "He'll do all the playing and you can do all the annoying little noodling you want with your volume way down."

Normally, Devon would put up an argument or simply denounce all that was being said, but after two hours of ear-deafening rock 'n' roll he didn't have it in him. "Whatever," Devon spat as he packed away his electric. "If both of you feel this way then go ahead and find someone. I'll see you next week."

Devon left with a grunt, leaving Morris and Slimy Ed relieved that it went down without too much resistance. Morris, indeed, had already approached someone for the job and had him on standby. He'd also given him updated tracks of their rehearsals, so the guy knew every song, which would make his entrance much easier on Devon's patience and pride. Morris was the master of rock 'n' roll diplomacy.

At their next practice, Morris introduced Wayne Willy to the twenty-minutes-tardy Devon Shires. After two hours of distorted noise and Devon slumping his grudging shoulders, Wayne became a permanent fixture of *Dirt*. Even Devon, who had sulked from beginning to end, couldn't deny that the guy was awesome at guitar and that their sound was thicker than it'd ever been. Morris even thought he saw Devon smile when they were leaving.

Soldier X by Devon Shires (Dirt: Dirt)

Chop my fingers
Chop my hand
Slice my arm in three

Rip my wrist
Tip your hat
Leg-drop me to your knee

It sounds the best
With Soldier X

Break my thumb
Fake your dumb
Hangin' in the trees

Take my pride
You little guy
You talk too much for me

But it sounds the best
With Soldier X

Their six songs were coming together and their sound was maturing with the guitar playing of Wayne Willy. Devon still had a few songs to write lyrics to, but after that *Dirt* would be ready for its next move. Morris had drawn up a business plan after he and Devon first got together. Being a great organizer and the undeniable brains of the band, Morris had written out a strategy for success. The first step was to form a solid band: Check! Second was to write and learn six songs: Almost check! The third step was to record a low-budget album consisting of the six songs: Next! With their own album they could spread the word of their abstract message. They could sell it or give it away to family, friends and fans (if they had any), they could send it to radio stations and record labels, they could book shows throughout the city and elsewhere, they could have reviews written up in music rags. The album would be their entry pass into the music industry.

Morris, of course, handled all of the scheduling. When they were ready to record, he found the best studio to work in and booked all the time they needed. Devon's parents, who were genuinely excited that their son was actually writing coherent songs and playing with a "nice group of guys," offered to fund the recording. It was "the least they could do." Devon, without pause, accepted their offer (and debated whether or not he should tell the others, thinking that he could use the old "let's split it four ways" scam and pocket the cash). He almost went through with the con, but right before they went into the studio, when Morris told everyone how much it would cost, Slimy Ed and Wayne both confessed that they had absolutely no cash (and Ed, to boot, was in debt). Not wanting to wait until Slimy Ed and Wayne earned enough cash to pay, Devon reluctantly shared the good news.

Dirt's recording sessions were fantastic. Devon felt like the rock star he had always dreamed of being. He took it so far as to not shower for the entire week and to smoke unearthly amounts of the Oregon Death Bud. Hearing his songs come to life was an amazing experience for Devon. Never before did he have the opportunity to listen to his own creations through speakers that cost more than a small car. Their sessions began at 6pm and usually went until 4am. When they got hungry, they simply ordered in sushi or cheeseburgers or whatever they wanted. When they were thirsty, the studio assistant would run out and get them a case of beer or a case of bottled water. Devon, the eternal night owl, was in paradise. He intently watched the engineers set up microphones and machines, experimenting with different placements and different settings, trying to achieve the best sounds possible (although a few times Devon thought that they were only procrastinating; "That sounds fine. Can we start now?").

He wore his favorite shirt all week thinking that it was good luck and if someone was taking pictures, then he'd look consistent in all of them. As he did with his body, he didn't wash his favorite shirt either. It was all about playing the rock star. Devon reasoned that if you played the part enough, then the part would eventually take over and before you knew it, you'd be there. Morris, even though he had his own minor rock star habits, disagreed completely and on the last day he forced Devon to shower and wear a different shirt. ("You didn't make me do anything, Little Man!") Devon felt at home in the studio and wanted them to get back as soon as possible. He figured it would require, perhaps, writing a bunch more tunes and waiting for the highly anticipated success of the current album to wane.

After asking a friend to do the artwork, Morris posted their self-titled debut album online. By the time they had the finished product, three months and five thousand dollars had been spent. As for Devon's parents, they were amazed that the cost was so low.

("The technology must be so wonderful.") Morris sent links of the album to the press and to clubs and to some local college radio stations. After a couple more months of calling and following up, *Dirt* managed to get zero radio play, one negative online review, and one gig at Lou's. All the friends and family who were given the album had the same reaction: "It's nice."

Despite the lack of encouragement from all directions, the four of them were excited about the one show they were able to book. Sure, it was at 11:30pm on a Sunday at a place you wouldn't recommend to the craziest person you knew, but it was a gig. And it was their first one.

Devon hated to admit it, but by the time that first show came around he had thoroughly exhausted his affection for their album. The benefit, though, was that both he and the other guys knew the material so well that they sounded more rehearsed than ever. There was no one in the audience for *Dirt's* first performance. In hindsight, it was a great way to break into the live scene. Because the club was empty, no one in the band was nervous (a few cold beers helped out, too). The soundman appeared disgusted with their music, but after Devon got him high on Sour Diesel he reconsidered his opinion and thought they "might be on to something" and helped them get another show.

A month later, *Dirt* played again, but this time in the 10:30pm slot on Sunday. Devon got the soundman high before they went on, and afterwards, the soundman graciously accepted a copy of their album in lieu of a tip. For six months *Dirt* played at Lou's, and they slowly moved up on the evening schedule. By the time they earned the 8:30pm slot, they had a slew of new material and a following of about three people.

Chapter Thirty-Seven

DEVON KNEW that success in the music industry came through hard work and dedication, but after six months of consistent gigging and promoting their album, *Dirt* still hadn't moved many souls. The new material he'd been writing was a departure from the first album, though it did retain much of its abstract nature. Devon had somewhat reined in his sound from the extremes and hoped more people would appreciate it (and maybe show up to their gigs). Altering "the sound" was a deep philosophical issue that touched the heart of Devon's existence, but a revelation dawned on him one afternoon: He wanted to be admired and respected more than he loved his abstract style.

"Are you selling out or what, man?" Slimy Ed asked after listening to Devon play a new song.

"You're getting old, dude," piped in Wayne (who was secretly thought to be over fifty).

"It's different… but yet familiar," Morris added, trying to hide his uncertainty.

Devon realized he must have brainwashed the band with his original vision (and wondered why he couldn't do that with anyone else). Perhaps now he'd have to do it all over again.

"Gentlemen," Devon began, "this is just the next phase. There's a five-phase process and our first album was the first phase. This new stuff, like it or not, is the second phase. It's too complex to explain, but I'm sure that you can see what I'm talking about."

Wayne started nodding his head in supposed understanding because Slimy Ed was doing it. Devon laughed and said, "So let's get going!" Morris, shaking his head after witnessing what had just gone down, kicked in with a drumbeat.

With the backing of the Shires family, *Dirt* once again returned to the studio. Devon had to use the "five-phase" explanation to ease his parents into funding the project (and he was certain that they, too, didn't understand it, but probably thought it was just the way the music industry worked). It was still apparent that neither Wayne nor Slimy Ed were passionate about the new material but Devon ignored them and held his stance. Devon wasn't enthusiastic about the songs either, but he was sure that with some studio magic they would turn out sounding great. The real truth, however, was that Devon just wanted to get back into the studio to remind himself that he was, indeed, a rock star.

Puppy Bitch by Devon Shires (Dirt: Dirt Dirt)

Brown eyes and wagging tail
Sloppy tongue breathing stale

You puppy bitch
You're such a hit
You puppy bitch
Sit, sit, sit

Frolic through my cash
Bite me a rabid gash

You puppy bitch
Got a spendin' feel
You puppy bitch
Heel, heel, heel

Barking blue into my ear
Unleash my sound for you to hear

You puppy bitch
Go far away
You puppy bitch
Stay, stay, stay

Devon immersed himself back into his studio habits. In addition to the usual one shirt, no showers, lots of sushi and an ounce of Kentucky Blue Bud, he also slept on the studio couch all week. On the third day, Morris brought him a toothbrush and a small toothpaste dispenser. Morris, thankful that the Shires were once again funding their studio experience, was willing to put up with Devon's antics and his new music, but he seriously questioned Devon's new lyrics.

"I didn't want to ask you in front of the others," Morris said after he led Devon out into the hallway, "but I just checked out your lyrics, and over half these tunes are love songs. What are you trying to pull here?"

Morris kept his voice down, but his concern was real. *Dirt* wasn't about love songs; that was a waste of radio space. They were about "abstractions." Devon was caught off guard by this interrogation but he also didn't think any of the songs were about love. Since when did anyone bother to read his lyrics anyway?

"What are you talking about, man?" Devon defended himself, but lacked anything else to say.

"You know exactly what I'm talking about! Now, I don't mind this new sound you're doing right now," growled Morris, "only because I'm waiting for phase three and I think that'll be cool. But we can't be getting soft, man. Not now. Not ever."

Devon wasn't sure how to react. He really didn't know if his lyrics had any love motifs flowing through them because he'd honestly never thought of that word while writing them. Morris was just trying to flex his power a little, Devon thought. Maybe he should let Morris feel like he had some. But then again, he didn't want to be talked to like that. So instead of saying something like, "Sure, Morris, my bad. I'll rewrite them," he went in for a bruising victory.

"You think this sound is soft?" Devon demanded, grabbing the authority stick away from Morris.

Morris paused before speaking, thinking that, perhaps, he shouldn't have brought this up. "Well… no, not really," Morris confessed, digging himself a comfortable hole.

"You think we're a bunch of folk-singin' pansies?" Devon roared, getting the attention of some studio workers.

"No," Morris weakly admitted and then tried to pick up his voice a little. "No, we totally rock, man."

"Damn straight, we do!" Devon yelled, getting himself fired up and luring Wayne and Slimy Ed out into the hall. "And what is love anyway!?"

Morris didn't know what to say, but Wayne was visibly excited.

"Yeah, we totally rock, dude!" Wayne said with blind certainty towards Morris, and then paused before adding a final thought. "We do!"

Morris, who now looked like a rock 'n' roll traitor, spoke out. "I know we do, Wayne. We're awesome… we're totally awesome."

Morris and Wayne looked at Slimy Ed, who appeared to be on the verge of saying something. Morris hoped that Slimy Ed didn't say anything, as Wayne had, to imply that he didn't think they rocked. Wayne hoped that Slimy Ed would shout our something inspirational like, "We're gonna rock the five boroughs, then the world!"

"It can't be defined," Slimy Ed said quietly to his shoes.

Morris looked at Wayne, who looked back at him, and then they both looked at Devon, who was a bit struck that Slimy Ed had spoken with such wisdom.

"What do you mean, dude?" Wayne asked his cohort.

"Love… it can't be defined," Slimy Ed said, again to his shoes.

Wayne tilted his head. "What do you mean, dude?" he repeated and then asked sincerely, "Are you okay, man?"

"Yeah, I'm fine, dude. That's just what I think," Slimy Ed said, perhaps opening himself up to the band for the first time.

Devon took that as his cue. "Which makes it abstract!" He only looked at Morris, victorious once again. "Now let's rock!"

That got both Wayne and the relieved Slimy Ed fired up. They marched back into the recording studio cheering and pounding the walls. Morris stood there for a moment as some cloudy thoughts breezed by and then nodded a confident nod. "Let's do it," he said and followed them in.

Devon's optimism was strong that *Dirt Dirt* would help catapult *Dirt* into the New York City music scene. He couldn't even imagine the possibility of that *not* happening. When they finished up in the studio, Tall Mickey, the engineer, took Morris aside and told him that he appreciated their business but he couldn't foresee

Dirt working there again. Morris handled it well (fully understanding the unspoken message) and kept it to himself, hoping that the highly anticipated phase three would see *Dirt* moving on to something else.

Upon the release of *Dirt Dirt*, the band received the same feedback from family and friends: "It's nice." They received the same negative response from the same online reviewer and they received the same opportunities from the New York clubs: another show at Lou's. But this time, Lou offered them a 11:30pm show on a *Saturday* night, which was encouraging. Morris was fatigued from all the effort he had exerted, desperately trying to promote the band, and although they were given a Saturday night slot, it wasn't enough for him. But watching the others strut around, proud of their upcoming show (and with Devon feeling more and more like a rock star), Morris decided to stay silent. He did, however, hound Devon for the details of the mysterious phase three, which always ended with Devon saying, "Be patient, Little Man."

After gigging once a month for six months at Lou's, *Dirt* had only earned their way to the 10:30pm slot (after which they were promptly moved back to 11:30pm). Their fan base reached a record fifteen one night, although eleven of them thought *Dirt* was a different band. It became clear to Devon that the others were becoming frustrated. The good times they'd had were turning into hostile evenings (even Slimy Ed and Wayne were jawing at each other). Most importantly, Devon saw Morris' ambition decrease. Devon would never publicly admit that he needed Morris' drive to keep the band afloat (nor would he ever tell Morris that in private), but he knew it to be true, and he also knew what that meant: It was time for phase three. Now all Devon had to do was think of what it was.

Chapter Thirty-Eight

"ALL RIGHT," Devon said, handing each of the guys a cold beer and a bag of Cheese Chunks as they made themselves comfortable in his apartment. He had done some soul searching, some musical scouting and some strategic planning: He had devised phase three. "I thought it'd be better to have a little band meeting than to practice tonight... because I think we need to talk about something."

The rest of the band sat quietly, unenthusiastic about everything in their lives, especially the band called *Dirt*.

Devon used the silence to his benefit and continued. "For starters," Devon solemnly said, "we suck."

That got everyone's attention and they all looked up at him.

"Secondly, our songs suck." Devon said as if it were a confession, letting the guys know that the fault was probably his own (being the only songwriter in the band). "Thirdly, our attitudes suck."

At that, they all looked back down, perhaps aware it was true.

"Fourthly, no one likes us," Devon said as if he cared (which he secretly did). "And no one wants us to play at their club, and no one wants to buy our music, and no one wants a free copy either." Devon paused. "And do you know why?" He waited until he had made eye contact with each of them. "Because we *suck*."

The band kept staring at the floor with their beers untouched. Slimy Ed appeared to be shivering. Devon was already on his second beer. It was time to push them. "We suck *hard*. We do nothing right. In fact, we're *beyond* sucking."

Sip.

"We're pathetic. Chicks are afraid of us. We're total losers."

Sip.

"We average one person a show." Sip.

"We're boring. People would rather listen to air than to us."

Gulp.

"It's been almost two years since we've started playing… in fact, cheers."

Gulp.

"Which makes us suck all the more."

Gulp.

"Morris, you do all the business stuff."

Gulp.

"But you suck. Wayne, you're a great player and have great energy."

Two gulps.

"But you know what? You suck, too."

Devon cracked open a new beer.

"And, Ed, you just flat-out suck."

Chug.

"And what about *you*?" Morris braved the question with a breath of anger, as Devon hoped someone would.

Wayne followed Morris' lead. "Yeah, what about you?"

Then even Slimy Ed muttered something. "Yeah."

Morris, with the power of three, let it all out. "You're talking about all these things, but you're not talking about yourself! What, are we the only ones who've been screwing up? We've all worked hard at this and it's not fair and it ain't right for you to go off like that."

Slimy Ed whimpered, "Yeah." Wayne was getting anxious with the mutiny.

Morris continued, though not quite looking at Devon. "Yeah, we all could've done more, and we all could *do* more, but don't lay all of this on us. We're a band. Maybe not a great one, but we're still a band, and that means we're a team. There's no blaming one person, that's not fair. And you're not even looking at yourself."

Slimy Ed added another timid, "Yeah."

Then Wayne took the baton. "A lot of what you say is right, dude. You're right on about our music and our gigs and stuff. And yeah, man, maybe we do suck…"

Morris, who felt he was on a roll, cut Wayne off (which upset Wayne because he had just conceded that they sucked, which wasn't his point). "We've all put in a lot of time and effort and sweat to make this thing real, to make it happen. It's all of our faults, not just one of us. We're not having fun anymore because we're all blaming each other for anything we can think of. But there's nothing wrong with what we're doing. I think we're doing all right. We just got to keep at it. We just got to keep rockin'. You know? One day we'll do it, I know we will."

Wayne had been impatiently waiting to finish his thought but momentarily lost his desire to say anything, as did Slimy Ed and Devon. They were wondering what was happening to Morris. He was talking like he was in some movie of the week. Devon, trying not to laugh, sipped his beer every time he was about to smile.

"Why are you looking at me like that?" Morris asked with a touch of paranoia.

Wayne took over, relieved he could finally finish his point. "I didn't mean that we do suck… that's not what I meant, dude. But maybe we do," Wayne said but then paused. "Damn it, man, I forgot my point."

Slimy Ed spoke. "I don't think any of us suck, dude."

"Oh yeah," Wayne recalled. "What I'm saying is that, yeah, we really haven't done so good… yet. Devon, man, you're right about some of the things you're saying but, dude, if we all suck then what about you, man?"

"What about me?" Devon challenged, forcing everyone's eyes back down. Sometimes he just couldn't believe these guys. Devon gulped more of his beer. "What are you saying, Wayne? What about me?"

No one looked up (and still no one had touched their beer).

"Well, then you suck too, man," mumbled Slimy Ed. He said it carefully and more to himself than to Devon, but the quietness in the room allowed them all to hear it.

Wayne glanced at Slimy Ed, proud that his cohort said what he had tried to say and contributed a soft, "Yeah." Then Morris did the same.

Devon was hoping for a machine gun attack, but in hindsight he knew he shouldn't have expected anything more than what they'd thrown at him. A riotous uproar would have segued perfectly into his proposed solution, but now he would have to just come out and say it. How anticlimactic.

"Well, you guys are right," Devon said and let it sink in for a while. "Now all of this has been the bad news, and if we're done with the bad news then maybe we could move on to the good news."

One by one, the others lifted their heads and looked curiously at Devon.

"What good news?" Morris carefully asked, trying to contain his piquing optimism.

"Gentlemen, the good news is that *Dirt*, if all of you are still on board, will, from this point forward… be moving into phase three."

Jaws dropped. The long-fabled phase three was upon them. Devon hadn't mentioned anything about it in months, and the belief that phase three even existed had vanished. But now phase three represented a spark, a speckle of hope that their dreams were still attainable, that maybe there was still a chance.

Devon waited until the giddy murmurs subsided. "Phase three starts with us taking what we've learned as a unit, and starting fresh with that knowledge."

Devon had their attention and he hoped they'd go for his plan. "The first thing we do is throw out all of our old songs and all of our old albums. There'll be no need for them now."

There were no objections to that.

"Second thing we do is come up with some new material." Devon thought he heard Morris grunt, but he ignored it.

"And I've already taken care of that," Devon said with some satisfaction. "It seems that from the start I've focused on the abstractions of sounds and songs. By doing so, we've distanced ourselves from any audience whatsoever. And now, after all these years, I realize that I had the wrong approach all along."

The others were listening intently as their leader preached.

"I have written ten new songs," Devon declared, then paused. "And they're of the pop persuasion."

Wayne dropped his beer, but rescued it before it spilled on the Oriental rug.

"Now, I know what you're thinking, but let me finish. We're going to take these ten pop songs, and when I say pop I don't mean like bubble gum, teeny-bopper trash." Devon heard Slimy Ed let out a deep breath. "I mean like rock pop. You know, a little catchy and a little easy to follow."

That still didn't please his bandmates but Devon was sure that they'd understand and agree with his new strategy. "We're gonna take these new tunes… and cut 'em up and put 'em back together again."

Questioning faces surrounded him, but Devon didn't hesitate. "We're gonna take the verse of song five and put it together with the chorus of song eight and mix in the bridge of song seven. You see what I mean? We're gonna mix it all together! We're gonna play on their field, but by our rules. You know what I'm talking about?"

Their eyes were widening and Devon knew he had them.

"Yeah, dude! That's totally cool!" Wayne exclaimed.

"Wow, man. All right," Slimy Ed said in deep appreciation.

Devon looked to Morris for approval, knowing that it would be imperative (at least at the moment).

"That's not a bad idea," Morris began, more to himself. "That could really work."

Wayne and Slimy Ed looked at Morris, beaming with excitement.

"We'll show everyone what abstraction is all about!" Devon yelled, rousing his troops for battle, and they cheered and hollered and chugged their cold beers. He waited until their excitement died down some before he continued. "And thirdly," Devon said, hushing his crowd, "we're changing our name."

The others looked at each other, mouths closed but nodding their heads in approval.

"A new start means a new name. And this time, we'll *all* help out." Devon figured that the democratic sharing scheme would be valuable for their morale. "We will all think of a word. Just one word. Then we'll write it down on a piece of paper, put them all in a hat, and then one by one take them out. And that'll be our new name."

Again, there were no objections, so Devon ripped a piece of notebook paper into four and handed everyone a slice. After ten minutes, the four scraps were in an old hat that Devon had lying around. Devon handed the hat to Morris, diplomatically delegating authority. "Alright, Morris," he began, "What is our *new* name?"

Morris pulled out the pieces of paper one by one. "Our new name is Phase... Electric... Phase? ...Beer. Our new name is *Phase Electric Phase Beer*."

Morris didn't seem too thrilled with the results but Wayne and Slimy Ed were grinning wide, excited about the name and more excited that they had both put in the same word.

Devon had a feeling they'd do something stupid like that, but knew their happiness was worth the price. Morris had scored well with *Beer;* that definitely had potential. And oddly enough, after chugging his own beer, Morris began to appreciate the new name.

After everyone calmed down some and a few more beers disappeared, Devon concluded his plan. "And finally, my abstract rockers, the last part of phase three is that we will be playing somewhere new."

They all looked at him, stunned in disbelief. They were all very aware that they hadn't been able to get a show anywhere besides Lou's (and Morris' sister's 25th birthday party, which at the last moment was cancelled; the gig, not the party, for reasons unknown). But this was Devon's crowning achievement. "In one month's time, my surreal minstrels, we shall be playing at... The Pit!" Devon heard gasps echo throughout the room and let them subside before announcing the coup de gras, "On a Monday night."

"Yeah, dude!" Wayne yelled, as though his favorite team had just won the championship.

They hugged each other and jumped around the apartment until a neighbor came up to complain.

Morris was still in disbelief. "How'd you get that?" he kept asking, but Devon only responded with a smile; it was his own little secret.

The band left his apartment with renewed spirit and determination. Devon knew they'd have to do a lot of practicing to be prepared with the new material, but he was looking forward to it. He thought he might not ever tell Morris how he got them a Monday night show at The Pit. But it wasn't much of a mystery. One can accomplish a great deal with good manners and a bag of South African Sinsemilla.

That's Not You (It's Me) by Devon Shires (Phase Electric
Phase Beer: Track & Field)

Stoned daddy sippin' scotch
Grabbin' ass and grabbin' crotch
Cigars and cars and workin' wench
Pigeon-holed on another bench

That's not you
It's me
It's not you
It's me
Not you
Me
'Cause you suck

Mad-ass mango fruity mama
Tears and beers and sweet gelata
Football dogs and pimpy coats
Diamond flesh and a pack of smokes

That's not you
It's me
It's not you
It's me
Not you
Me
'Cause you suck

Back off, baby
Watch your step
Don't mess with Mister Handy

Nothin', nothin', nothin' nice
Pellet guns and chicken spice
Eat my feet on razzle-dazzle
Walk with me through a herd of cattle

That's not you
It's me
It's not you
It's me
Not you
Me
'Cause you suck

The result of mixing and matching different parts of his songs was an awkward pop rock sound. Uncomfortable key changes and tempo shifts lent themselves to songs that were hard to follow. The band "mostly" learned the material, but Devon didn't mind; it just confirmed their abstractness. They played the opening slot on Monday night at The Pit, although to Devon's momentary disappointment they were billed as *Dirt* (Devon had booked the show before the phase three meeting). Despite Slimy Ed and Wayne being visibly terrified on stage, they played pretty well as a band. Their complete lack of fans and their strange brand of rock 'n' roll helped them immeasurably, as did the second half of Devon's pot promise to the bartender, and they were offered another Monday night.

They recorded *Track & Field* a few months later in a different studio and, again, with the Shires family funding. This time, however, they managed to get someone at a New York music rag to review it and the primary comment was that it '*wasn't so bad.*' They didn't sell any albums, but they did give a lot away at what had turned into a monthly Monday night show at The Pit. There was even one time when someone in the audience yelled out a request. Best of all, *Phase Electric Phase Beer* had earned the 11pm slot (bypassing *Whette Dawguh* for the honors). The chemistry amongst the ranks was incredibly peaceful, and they all felt that progress had been made.

Chapter Thirty-Nine

NO ONE in *Phase Electric Phase Beer* had eaten dinner and they all tried to avoid staring at Libby's giant beef burrito. A liquid dinner would suffice as it usually did on gig night, especially with drink specials for every band. The 7pm band, *Hub Cap Hubert*, had just cleared their equipment off the stage and *Hitch, Bitch & Ditch* was getting geared up. They, along with *Phase Electric Phase Beer* and *Whette Dawguh*, had been playing on Monday nights together for almost a year now. Devon had made out with every girl in *Hitch, Bitch, & Ditch* and had slept with two of them. Wayne had hooked up with one of them as well. Devon was certain that two of the three guys in *Whette Dawguh* had also been with some of them, too.

The gals played their typical set, but adding an unmemorable new song at the end. Devon, like many of the men there and some of the women, didn't concentrate so much on the actual music. He couldn't help but reflect back on the crazy sex he'd had with Candice, the bass player, and then the ultra-crazy porn sex he'd had with Lolly, the drummer, He wondered if anyone else had had the same experience. The girls were never down for any sort of relationship; they were rock 'n' roll girls who enjoyed their rock 'n' roll lifestyle. Devon would never bring it up with the band, but he had once thought about dating Candice (because, though he hated to admit it, Lolly wasn't his type).

A line started forming as the bartender began pouring dozens of shots.

"Wanna do a shot with me?" Candice asked, as if Devon had a choice.

"Yeah, sure. Nice set," Devon complimented.

"Thanks, next time we're gonna try to do some more new stuff."

"Cool," Devon said as their shots arrived. They threw them back and ordered more for the others. The sounds of *Whette Dawguh* were a bit annoying but everyone was so used to it that no one had much difficulty speaking over them.

"Hey! We should have an orgy!" Lolly yelled. Slimy Ed, who had turned a shade of green after drinking his shot, turned a shade of red after hearing that. Everyone yelled, "Yeah!" in response, and Lolly got to work on the planning. It wasn't the first time she had suggested it but it had never happened. Maybe one day, dreamed Devon.

After two more shots and two more beers and an unusually long conversation between Devon and Candice, *Phase Electric Phase Beer* took the stage. Mel announced them and relayed that the drink special was dollar drafts. Feeling good, if not a little wobbly, Devon and the band played a decent set, rocking about half the songs from *Track & Field* and a bunch of newer tunes. The crowd was energetic and seemed to genuinely enjoy the music. When they were done, Devon went back to the bar for another drink with Candice and the gals. The rest of the band soon joined him and they ordered a round of Manhattan's, the drink special for the next band. The standard closing band, *The Liberators*, went on at 1am. By then, there were no sober patrons. Devon and his cheerful crew (and everyone else in The Pit) sang along with all of *The Liberators'* anthems. It was downright joyous.

Hard Candy by Devon Shires (unreleased)

Sweet treat
Boiled heat
Rotted teeth
Goo

Sugar smile
Crocodile
Burning mile
Roo

But I'm thinking of you
And my hard candy

Lasting suckers
Up and puckers
Super chuckers
Boo

Sass-a-frass
Black molass
Sunday mass
Foo

But I'm thinking of you
And my hard candy

The phone woke Devon. He focused on his clock until his sleepy eyes cleared. It was 5:30pm. He had somehow ended up back in bed. The phone kept ringing and it took Devon several moments to find it.

"Hullo," he said in a worn voice.

"Oh, Devon, dear, did I wake you? What time is it? Oh, my!" His mother was ever-loving, checking up on him whenever possible.

Devon snapped into awareness, not wanting to convey the idea that he slept this late. "No, Ma. I was just taking a nap. I was up before. We had a gig last night."

"Oh, that's wonderful. How'd it go? How's Morris?" she asked. She adored Morris, thinking he was just the cutest little thing.

"It went great, Ma. We did really well. I was up before but I guess I was really tired. You know, these shows (not to mention alcohol and various tobacco products) can wear you out," Devon said, subtly defending himself.

"Did you sing well?" his mother asked, knowing that once upon a time he wasn't the most pleasurable vocalist. But she also knew that he had worked at it and was proud that her son was the star singer.

"Yeah, I did pretty well, I think. It felt good. Everyone did well."

"Well, that's wonderful, dear. You know, your father and I would love to see you play sometime… and I know I always say that. So we really want you to have a show out here soon."

Devon could not begin to imagine his parents at a *Phase Electric Phase Beer* show and didn't want to try. "Okay, Mom," Devon said, like he always did.

"And I just wanted to remind you about your cooking class tonight."

That's why she was calling. He had missed last week's class, and she wasn't very pleased about that. The class was her idea because it'd be good for him to "expand his horizons" and it would "help his music," and she was paying for it, too. He didn't mind going so much, at least when he remembered to. If the music thing didn't work out, then he supposed he could be a breakfast chef in the mountains somewhere.

Devon quickly recovered from his memory lapse. "I know, Ma. I'm looking forward to it," he said with a smile.

"Good, dear. Maybe you can show me some of the things you're learning?" she cleverly proposed.

"Okay, Ma," Devon said, as if she were embarrassing him. "But, hey, I should start getting ready. I need to take a shower and stuff."

"Okay, dear. Well, have fun and let me know how it goes and we'll talk later this week and I love you," she said all in one breath.

"Love you too, Mom." Devon hung up the phone and sat still for a while. It was approaching 6pm. He casually looked over at his guitar, and then at his notebook, and then at his coffee mug on the small table. An illogical thought passed through him and he tried to understand it. When he realized he couldn't, he grabbed Francis the mini-bong and toked-up a batch of the tasty New York White. He then stood up, smiled at nothing in particular (like a true rock star would), and got in the shower.

Chapter Forty

THE MARBLE counters sparkled in the famed cooking class kitchen. John and Natasha sat at the small table at the front of the room and talked about food, amongst other things. When John looked into her eyes he could see a reflection of himself; someone with purpose, someone fulfilled, someone content. He could see peace.

John uncorked a bottle of Pinot Grigio and they enjoyed a glass while waiting for "the kids." Wine had never tasted so good. With each sip, John thought of another reason why he loved the woman sitting across from him. He turned on the portable radio on the back counter and tuned it to a classical station. The sound had some static but it livened up the room. John and Natasha felt like teenagers again, unchaperoned and up to no good. Everything was amusing, and they laughed out loud as they embraced the phenomenon.

They began dancing to some mediaeval march, twirling each other around in circles, weaving in between the rows of counters. They were royalty at the kitchen ball.

"So, are the kids good cooks?" Natasha asked, trying to be serious for a moment. But she was smiling too wide and couldn't hold back the giggles.

John started laughing again, too. "Yes, they're excellent," he said, barely getting the last word out.

After another dance, this time a regal waltz, John and Natasha found their places at the small table again. The sun was still out but had begun its descent, casting golden rays of light through the windows. John knew it was the summertime and the entire day had felt like a summer day, but right then, due to the good cheer or something similar, it felt like the winter holidays. For a brief moment, it was the middle of December.

"Hello?" Amanda asked.

A bit startled, John came out of his trance. "Ah, Ms. Myers," he said after remembering her name. He didn't think he could fall into teaching mode tonight; there was just too much going on in his head. "Amanda," he continued, "I'd like you to meet Natasha. Natasha, this is Amanda."

"Very nice to meet you, Amanda," Natasha said with a grin.

"Nice to meet you, too," Amanda echoed with her own grin. She had quickly surmised the situation. It was most apparent that Mr. Sebastian had the disposition of a five-year-old and that he and this Natasha lady had started some sort of sandbox club: She saw a man in love. She wondered if she, too, would have to wait until she was fifty. That was a long time, but judging from her cooking teacher's behavior, it might be worth the wait.

"There are glasses in the back," John offered. "Have some wine with us."

"Great," Amanda chirped and fetched a glass.

John poured her some wine as a symphony fought through the little radio speaker in back. "To food!" John toasted, and wondered if Amanda thought him to be a little goofy.

"And love," Amanda sneaked in, amused by her random toast-filled evening.

John looked at her and then at Natasha and simply said, "Yes."

They each had a sip, and the sips turned into smiles. Though her blind date had been a disaster, Amanda felt a bit warm and fuzzy inside. Seeing a couple in love made her feel unusually sentimental. She was just happy for the ones it happened to (although later that night, she knew she might shed a tear for herself).

Just then, Clyde strutted in, seemingly to his own theme music. "Yo," he said and instinctively got himself a glass.

Everyone else shrugged their shoulders.

"So what are we cooking tonight?" Clyde asked.

"Chicken," answered John.

"All right," Clyde said and playfully winked at Natasha. This class is great, he thought. No one knew him as the Porn King, so he could just be the harmless geeky punk he was and there'd be nothing but cheerful faces. "Then I propose a toast to the power of poultry," Clyde said and lifted his glass above his head as if praising a higher spirit. He knew he was being a little silly, but after being locked into an "I'm Da Man" persona every day, it felt unbelievably liberating to be a little silly.

"And to all other foods," John reminded.

"And to love," Amanda concluded with mock, but kind of real, sincerity.

They all drank their wine and started gabbing away. Amanda talked with John and Natasha, inquiring as to how they met and how long they'd been together. Clyde, however, pondered if Amanda was single and how he would ask her out if she was. After a few minutes, Paulson and Dana walked in with Devon a few steps behind. The room greeted the three with a "Hey!" and instructed them to grab some glasses. John introduced Natasha as two more bottles of wine were uncorked.

"It's very nice to meet you," Paulson said sweetly to Natasha, who returned the sentiment. "Mr. Sebastian is one lucky man," he added with a sigh.

Dana inched closer to Clyde, thinking he was pretty cute, and started talking to him about her audition, which surprised him because he didn't recall asking about it. He was still thinking about Amanda, wondering if she would say yes if he asked her out. But then he thought she might say no and wondered how strange that would feel.

"We need another toast!" Clyde declared, trying to avoid both his analytical mind and further conversation with the outgoing actress.

Paulson was quick to respond. "A toast to a very lucky man!"

Everyone raised their glasses and the toasts started going around the room again.

"And the power of poultry," said Clyde in a veritable whisper, now fully aware how ridiculous a thing to say it was. He figured he had to say it, though, because the new round of toasting was his idea. He hoped Amanda didn't think he was a loser.

Dana then decided to add her own toast. "And to my great audition!" she squealed. The room went silent. The radio station was airing a car commercial, making the moment that much more awkward.

"And to food," John said, trying to break the spell. It worked, coinciding with the return of a symphony on the radio, which seemed to lift everyone's glass a little higher. Pleasurable howls echoed throughout.

"And to love," Amanda said softly, and "Ooh's" and "Ah's" took the place of the howls.

Natasha, smirking at John, sipped from her glass. She could see why he was so dedicated to his cooking classes. There must be quite a difference in personal gratification, she thought, between feeding an old grumpy businessman at a restaurant and teaching an eager student how to cook. She was glad that he now belonged to her.

Dana yapped on to Clyde about her audition and he was becoming irritated. Thoughts raced through his mind: Why did she pick me to tell her life story to? How can I get away from this chatterbox? How can I approach that Amanda girl? Has she been in this class from the start? Would she go out with me despite my lame toast? Is she good in bed?

Paulson approached them and joined in the discussion. He already knew the gist of Dana's day (between the building entrance and the classroom door, Dana had given him all the information). As it turned out, and much to Dana's delight, Paulson was a fan of her father's films (although he'd only seen a few). His favorite was *Who Called The Cops This Time?*

Devon hovered around the outside of the group, smiling and nodding his head. He was incredibly stoned. The bong hit he took an hour earlier had taken control of his body. It gripped him from head to toe and wouldn't let go; just the way he liked it. He was not a prolific socializer with people he didn't know very well, but he could hold his own when he needed to. Sometimes, though, he preferred to watch from the perimeter. Scanning the room, Devon decided to play "Who Would I Hang Out With?"

He was unsure of most of the names so he made up his own. He began with John and Natasha, naming them "*Teach*" and "*Pet*," and soon determined that he'd "Hang" with both of them, but only once a week. Standing near "*Teach*" and "*Pet*" was Amanda, who Devon thought of as "*Kitty Kitty Meow Meow*," and she totally earned a "Hang Out." Then there was Paulson and Dana, who were given the names "*Sweetz*" and "*Deetz*," respectively. They talked way too much and made his equilibrium malfunction, so neither of them received a "Hang Out." Lastly, there was Clyde (who had somehow escaped Dana's company and was now walking in Devon's general direction). Devon named him "*Nerd*" and was still debating his "Hang Out" status.

"How ya doing?" Clyde asked a disappointed Devon, who calculated he was about two seconds from issuing a verdict.

"Good, man, good," Devon said, still trying to rate Clyde (which was difficult to do while you were conversing with your subject). "How ya feeling?"

"Pretty good," Clyde answered. "Feeling pretty good. You're Devon, right?"

"Yeah," Devon said unenthusiastically. "*Nerd*" was close to earning a "Not Hang Out" badge.

"Yeah, cool. I'm Clyde," Clyde said, turning to face the others as Devon was. Devon remembered the name, "Clyde," for exactly half a second and then completely forgot it.

"So what do you do again?" Clyde asked, but having never known in the first place, which was what Devon was thinking.

"I'm a musician," Devon said somberly, hinting that it wasn't the best time to talk about it.

"Hey, that's great. "So what instrument do you play?"

Devon's head dropped a couple of inches as he looked at Clyde. He didn't want to talk to him about this, and to his great pleasure Clyde seemed to pick up the signal.

"So, you like to cook?" Clyde asked. The music discussion, for some reason, didn't feel right so he changed the topic. He thought this Devon character was a bit of a knucklehead, but their forced conversation was more soothing than Dana's willingness to gab on about her audition. Besides, all he was really doing was procrastinating. The only thing he was thinking of was how to ask out Amanda.

"Not really," Devon replied to no one in particular. He was thankful that "*Nerd*" moved away from the music talk. (Devon despised talking music with anyone who wasn't in the scene, and "*Nerd*" definitely wasn't in the scene.)

"Yeah, me neither," Clyde confessed and actually laughed for a second. Devon, however, was not at all amused. In his stoned thoughts, he pictured a stand-up comedian repeating their dialogue and it still wasn't amusing. "*Nerd*" was just a little out there, he concluded.

Amidst another toast to the same subjects, Ginny walked in. She looked at everyone in amazement and quickly added, "And to me, damn it!" to which everyone howled. She scanned the room for Will, but seeing that he hadn't yet arrived, she got herself some wine. She slammed down her first glass and had a second one in hand before Devon could have a sip of his first. (Devon, who had been studying her, named her "*Scrappy*" and gave her instant "Hang Out" status.) The argument with her mother lingered, as did her semi-vicious spat with Will. She felt bad about lashing out at him and hoped that he'd get there soon. She just wanted to hug him. After pouring her third glass of wine, she finally went up to John and Natasha, who were still sitting at the small table.

"Hey, Mr. Sebastian," she greeted.

"Ginny, good to see you. This is Natasha." John was a bit more relaxed now that most of the introductions were complete (and a few more glasses of wine had disappeared).

"Nice to meet you, Ginny," offered Natasha.

Ginny could immediately feel the energy between John and Natasha, which provided her temporary refuge from her own frustrations. "There's a lot going on here, huh?" Ginny asked. John turned a shade of red and looked down at his glass before Ginny amended her statement (just to make him comfortable again). "Yeah, everyone seems to be in great spirits," she said, looking around the room.

"Oh, yeah," John concurred. "It must be the weather we're having."

Ginny smiled and casually shimmied away. She eventually found herself next to Dana and Paulson, who were still discussing

Dana's audition. Ginny stood by for a few minutes, listening to some story about "Daddy's Little Girl." When there was finally a lull, Paulson turned to Ginny and asked if she'd seen the movie *Mumbo Jumbo Mama*, and told her that Dana's father had made it. Ginny found that to be interesting but said that, regretfully, she'd not seen the film. After a brief discussion about New York City real estate, Ginny decided to move on. She went to the back counter and replenished her wine.

Devon, who thought Amanda was blazing hot, tried to smoothly introduce himself as she walked by. "Hey, I'm Devon and my favorite food is beer."

Amanda laughed at his quirkiness and thought about her own favorites. "I like fruit," she said, much to Devon's surprise, but it was the first thing that came to her mind.

"Fruit?" Devon asked, confirming that she had indeed said that.

"Yeah," Amanda asserted.

There was a brief moment of silence which was interrupted by Devon belching. "Ah, excuse me," he said, more amused than polite. The smell was a combination of wine and marijuana and it took Amanda only an instant to detect the fragrance. She rolled her eyes, laughed and walked away, leaving Devon to himself, upset that he might've just struck out.

With most of her concentration on trying to stay clear of the audition gal, Amanda bumped into Clyde. A few drops of her wine splashed onto Clyde's T-shirt and a few more landed on her blouse. Instead of apologizing, though, like she normally would have, she just stood there. Just then, the classroom door opened and Will walked in. Amanda's eyes shifted the other way as she saw Ginny put down her wine and go up and hug him.

Paulson retreated to the back counter to fill his glass and joined the favorite-food conversation with Devon, who had become upset once again because he thought he might've had a chance with Ginny. Will greeted John and was introduced to Natasha. Amanda then heard, "Pizza!" and didn't need to look to know that it was Paulson declaring his favorite food. Yet with all this action surrounding her, she still hadn't moved. Nor had Clyde. When she realized this, she became nervous and had to take a deep breath before she could look up at the man standing two inches away from her. Clyde, who seemed to have been equally distracted by the events around them, looked at Amanda at the same time. Letting go of her nervous reaction, Amanda smiled when they made eye contact. Clyde tried to smile too, but he felt like he was snarling.

"Hi," Clyde finally said.

"Hi," replied Amanda in a voice, she proudly noted, that wasn't too nervous, too excited, or too disinterested. Who is this guy? She kept asking herself, waiting for an answer, but none of her intuitive powers were working. She was two inches from this stranger, someone she'd only seen a few times, someone she'd never talked to beyond, "Hey, how's it going?" She knew nothing about him and yet she felt she'd known him before. This was all too bizarre.

"I'm Clyde." Clyde barely managed. Was she the one he was destined to meet at this Tuesday night cooking class? Was she the one who would change his life? Was she the future *Mrs. Hot Pants*? Was she really the one? Clyde felt like he was falling into a volcano.

"I'm Amanda," said Amanda, once again in that "not too anything" voice. She was in a most unusual comfort zone and felt she could stay there for a very long time.

"To pizza!" barked Paulson in the background. The rounds of toasts circulated the classroom again. Clyde refrained from his "power of poultry" toast, which he had retired for the evening.

"It's nice to meet you," Amanda said after the melee. Standing in the middle of the crowd, enveloped by glasses clinking, toasts being announced, random foods being yelled out, high-speed gabbing, and a static-laced classical soundtrack, both Amanda and Clyde had the unique sensation that they were in the eye of quite a peculiar storm.

"Nice to meet you too," Clyde replied. Time was lost in both their body clocks. In the distance, Amanda heard Devon secretively say (though he was far too high to be inconspicuous), "and *she* said 'fruit.'" Amanda grinned at Clyde, who had heard as well and grinned back (with a little less snarl this time).

Fruit was not such a bad choice, he thought. "I like bacon," Clyde confessed.

"Baby," Ginny pleaded with a three-drink buzz, "I'm *so* sorry about today, but can't we just talk about it later." She didn't want to talk about their argument, or about Will's indifference. Nor did she want to bring up the battle she'd had with her mother even though she kept alluding to it in her tipsiness.

Will was surprised, and very pleased, to see that Ginny had showed up (it helped him remember how much he enjoyed hanging out with her). He was also frazzled, though, by her state of mind and he wanted to know what happened with her mother. Hoping it might make her feel better, he told her more about his father being cooperative and said it wasn't that difficult at all. With every word he spoke, though, she drifted further and further into misery. She couldn't let go of the fact that she had achieved the opposite results. Noticing Ginny's sunken reactions, Will kept pressing for the truth.

Paulson brushed by, but judged their expressions and opted not to say hello. Instead, he strolled to the small static-filled radio and spun the dial until he found something funky. Feeling it, he immediately started dancing. Much to his delight, almost everyone else did, too, including Ginny, who noticed that the music was coming from a portable radio, which somehow reminded her of a portable beach, and it quickly shook her sour mood away. A moment later, Will joined her, wanting to take advantage of the happy wave. Clyde and Amanda remained in the center of the dance floor, still inches apart, and still very curious about each other. Devon, with an unusual burst of love, started tapping his feet. Paulson, who took center stage, started showing off his self-invented dance moves, including the "Sun in My Eyes" and the "Dangerous Diver." Dana, who was pleased that someone had turned off the boring "cartoon music," was performing her own interpretation of the "Forbidden Dance" (a little too close to Will, thought Ginny). Will and Ginny were content with their own style of dancing, even though it looked like they were dancing to easy-listening jazz. Paulson soon boogied his way to the other end of the classroom and got down with Dana (much to Ginny's relief), and they started a passionate ballroom spectacular. They gave each other mock looks of drama, acting out a jealous love triangle with the third party missing. Even Clyde and Amanda were swaying to the funk by the time John reached the radio and switched it back to the classical station. The class exhaled a unanimous moan while John sported a spoiler's grin. Paulson and Dana, however, continued their ballroom dance, which was entirely more appropriate with the classical music, and everyone gathered around them and cheered. The headline, COOKS CAN DANCE, flashed through Will's head as he clapped and stomped to the symphony.

"All right, class," John said over the music, "I think it's time to get started."

Paulson and Dana completed their last move and everyone gave them one last ovation. They now awaited orders from their teacher.

"I want everyone to get four small bowls from the back," John began, "and fill one with flour, one with two eggs, one with two cutlets and one with string beans." John scanned the room to see who was confused and who wasn't. From what he saw, John thought they had only processed about half that information. He decided to make it a little easier.

"Okay, we'll do it like this: Amanda, you're in charge of divvying out the flour. Paulson, you're on the eggs …two each. Clyde, you do the chicken. Ginny, you're in charge of the string beans, and… Will, you can get all the bowls out. You'll find all the ingredients in the back cabinets and refrigerator." John made sure his recruits seemed confident about their duties before addressing the others. "In the meanwhile, everyone else should go to a workstation and fill a medium-sized pot with a couple inches of water. Also, get a bottle of wine for each counter." John paused and then added, "And take your time."

The class scattered, the gabbing resumed, and the orchestral sounds of the kitchen complimented the classical music on the radio. John returned to his seat with Natasha, hoping she wasn't bored.

"Classes usually aren't like this," he said, although he wasn't sure if he'd used a convincing tone. "I don't know what's gotten into them." He was truly puzzled.

Natasha gazed at him with her soothing eyes and smiled, "Maybe it's you."

Bashful John looked away, not knowing what to say. "Not too much flour," he projected towards the back, and Natasha laughed at his avoidance. "Or maybe it's you," John said and then laughed at himself.

"I am so happy," Natasha whispered.

John stared at her, not knowing what to say, but knowing that for the first time in his life, he felt the same way. "Me, too," was all he could get out. From this day forward, he realized, he'd be traveling to a new world and learning everything all over again. "Who wants to chop up the parsley?" he asked the room before he could drift into deeper thought.

"I'll do it!" Dana yelled in a rush, causing John to rethink the idea. After some wine, he wasn't sure if he wanted anyone but himself to handle sharp utensils.

"Actually, Dana, you know what? I think I'll do it," John said, and then added some sugar. "It'll just be faster… but you can get it from the fridge and rinse it if you like."

Momentarily hurt, but then excited again, Dana charged to the refrigerator and started her chore.

"Good choice," Natasha said, holding back a laugh.

At the only counter space left in back, John quickly chopped enough parsley for three classes. Those who stood nearby were mesmerized by his fluidity. Devon, who was still incredibly stoned, thought it was the coolest thing he'd ever seen.

"Devon," John said, seeing how intrigued he was, "can you get out some little bowls and fill them up with this stuff and put one at every station?"

"Yeah, totally," Devon replied. He was fired up to help but wasn't really sure why.

As all the preparation duties were being fulfilled, John took his space at the head workstation facing the others. Everyone eventually found their own workstation, each with their own bowls of ingredients and a glass of wine. Waiting for the chatter to subside, John noticed that one workstation was empty. His memory wasn't as good recalling the names of absent students as it was with those he could see.

"It seems we have one missing," John announced.

Everyone looked at the empty space in the middle counter. Devon was a moment behind even though it was to his immediate right.

John then had an idea. "Natasha? Would you like to sit in?"

"Really?" she asked, a little shy.

The students hollered their approval and John playfully added, "Yeah, we need you."

Natasha nervously left the small table and stood in front of the vacant workstation. Devon nodded with approval as she studied the ingredients before her.

"Okay," John spoke, holding his hands up to the class, attempting to cut through. "Before we get started, I think I'd like to make one final toast."

"Pizza!" Paulson boomed.

John shook his head as the tipsy class got involved. Maybe that was the wrong thing to say. The wild celebration of toasts continued as glasses clinked and smiles spread and dancing resumed. John looked at Natasha in comic disbelief as he waited for the excitement to cease.

When it had, he held up his hands until he had everyone's attention. "But *I* would like to make one more toast." Again, he shifted his gaze towards Natasha and then paused, not wanting to make a hasty mistake. "I would like to make a toast," he began, "to our newest student."

The class erupted yet again with more clinking glasses, wide smiles, and extravagant dancing. Devon even played some air guitar.

John, however, had not moved. His eyes were fixated upon Natasha's and they hadn't strayed for a second. She gave him a small smile, with her eyes as much as her lips, and he knew he'd never forget that image. His own smile slowly widened and a minor laughing fit ensued. "All right!" he bellowed out to the class. "It's time to cook."

CPSIA information can be obtained at www.ICGtesting.com
Printed in the USA
LVOW04s1725240815

451328LV00010B/141/P